"God's holy mercy!"
she whispered. He was naked as the day he was born!

Eyes wide with fascination, she watched MacBain as he checked the horses for injury and resettled the packs on their saddles. The man had no shame whatsoever!

Of course, he thought there was none to see him save his manservant, who appeared to be sleeping, Mairi reminded herself. But did he not remember that she must come out of the woods soon? Did he *want* her to see him so exposed?

Her face flamed at the sight, but she could not tear her gaze away. What muscles he had, she thought as they flexed in his arms, shoulders and even his backside. Ah, that backside *was* something to see!

Her hands clenched, imagining the smooth feel of all that sun-kissed skin. The desire to touch him all but overcame her....

Praise for a few of Lyn Stone's previous works

Bride of Trouville
"I could not stop reading this one....
Don't miss this winner!"
—*Affaire de Coeur*

The Knight's Bride
"Stone has done herself proud with this
delightful story...a cast of endearing characters
and a fresh, innovative plot."
—*Publishers Weekly*

The Wicked Truth
"Stone has an apt hand with dialogue and
creates characters with a refreshing naturalness."
—*Publishers Weekly*

The Highland Wife
Harlequin Historical #551—March 2001

THE HIGHLAND WIFE

Lyn Stone

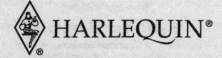

HARLEQUIN®

TORONTO • NEW YORK • LONDON
AMSTERDAM • PARIS • SYDNEY • HAMBURG
STOCKHOLM • ATHENS • TOKYO • MILAN • MADRID
PRAGUE • WARSAW • BUDAPEST • AUCKLAND

ISBN 0-373-29151-5

THE HIGHLAND WIFE

Please address questions and book requests to:
Harlequin Reader Service
U.S.: 3010 Walden Ave., P.O. Box 1325, Buffalo, NY 14269
Canadian: P.O. Box 609, Fort Erie, Ont. L2A 5X3

Special thanks to my son, Eric, for providing
inspiration and informal signs,
to my daughter, Pamela, for her encouragement,
and to my husband, Allen, for everything.

Chapter One

The Highlands
Summer 1335

What the devil was he doing in this place? He did not need a wife this desperately, Robert MacBain told himself. Yet here he rode, into the very heart of the unfamiliar. Into these alien hills, to wed an unseen betrothed who was likely more apprehensive than he was about the whole matter.

Yet he was obliged to carry through. Thomas de Brus had traveled far and spent half a year arranging this marriage, urgently driven to it because his sister had spurned Rob and broken their lifelong betrothal. Rob had not the heart to refuse his friend and leave him with that guilt, but now he wished he had waited for Thomas to recover and come with him. The date of Rob's arrival had been agreed upon, however. His bride awaited.

So here he was, facing the only terror that ever plagued him. The unknown. The makings of his worst nightmares. This was not a fear he would ever admit aloud. Nor a thing he would avoid.

He glanced around and up at the harsh gray peaks that defined the Highlands. This forbidding region looked so different from the Midlothian he called home. Neither did it bear any resemblance to the various places on the Continent he had visited to participate in tournaments with his brother Henri.

Rob had no wish to be in this place, yet its peculiar scents and incredible beauty fascinated him nonetheless. He decided he must dwell upon the favorable aspects of this journey instead of his dread.

Would his Highland bride hold true with her surroundings? Would she differ so greatly from the women he had explored in the past? Would she beguile, or repel him? Or perhaps do both at once, as did her homeland?

The sharp blade of anticipation sliced through his apprehension. While that did not banish it altogether, it certainly made it more manageable. The woman might make all this worthwhile. Thomas had promised she was quite beautiful as well as congenial.

He inhaled a deep breath of the cool, crisp air and shook his head to clear it of the useless musing. Whether he liked the lass or not, she would be his wife. His family and Thomas would cease worrying about him then. Rob needed to get an heir from some woman. If he could not have the lady meant for him, he might as well take this one since Tom had gone to so much trouble.

His man, Newton, reined his cob and waited until Rob rode abreast. "Craigmuir's just through yon hills, milord." He pointed ahead, off to the right. "Would you care to rest? Tidy yourself?" Newt made a scrubbing motion on his chest and cocked his brow. "Your bride awaits!"

The merry grin Newton wore told Rob how begrimed he looked after a week's travel in the same garb.

"There's a burn up ahead we must cross to get there."

Rob nodded and rode past Newton. Their mounts picked up the pace to a trot, scenting the water.

His father had taught him that in any confrontation, Rob should appear as though he already conquered the world. Thus far, the advice had served him well. It would today.

"He comes! He comes!" cried the sentry on the wall. Corby was all but leaping about with glee as he pointed toward the south.

Mairi MacInness refused to play overeager. Especially when everyone else at Craigmuir acted as though Christmas mummers were expected. She supposed they had good enough reason for their excitement, with the feast and merrymaking imminent. For them it would be a grand holiday. As for herself, she would reserve judgment until she saw whether she had any good cause to celebrate.

Her father joined her on the steps to the hall. "Best you wait inside, dove," he advised her. "I would meet him first."

Mairi complied, but she did not go far, certainly not to her chamber to await being summoned. Instead, she went to the small chamber her father used to tally his accounts and store his books. From there, she would be able to see all that took place within the hall without being seen.

She wanted no surprises. If the man proved loathsome, this would allow her time to prepare a proper reaction when they were introduced.

While waiting, Mairi once again straightened the neck of her chemise, smoothed her skirts, rearranged the belt, her chatelaine and the simple scabbard that held her eating knife. Satisfied that she appeared as presentable as possible, she then kept avid watch upon the hall door.

Her eyes grew wide with wonder when at last she saw him enter. Mercy, he did look impressive. Taller even than her sire, he was, and quite a contrast to her cousin Ranald. She had hoped never to see that one again. He'd arrived late, but there he came now, hurrying to catch up to her father and the newcomer as they crossed the hall.

Unable to quell her curiosity, desperate for a closer look at the stranger who had come to wed her, Mairi decided she would risk appearing eager after all.

They had halted at one side of the raised dais. Mairi approached just behind and to the right of her sire and remained silent and unobtrusive, as was proper. Her time would come, and none too soon to suit her.

Baron MacBain's emissary had arrived to make the arrangements two months prior to this. She had met him briefly, but had not known why the man was here until he had departed. After informing her rather curtly of the marriage plans, her sire had said nothing more on the subject no matter how she had plagued him about it.

Mairi had prepared herself to refuse the match if it was not to her liking, no matter that her father had already arranged her wedding down to the last ribbon on her gown.

Now she forgave him that, for it seemed he had done right well by her after all. Her mother would be proud of Da's arrangements and of Mairi's biddable acceptance, had she lived.

What a pleasant surprise that the intended was such a young and comely man, Mairi thought. Since she was four and twenty, a good decade past the age his kind usually sought in a bride, she had fully expected to meet a groom in his dotage, minus most of his hair and teeth.

That the man chosen was not a Highlander only counted in his favor. Leaving this isolated place would pose little hardship as far as Mairi was concerned. All her life she had craved adventure and travel to new places, even while thinking how unlikely she was to experience either.

She would miss her father, of course. Though most of the time the laird scarcely gave her more attention than he did his hounds, she knew he loved her well. Otherwise why would he trouble himself to chastise her roundly now and again and caution her to be more thoughtful and prudent?

Since she had never known her mother, he must feel obliged to make a proper lady of his only child. Mairi was glad he cared enough to bother.

At the moment Da headed her list of favorite people simply because he had chosen such a fine husband for her.

Aside from the occasional raids by the neighbors, life at Craigmuir proved exceedingly dull. Even those events possessed a sameness. Ride near, steal a few head of kine and ride out. Then her father's men would retaliate. Other than patching up the few minor wounds acquired and enduring the curses when a raid failed, none of it affected her own routine.

Now here stood her hope for great change. His light brown, sun-streaked hair had been neatly groomed, combed away from his wide brow. His dark gray eyes seemed to miss nothing, though he did not turn his head and gape as some did upon entering the cavernous hall. He must be used to even larger and better.

Mairi thought so because his exquisitely embroidered woolen tunic and tightly woven hose seemed richer, and his excellent weaponry more costly, than her father's. Or any other she had ever seen, for that matter.

Silver spurs and the chain he wore marked him as a knight as well as a noble, but she had already known that about him. One of the few details she'd been granted was his title of baron.

And how seriously noble he was. She smiled in welcome from her place just behind the laird, hoping for a ready response that would signify friendliness. Yet judging by his countenance, the man might have been approaching a hangman's noose. He gave neither her nor her smile any notice whatsoever. Of course, he did not know yet who she was, Mairi reasoned.

She clenched her teeth and maintained the smile, silently determined to not judge the man too swiftly. He must be as worried as she was about this first meeting.

Her father had yet to notice she was present, for she stood out of his sight. He had just greeted her cousin and was making introductions.

"Lord Robert MacBain, Baron of Baincroft, meet my kinsman and chosen tanist, Sir Ranald MacInness." He inclined his head toward their cousin who would be laird of the MacInness after him.

Ranald was a tall, stalwart man of thirty years who seemed cursed with a perpetual smirk. The sin-dark eyes examined their guest as intently as the man's silvery-gray gaze regarded him.

Though Ranald bore the sword, spurs and other trappings of a knight, Mairi knew he possessed none of the inner qualities required of one. Chivalry, humility and honor were unknown to him. She wondered whether that would be obvious to one who had never met him before. Lord MacBain's handsome face remained so unexpressive, she could not tell what he thought.

"Sir Ranald," MacBain acknowledged gruffly, her cousin's name sounding foreign upon his tongue.

He offered his arm and, after a short hesitation, Ranald clasped it briefly in greeting. "MacBain," he replied with obvious disdain, ignoring the baron's title. An insult.

Mairi felt a prickle between her shoulder blades. Ranald would bear watching, she thought. It was a safe wager the man had a purpose in being here other than to meet her bridegroom. He had requested that nebulous honor for himself with some regularity, much to her disgust.

"I regret I cannot stay for the nuptials," Ranald told her father. "I must return to Enslor before the morrow."

"Expecting trouble?" the laird asked.

"Nothing I cannot deal with," her cousin replied curtly. "'Tis little enough I have to do these days when I could be relieving you of many duties hereabout."

Mairi's father sighed. "Ambition is often admirable, Ranald. But I'm not dead yet, as ye can see."

This could degenerate into another family squabble, Mairi thought with mounting apprehension. What an embarrassment to them all, that would be. Her gaze leaped to Lord MacBain, who observed her father and Ranald with keen interest.

Ranald pressed a hand to his chest in mock dismay. "Ye mistake my offer of help, m'laird." He looked past her father and fastened his evil gaze on Mairi. "Just as ye mistook my frequent proposals to become as a son to ye."

Her sire snorted inelegantly. "Cousin is a close enough tie to suit me. The clan chose ye years ago, and ye'll have yer due, but not through me or mine."

Ranald looked Mairi up and down, then smiled his oily, suggestive smile. How often he had done this, silently promising her what would happen if he ever caught her alone?

Abruptly the MacBain stepped between them, purposely cutting off her cousin's view of her. Only then did Ranald halt his taunting of her and take his leave.

Thank God he did. The man made her skin crawl as though she were covered with leeches.

When they were finally free of Ranald's presence, her future husband turned and looked her straight in the eye, as if she were the only person in the world worth seeing.

Mairi's skin felt fine at that moment. A bit overheated, yet fine. 'Twas her bones that melted.

God save her soul, this man could charm the thorns off of thistles. She felt totally bereft when he looked away to focus expectantly on her father.

Today, for the first time since she had found she was to marry, Mairi MacInness felt the definite thrill of expectation.

Of course, she had another reason for that feeling. She had not even hoped that he would be this handsome or look so worthy, given her father's obvious reluctance to speak to her of the match.

"Lord MacBain, here is my daughter, Mairi MacInness," her father said by way of introduction, and drew her forth by her arm to stand immediately before her intended. "Yer bride."

Again she became the target of his full regard. The steel-gray, long-lashed eyes widened slightly with avid interest, mayhaps even desire. Mairi almost shivered.

Cautiously, as though he thought she might refuse the gesture, he extended one large hand, calloused palm upright. Mairi offered her own and watched as he lifted her fingers to his lips. He had wonderful lips. She sighed.

His eyes never left her face as that finely shaped mouth nearly touched her knuckles. She felt his breath warm upon them. That sent tingles up her arm and they did not stop at her shoulder.

"My lord," she acknowledged. She wished she had not sounded quite so breathless, but indeed she was. His size and very presence quite overwhelmed her. But in the most wonderful way she could imagine.

"My lady," he murmured in a very deep voice completely devoid of inflection.

She could not decide whether she liked the sound of

him. However, the rest certainly left no room for complaint. He bore the scent of costly spices from the East. Cloves, she decided, drawing another deep breath. And cinnamon, which she dearly loved. That boded well, Mairi thought, used as she was to men bearing only the smells of sweat and horse.

Her father cleared his throat. "Coom, sit and rest yerself," he commanded loudly, and motioned across the hall toward the low-burning fire. "Bring us ale!" He nearly shouted the words at the servants now bustling about the tables, readying them for the evening meal.

"Da! Please, speak more softly," Mairi reprimanded quietly, patting her sire's arm.

He merely grunted in a very low voice, not moving his mouth, "'Tis lack o' hearing, lass. Sad to say, but ye must have pity and patience. I should ha' mentioned it before."

Mairi sighed, troubled, but not overmuch. Such a loss was to be expected in a man of her father's advanced years. Yet he did not have to treat everyone as though they shared his affliction. Still, the young baron seemed not to have taken umbrance at her father's loud barking. Mayhaps he understood.

To her surprise, her intended bypassed the comfort of the only two cushioned chairs, leaving these softer ones for his host and hostess. Deferring to a lady and an elder spoke very well for the man's manners, she thought.

Why, then, did her father look so uneasy? Not fearful, exactly, but certainly wary. There was little that ever disconcerted him. He probably worried she would disgrace them all.

Not so, this time. She'd put her rash, impulsive ways behind her. Never again would she rush into an action or for a judgment, forsaking caution and good thought.

Was she not proving this even now? Each move the

baron made, she evaluated with great care. After all, her very future depended upon how well they got on together.

Mairi modestly bowed her head and busily arranged her skirts as she asked pleasantly, "Were yer travels here remarkable, my laird? The hills are bonny this time o' year, aye?"

He disregarded her completely as though she did not exist, his full attention still focused on her father.

"I wondered whether ye encountered any difficulties along the way, or if the trip proved an easy one," she continued softly, waiting, unmoving, determined to get a reply of some kind from him.

He gave her none, but kept his eyes trained upon her sire as though expecting him to reproach a forward daughter for speaking freely. Da did grimace at her in warning when she glanced at him. "Hist, lass," he muttered, shushing her.

That turned MacBain's attention. He inclined his head to her slightly as one might to notice a bug upon the floor.

"You think me impertinent for speaking?" she prompted the baron yet again. Daring him, really.

That gained her an almost imperceptible shrug. Barely there and then gone. His lips curved, but it was not a smile. More like a gesture of mild annoyance.

And she had thought this man mannerly? How churlish of him, deliberately refusing to answer her. Contentious knave. Did he think so little of females in general? Or was it *her* in particular he found offensive? Had she mistaken his former look of interest after all?

When he did speak, it definitely was not to her. He had ceased looking at her and addressed her father.

"When may we wed? I must go home," he stated very slowly in the same low, brusque tone that did not vary up or down.

Each word, he presented distinctly, as if it would stand alone. Did he think her father a lackwit? Or did he mock him as a Highlander who was unused to comprehending correct English? Either way, he had no cause to insult. Craigmuir might be isolated, but its laird was certainly educated, nonetheless. The MacInness had traveled widely in his youth and was well read. He had even insisted that she be taught to read and cipher.

Her father sighed sorrowfully as he replied. "Ye must wed soon, I suppose, since we've settled upon it." Then, as though he had not yet answered, he forced a smile and raised his head as well as his voice. "Soon. Ye may marry this week."

"This week?" Mairi exclaimed. She glared at her father, willing him to heed her. Did he not realize that she must get to know this man before the wedding? If, indeed, there was to be one, she thought diffidently. Fine, young and wealthy as the man appeared, Mairi was not certain she liked him at all.

With a succinct nod, MacBain then turned to her. "Do you agree?"

At last! He deigned to notice she was present for this conversation, could one even call it that. It was likely to turn to an argument if he did not change his ways on the instant. If there was anything she detested, it was to be ignored.

Mairi smiled sweetly at him. "Ye jest, surely, my good laird! Have ye ever known any maid of my age to cry off a marriage? However, I feel *you* might wish to think twice on it, ere ye get more than ye bargained for!"

"Mairi!" her father gasped. "Mind yer tongue!"

She rose and turned on him then, giving the pompous baron her back. "Well? I *am* four and twenty, Da. Not that anyone has bothered to notice my aging these past dozen years. Now ye invite this man to take me off yer hands? Paugh! He can scarcely stand to look at me! He will not even reply to a common pleasantry!''

Her father grasped his chest and rolled his eyes as though caught in the throes of apoplexy. Not that she believed that for a moment. 'Twas an oft used ruse to raise her guilt and gain an apology. Well, he'd not get one now, she decided. Not after trying to match her to this surly scoundrel.

"Do excuse me, Father," she said as haughtily as she could. "I would retire and leave ye to *your* guest! I am certain he willna be missing *me.*" With chin high and without another glance for her erstwhile betrothed, she stalked off toward the stairs.

Handsome the man might be, but damned if she would shackle herself to one who had likely been bribed to wed her. From the look of him and the way he behaved, her father had not paid nearly enough to make the haughty wretch glad of the transaction.

She had done without a husband all these years and fared well enough. Why take one now who did not consider her worth a smile, a kind word or even a second glance? Rot him, then. She would stay a maid.

Rob appreciated the swing of those slender hips as the fair-haired lady took herself away. A pity he could not grasp one word in ten of what she said or he might guess the reason for her leaving.

He found any Highlander's odd speech hard to ken, especially when one spoke as rapidly as did she and with hardly moving her lips. The old laird made an effort on behalf of Rob's understanding, but the woman did not. Possibly, she did not yet realize she needed to.

Could that be? Had they not told her? Thomas said he

had insisted that she know. Rob had made it a firm condition before his steward set out on the quest.

He shrugged off the worry. Thomas would never lie, not about that. The woman knew about him. She simply did not understand how to deal with it yet. That could be taught easily enough.

Mairi MacInness was a lovely woman by any man's standard, not at all the timid girl he had feared he might find. Thomas had not told him her age, but Rob guessed she had passed twenty. That suited him.

Anger at her sire had added color to the smooth cream of her cheeks. The blue eyes had sparked when she had included him in her fit of pique. Whatever had caused her displeasure, he was glad that she showed some spirit. She would need it.

Again he faced the laird. "You *did* tell her?"

"What?" the old man asked warily, his gaze darting here and there, avoiding Rob's.

Rob eyed him steadily, waiting, not bothering to define what the man already knew but was obviously reluctant to discuss.

"Aye, I told her, but I was brief." He ducked his head, then looked up again. "And I left it late," MacInness admitted.

"Late?" Rob repeated, sorely afraid he now understood the woman's anger all too well. "How late?"

The laird looked shame-faced and ran a hand through his graying hair. "Today. Just now."

Rob exhaled sharply and shook his head. "Damn."

"She'll grow accustomed," MacInness said hopefully. "Mairi is a guid lass. Kind," he added.

"When you told her," Rob asked, hiding his apprehension, "she was angry?"

Rob did not want her to reject him, he realized. With

others, he had not cared so much. Except for Jehannie. Her betrayal had nearly destroyed him. Since she had broken their long-standing betrothal, he had cared not one way or the other whether he ever wed anyone.

If he had not needed to produce an heir for Baincroft, he would never have agreed for Thomas to contract a match for him. He had felt no great rush to wed anyone. Not until he had seen this woman...

"Nay! Nay. 'Tis not *that* which angered her," the laird assured him, shaking his head. "She but wants courting, I think. All women do."

Rob nodded. Courting, of course. He should do that, yet he had little time or inclination for it. Nor did he think it necessary in this instance. The betrothal contract had been signed. The woman was his. All that remained was signing the marriage documents and repeating the vows. And the bedding, of course. Not likely he would forget that now that he had met her.

He chewed his bottom lip for a second, caught himself doing so and quickly smoothed his features. If he did not court her properly as her father suggested, *she* might be the one willing to forget that final detail of the ceremony that Rob so looked forward to accomplishing.

She could cry off the match and he would never touch that fair, smooth skin of hers the way he wanted, or inhale fully that subtle scent of roses she wore. Not to mention the other pleasures he now anticipated.

Fine, then. He would court, but he would not prolong it. Now, he only wished to wed and go home again.

Once they reached Baincroft, the lady would soon see that she had no reason to doubt his ability to care for her and the children they would make together. There, among his people, lay his best chance to impress a wife.

However, if she wanted constant courting and sweet

words daily after their marriage, she might go lacking. Rob had tried being courtly with his first betrothed as soon as she'd grown old enough for it. That had come to no good end.

His beloved stepfather and brother had been right all those years ago to caution him against showing any gentler feelings he might have. They had said he must cultivate a stern and commanding demeanor in order to gain respect.

Though both had spoken of Rob's dealings with other lords, knights and men of business, Rob wondered if the advice might not hold true for women he wished to respect him.

Should he play the smiling, teasing courtier with this one as he often did with the women he sought for pleasure? Or ought he to remain somewhat aloof, since she was a noble and about to be his wife? He wished Trouville or Henri were here to advise him in this.

He did not like to be away from Baincroft, especially in these strange surroundings where he knew only the four men who rode with him. Because of their low rank, he could not keep them close by in these delicate encounters with his future bride and the MacInness laird.

Had Thomas come with them to speak for him, matters might be proceeding more smoothly. Then this would not be so difficult because Thomas already knew these people. Unfortunately, that one lay abed back at Baincroft with a broken leg.

Rob damned his luck, losing the services of his friend and factor at such a critical time. The loss of his usual self-confidence plagued him. Jehannie's doing, of course.

Only once, as a child needing the love of a father, had he given any particular care at all as to what a person thought of him or his abilities. Until Jehannie had refused to wed him.

Since that time, self-doubt had increased with every new acquaintance he made. He must somehow recapture his early certainty of his worthiness. His mother had worked too diligently to instill that for him to lose it forever. But he much doubted he would regain it here and now amongst these people.

Was it lack of courting alone that had put the Lady Mairi off? No matter how much he might wish that were the case, Rob found it hard to believe. Especially in view of what she had only just learned about him. That surely must play a part.

Well, it was her misfortune, then, if she could not deal with her lot in life. The bride price was paid. She must honor her father's contract. Rob *would* have her.

The laird looked miserable, he noticed. Sad to be losing his daughter, Rob surmised. Losing her to such a man as the MacBain could not be easy for him.

Rob admitted he might feel the same way in like circumstance. Thomas said that he had explained everything in detail to MacInness. Since the laird had only told her just now, she would not have those details as yet.

Would she be consoled to know that Rob's deafness would not pass down to their children? His mother assured him this was so, since he had been able to hear for a while after his birth. A fever had stolen the sounds.

Would it help her to know that he could hear some things? He scoffed at that as soon as he thought of it. Heavy drumbeats and shrill whistles did not count for much when nothing but muffled silence existed between the two extremes. No, she likely would not care about the fine points of it. To all intent and purpose, he was deaf as a stone and that was that.

The contract had cost him dearly because MacInness had not wanted to let Lady Mairi go to him as wife at first, so Thomas had said. However, the laird had needed to see to his daughter's future now that he was growing old. Rob might not be able to hear the lass, but he could make her a very wealthy woman.

In return for the bride price, Rob would gain a crumbling estate near the border as her dower. A bog around rocks, that place. He had gone out of his way to see it on the way here. He might as well have accepted the woman dowerless for all the good that useless property would do him. But he knew such was not done, even among the lower classes, though Rob would have been well content with only her person after having seen her.

Rob needed a son to inherit sooner or later. Considering his deafness, it was not likely any other family of nobles who learned the truth about him would trust him with a daughter. He supposed he must concede something to MacInness for extending that trust.

"For two days, I court," he promised MacInness, holding up two fingers for emphasis. "Then we wed and go."

The laird slumped and nodded, then pushed heavily from his chair and flung a hand idly toward the tables at the head of the hall. "Come, eat."

Rob took his seat in the place of honor. The Lady Mairi did not come to table at all.

The laird said nothing more to him until they had finished their meal. Then he turned and faced Rob with a frown. "Will you be good to my Mairi? Did you like her at all?"

Rob's heart softened in spite of himself at the parental concern evident in the old man's eyes and offered what reassurance he could. "Aye, sir," he affirmed, attempting to remain brusque and failing miserably. "I like her."

Chapter Two

The next morning Mairi approached the situation more pragmatically than she had the evening before. If she did not marry this baron, nothing would change for her. She would spend the rest of her life counting the linens and shining Craigmuir's meager collection of silver, upbraiding unruly servants and ordering goods for the keep. Yet, should she accept the man as husband, she at least had some chance of establishing a family of her own, of having children who would love her.

And, at last, she would see what lay beyond the sparsely inhabited hills and glens of the Highlands. More than anything, she longed to see a city, any city. She wanted to travel, to meet new people and hopefully have an adventure along the way. Just one would be enough. Simply wedding the MacBain might provide that last wish, Mairi thought with a hidden grin.

He might not bother to speak to her any more than was strictly necessary, but she had to admit he was not hard to look upon. Given time, she could surely coax some semblance of geniality from him.

Once she accomplished that feat, Mairi suspected that their bedding together would be no unpleasant chore. She believed she had felt his brief assessment of her for that purpose, if none other. She supposed it would have to suffice unless they could find some other common ground. Many marriages had not even that to recommend them.

Determined to show him that she could provide interesting company, Mairi headed to the kitchens soon after Mass and put together a basket of cheese, cold meats and bread fresh from the ovens. She added a flagon of wine and set out to find her betrothed, who had not bothered to attend either Mass or the informal breaking of fast afterward.

She found him in the stable, grooming his steed. "Good morn, m'laird," she said, summoning her brightest smile.

He smiled back at her, a blindingly sweet expression that stopped her right in her tracks and made her suck in a sharp breath. God's mercy, the man could spellbind when he put his mind to it, Mairi thought, absently patting her chest with one hand. Her heartbeat had speeded to a dangerous pace and she felt quite giddy of a sudden.

Just as rapidly as it had come, his smile faded. The taciturn baron frowned as he regarded the basket she carried. That left her wondering if she had merely imagined his greeting. Wishful thinking?

Her wits returned, Mairi lifted the cloth on the basket to show him. "I brought food. There's a wondrous place I could show ye, if ye'd like to ride." She then lifted a bridle off its peg and handed it to him, nodding toward her mare.

"Ride?" He glanced around them and back at her. "Alone?"

She grinned and cocked her head to one side. "Why not? We *are* betrothed. Who's there to censure us? None, that's who!"

With a shrug of uncertainty, he reached for her saddle.

Mairi felt content to simply watch him move as he readied her mount and then his own.

Grace in motion, she thought, impressed by the economy of his every action, the play of muscles just visible through his well-fitted clothing.

Rude or not, he stirred her blood, this man. He was the first to do so, and so she half forgave him for his inattentiveness last evening and the lapse of that enchanting smile just now. Mayhaps he was only shy, or had never been taught better manners.

She could teach him. For a first lesson, she waited expectantly for him to assist her in mounting. After a hasty perusal of her person, he grasped her waist, lifted her as if she weighed no more than the basket of food and plunked her atop her mare.

Had those braw hands of his lingered longer upon her than necessary? She thought so. A good sign, that.

He quickly mounted and they rode in silence for a while with Mairi leading the way. Her special place awaited them, a lovely clearing in the wood where a stream pooled beneath a shallow fall. The ferns and flowers growing there made it seem a faerie glen. They could spend a few quiet hours away from the keep, becoming acquainted.

Not that she would allow him any liberties. He would know better than to attempt that before the wedding, certainly. Or would he?

Mairi smiled to herself, almost wishing he would abandon propriety. Many a couple anticipated their final vows. Not that she would countenance such doings, of course, even to turn him up sweet. A lady must have limits. Da said so.

So many times Mairi had wished to speak with another woman about these matters. Her mother was long dead and the few females left at Craigmuir were not the sort she'd ask for advice of that nature. Most were right free with their favors and made no secret of it.

When they reached her destination, MacBain remained mounted and spent quite some time observing the surrounding woods. She could have sworn he checked the grassy ground for tracks and sniffed the air for trouble. Did he believe she had invited him into a trap of some kind?

"I like it," he announced finally as he dismounted and came to assist her off her mare.

Then he bent down and quickly gathered a fistful of wildflowers. "For you," he said, all but glaring as he held them out. Mairi chose to believe he merely worried whether she would appreciate the offering. She decided to ignore the intensity of his regard. God's truth, he rarely blinked.

"I thank ye!" she muttered, quite taken aback by the gesture, perfunctory as it was. He certainly wasted no time. Or tenderness. However, he had made an effort and she would give him the credit for it.

"Coom with me," she ordered, reaching for the strong hand she had just emptied of the blooms. She grasped it and pulled him along toward the bank of the stream, set upon making friends with the man, no matter how rough his manners.

He dropped to a sitting position, gently pulling Mairi down with him. Once seated, he glanced at the water, shot her a look of daring and began to remove his boots.

Intrigued at his unexpected hint of laddie-like behavior, she took the dare and did likewise, tossing her shoes and hose over her shoulder onto the grass. In moments, they sat side by side, bare feet slowly swishing in the cold, clear water.

"Ah, here's a pleasure, in't?" she commented, lying

back upon the lush carpet of green behind her. "Have ye such a place near yer home? Somewhere special to ye as this one is to me?"

Though he did not answer, he reclined on one elbow, leaned over her and fixed that avid gray gaze upon her face. For a moment Mairi thought he might kiss her, but he only reached for the flowers she still held in her hand and chose one.

"Beauty," he whispered gruffly, teasing her nose with the petals. "Here," he said, dragging the flower across her lips. "Here," he repeated, drawing it down her neck to the edge of her chemise that peeked above her gown. "Hiding," he teased, trailing the small bloom across the fabric covering her breasts and stomach.

Heat flared within her. More than anything, she wished to see that smile of his. She had surprised it out of him once at the stable. Could she do it again?

"Kiss?" she murmured coyly, adopting his peculiar habit of brevity in speech.

As an answer, he simply lowered his mouth to hers. After a moment's gentle press of his lips, he eased hers open with his tongue. She'd never been kissed so in her life. More's the pity, Mairi thought, enjoying the sensation immensely. She quickly responded to his exploration with a foray of her own.

She met the hot, wet warmth of his mouth, tasting his heat as her own increased. Encompassed and loving it, Mairi saw no need to withdraw. They gave and took with an abandon that sent a trail of fire down her middle, a consuming blaze she could scarcely control. Her heartbeat thundered in her ears as sparks danced behind her eyelids.

When he drew back, breathing as heavily as she, Mairi blinked up at him in wonder, realizing that nothing save their mouths had touched. If he could wreak that sort of havoc with only lips and tongue, whatever might he do with the rest of him? She released a heavy sigh and closed her eyes again, just imagining.

"You want me?" he asked. And sounded *serious*.

"Is the sky blue?" she replied wryly, eyes still shut, a silly grin stretching her lips wide. "What do ye think, ye foolish lad?"

He laughed. A strange sound, she thought. Too loud and abrupt, as if he did that rarely and it had caught him unaware.

Mairi rather liked his laughter the more because it was not planned. Because she had surprised it out of him. Surely a man could love a woman who made him laugh, especially if he had little laughter in his life.

She would provide that for him, Mairi decided on the instant. Laughter and children. Both, in abundance. She laughed, as well, delighted by the notion.

He seemed easier to be with now, more comfortable in her presence after their kiss and her bit of teasing.

For what seemed hours, they lay side by side, the fingers of her right hand interlaced with those of his left. Now and again, he would turn his head to look at her—sometimes quizzically, other times with satisfaction—but no words passed between them. She detected a ripple of uncertainty beneath his calm, as though he wished to speak of something, but held back.

What a mystery he was! Why did he not ask questions of her or tell her about himself? Mairi longed to know about the home he planned to offer her and the route they would take to reach his keep in the Midlothian.

She kept waiting for him to say something first, so that she would not seem too forward as she must have done last night. But he appeared content to simply lie there, soaking up the errant rays of sun that stole through the foliage of the leaf-laden branches overhead.

Despite her eagerness to learn more of him, there was much to be said for this silent reflection, Mairi thought to herself. Somehow she felt a kind of peace had sprung up between them so that now they might go on from here to some sort of closer communion. It could only bode well for their marriage, their getting on this well after so short a time.

She felt badly for misjudging him last evening and treating him to that wicked temper of hers. Her worst failing was to judge too quickly. He was not the first to suffer for it, but she would make amends.

Likely he had only been tired and out of sorts from the long journey. And very shy, of course. Mairi was firmly convinced that was his greatest problem. Nothing she could not alter, of course. Anyone would vouch that Mairi MacInness harbored not one shy bone in her body.

In a while he got up, replaced his boots and found her shoes and hose for her. While she donned them, he left her to fetch the basket still lashed to her mare's saddle.

Silently, speaking only with their eyes, they ate, relishing the food and imagining each other's thoughts.

He held out a sliver of cheese. Mairi leaned forward and accepted it, grazing the tips of his finger and thumb with her lips as she did so. The heat in that gray gaze rekindled the fire inside her his kiss had first ignited. She carefully banked it for now. There were the vows to say yet and he mustn't think her wanton.

What a strangely intimate meal it was. Now that they had kissed, MacBain's eyes spoke clearly of what he would rather be doing. Yet he restrained himself, as did she. She chose to believe he did so out of respect for her and applauded that, even as she regretted the rightness of his restraint.

"We should go back," she said slowly, reluctantly, when they had finished the meal.

He nodded and began to help her gather up the cloths and cups and place them in the basket. Then he rose and offered her his hand.

The instant she gained her feet, he drew her into his arms and surrounded her with his strength. Mairi could feel the warmth of his lips brush the crown of her head.

Never had she felt so protected. And wanted, too. She could hear his heartbeat against her ear when she pressed her head comfortably against his chest. Mairi decided she could stay where she was forever and be content.

The sound of distant thunder distracted her. Puzzling. It had not rained for several days and she had seen no clouds anywhere this morn.

Suddenly he tensed, his hands grasping her shoulders as he set her away from him. When she looked up to question him, she saw how watchful he had become, how alert and still, as though expecting danger.

His nostrils flared as if seeking a particular scent. Then he looked down at her. "Do you hear?"

"Only thunder," she replied with a shrug. "Still far away, though. It will not reach us for some time yet, but—"

He placed two fingers over her mouth. "Listen."

Mairi obeyed, tuning her full attention to the rumbling noise. "*Not* thunder!" she whispered in awe, clutching his forearms. The sound did not abate or vary, but was constant and growing louder. "Hoof beats!" she cried, pushing him away, toward their mounts. "A raid! Coom, we must hurry!"

But MacBain rushed ahead of her. He leaped onto his

horse and drew his sword. "Wait here!" he commanded, whirled his mount around and set off at a gallop.

Mairi led her mare over to the same large stone she always used to remount when she came here. In moments, she was right behind him, careful to keep a few lengths distant in the event he would turn and order her back to the glade for safety.

Even some distance away, she heard the shouts and cries and clang of metal. *Swords!*

When she drew closer, Mairi realized this was no neighborly raid to filch a few of her father's cattle. Craigmuir was under serious attack.

Rob charged through the open gates of Craigmuir and found hell itself.

Unable to distinguish friend from foe in the melee, he quickly searched for his own men. Markie was down, a dirk in his chest, eyes staring sightless at the sky. On the steps lay the hefty Elmore in a pool of blood. He did not see Newton. Or Wee Andy.

His fleeting gaze snagged on a dark blue mantle spread like wings upon the ground near the well. *The laird!*

Rob surged toward the attacker towering over his host and slew the raider with one swing of the blade. A small figure darted past the body even as it fell.

"Mairiee!" Rob shouted and swung off his mount. Damn the woman! Had she not heard his order to stay in the wood? Another enemy rushed at him the moment Rob grasped Mairi around the waist. Just in time, he twisted sidewise and thrust his sword up, spitting the oncomer. The opposing blade just missed striking her face.

He roared as he kicked the body off his weapon, furious and frantic to get Mairi to safety. In desperation, he backed against the well wall, trapping her behind him.

"Stay!" he commanded.

Instead she wriggled right past him and ran to her father, who had managed to get to his hands and knees. Rob dispatched another who would have cut him down and then joined her.

Half dragging the laird, he sheltered the two in a corner betwixt the castle wall and the armory and stood guard against any who would do them harm.

He chanced to spy Wee Andy on the parapet wielding his short bow with a vengeance. The stout lad made his next shot, waved Rob's way and pointed to a tangle of bodies around the gate. He raised one hand and rotated his fist, Newton's name sign, given for his expertise with a flail. Then Andy held a palm up and quickly turned it down. *Newton, dead. Damn!*

Rob nodded to show he understood. Of the contingent who had come to Craigmuir with him to fetch his bride, only he and Andy were left. He could not wait to quit this cursed land, to take his bride and go from here.

Had the tournaments taught him nothing? He'd been too long away, that was the problem. Soft, he was becoming. Like the gentle lad he'd once been, harboring that profound reverence for life his father had warned him against revealing to those who might do him ill.

Trouville had encouraged him to travel the Continent with Henri, and thereby caused Rob's absence when the boy king from England had thrust into Scotland two years ago. Now Rob wished he had been there. He sorely lacked experience in this.

Here was no mock battle with rules set by the marshal and a horn to sound the end. Men were dying, three by his own blade thus far! Mairi's death had been a very near thing and his own barely avoided. While he did not fear death, neither did he welcome it just yet.

The time had come to steel himself, to banish again any empathy or sympathy that would mark him as weak. To be the warrior he had trained so diligently to be. To kill and kill again, or else be killed.

Rob pulled in a harsh breath and observed the fighting, searching for identifying characteristics in the combatants. The few men he did recognize from the evening before in Craigmuir's hall looked a sight more refined than the great, hairy, half-naked brutes who fought them. A ragged, unwashed band, these raiders who had come to do battle.

And at the moment, they were prevailing.

Quickly he turned and pulled the wounded laird to his feet. "Go in!" he shouted to Mairi. After a quick glance to insure the armory was empty, he shoved her and her father inside. "Bar the door!"

Satisfied that they would be safer there than anywhere else in this godforsaken place, Rob drew another deep breath, dashed forward and fully engaged in the slaughter.

When the clangs and shouts of the fight finally diminished, Mairi heard a frantic knocking. Hurriedly she peered through a crack between the boards and threw open the door. Young Davy, her father's foundling squire, rushed in.

"Did ye see him, m'laird?" the lad asked as he dropped to his knees on the dirt floor of the armory beside his master. "Afore ye fell, did ye see?"

"So it's over then?" Mairi asked absently, shoving the gangly bairn out of the way.

"Aye!" young Davy answered, his voice full of awe. "The handful left standin' turned and ran just now. Laird MacBain gives chase! God's nails, he's ruthless, that one!"

Then his gaze dropped and focused upon his master's wound. "Ach, sire, 'tis verra bad, this here!"

Mairi motioned him back outside. "Get some of the men. We must move him into the keep. 'Tis too dark in here to treat his wound." Mairi pressed both her hands over the gaping gash in her father's side. "Make haste, Davy!"

Her sire might not live the night, she reckoned, but she would not give him up just yet. "Hold on, Da," she whispered, struggling to imbue her voice with hope.

His wan smile worried her more than a gruff reprimand would have done. One of his huge paws wrapped around her bloody wrist. "Lass, get...get you from Craigmuir, lest Ranald find you here when he comes back."

"Ranald?" Mairi's disgust made her grimace. "Aye, I should have guessed this was his doing," she growled. "Greedy wretch! Th' cowardly bastard didna swing his own sword today, I'll wager ye that!"

"Nay, he'll be elsewhere so he can look innocent of it. But he'll come once he hears I'm dead, daughter. He *is* my tanist, God rot his hide."

Mairi tossed her head in disgust. "We can hold Craigmuir against the likes of him anyday."

"Nay, he'll have my place here, Mairi. The clan decided that years ago," he argued, gasping. "But he'll no' have my lass. I told him so...our kin's too close."

"Greater reason than that not to have him!" Mairi exclaimed. "I'd die first!"

He clenched his eyes shut and grimaced. "Wed MacBain this night, Mairi...and begone afore it's too late."

"Hist!" she said to hush him. She would wed, but she'd not leave. "Ranald sent those men to do murder, Da. He should be punished for it, not rewarded with Craigmuir!"

"May be, but he…he will have it nonetheless," he insisted. "Just marry and go, hinny. Please!" he gasped the word and groaned.

"As ye wish, Da." She'd not leave, of course. She could never desert her father when he lay mortally wounded. Nor would she abandon her home as a boon for that dastardly cousin of hers. But she *would* wed MacBain as soon as someone could fetch the priest. Not only to fulfill her father's wish. She wanted to.

Ranald MacInness would never claim her as his wife if she had to wed the devil himself to prevent it. Fortunately, it would not come to that. She had a perfectly good husband-to-be at hand, thanks to her father's foresight.

When the men—grimy from battle and grieving for those lost to it—had moved the laird into the hall, Mairi made him as comfortable as she could. Someone had brought a pile of blankets and furs from his bed abovestairs and placed them upon one of the long oak trestles used for meals.

It looked to Mairi like a bier, which she realized it soon would be. She had stopped his bleeding at long last, but not quickly enough to save him.

His tunic, the blankets that covered him and her own sleeves were soaked with his blood. Her father was not long for this world, she knew.

"I am with ye, Da," she whispered. "I'm here."

The priest had come and administered rites. He now stood by, praying silently for his old friend and laird. There would be further duty for the Father Ephriam if only her betrothed would get himself within the hall.

Where was MacBain? Mairi wished with all her might that he would arrive in time. Her father would rest so much easier if he could witness the wedding and know that she had at least complied with one part of his behest.

Seeing the marriage accomplished would give him peace in his final hours. There was little more she could do for him, other than grieve for him when he was gone, and then avenge his death.

That, she vowed she would do. It was her duty as well as her heart's wish. Ranald MacInness would die a gruesome death for this day's work. She could envision his dark hair whipping in the wind, that smirk permanently frozen on his face when they mounted his head upon a pike outside the gates of Craigmuir.

A scant hour later, when she had almost given up, MacBain strode in, followed by several of her father's men. No decently groomed lord now, he wore a savage look upon his face and carried himself like the victor he had proved to be. Her father had chosen wisely for her. And for Craigmuir.

When MacBain stopped several feet away and remained silent, Mairi beckoned him closer.

"We must wed *now*," she announced clearly, fearing for some obscure reason that he would object to the haste. He merely looked at her, a question in his sharp gray eyes.

"My father is dying. He desires me safely wed to you without wait. I would have it so."

The baron turned to the priest, who nodded in agreement with her words. From his sleeve, Father Ephriam drew the parchments prepared long before MacBain had arrived, and handed them over to her betrothed.

Within moments they had signed them and the official deed was done. Even without the spoken vows to follow, they were contracted man and wife. All that remained were the words of acceptance and, later, the consummation. She grasped his hand, eager to proceed for her father's sake.

Her sire looked on from the table upon which he lay.

With great effort to suppress her tears, Mairi smiled at him, telling him with her eyes how dear he was to her.

No matter that he had been a gruff old father who reprimanded far more often than he praised. She could see his caring much more clearly now than ever before in the provision he had made for her.

"Lord Robert Alexander MacBain, wilt thou have this woman, Mairi MacInness, to wife?" the priest droned.

"Aye," his lordship answered gruffly, squeezing her small hand gently in his. Mairi noted bloody smears on both and shivered with dread that this presented a bad omen. Nay, she thought, this marriage was a good thing. The blood just spilled would bond them inexorably.

She watched the baron slip a gold crested ring off his smallest finger and slide it onto her third. A circle of fire it was, hot from the heat of battle, wet and slippery with sweat and gore he had shed for her and hers. She made a fist to keep the ring in place. A fist full of vengeful promises that must be honored.

"Lady Mairi MacInness, do you take this man to husband?"

She glanced up at MacBain—called Robert, so she had just learned—and caught a fleeting look of apprehension. Did he fear she would say nay?

"I *will*," she answered emphatically, and added a nod for good measure. Not for anything would she leave a doubt in anyone's mind. This was her choice. She was this man's wife now. As soon as humanly possible, she would make certain no man could alter that.

Strange and fearsome as he was, the man could fight. And he had done all he could to save her and her father during the attack. At the moment, she could think of no better recommendation than that for a husband.

Her new lord might not be a Highland man, but he was

a true Scot. And when the wedding and bedding were done, he would be family. Then he could do naught but marshal her father's men, give them their orders and lead them out to avenge the laird.

Ranald MacInness must die at his hand, and the MacBain must rule Craigmuir. She had decided. And no man—not even her father at his fiercest—had ever been able to sway Mairi MacInness once she had settled upon a true course of action.

The night through, Rob sat beside Mairi near the laird's deathbed. Now and again, she would lean forward and adjust the covers, caress her father's brow or pat his hand. Her strength and control impressed Rob. Not once had she wept for what was to come, though she surely knew.

Only once did she excuse herself to go abovestairs and then only for a short time. Long enough, however. The old laird roused himself and gave Rob orders to take Mairi away at first light.

He spoke haltingly, yet formed each word clearly and precisely. "Ranald wants her…and my place here. No matter what Mairi says, take her and depart."

Rob nodded in understanding and grasped the gnarled hand the laird offered him.

"Leave me to my men," MacInness instructed. "Travel light and swift. And watch your back."

Rob did not ask why. He did not need to. Any man who wanted Lady Mairi would not relinquish her easily. MacInness's tanist would follow. In his place, Rob would certainly do so. The woman was a treasure worth fighting for.

"I beg you, do not rest until my lass has seen her last of the Highlands. Never bring her back here. *Promise* you will honor my…my wishes! *Swear!*"

What alternative did Rob have but to give his word? A

last request was a last request, after all. And the laird was Mairi's father, and now also his, by marriage.

Reaching down, Rob grasped his sword and raised it enough for the old man to see. He bent his head and put his lips against the jeweled pommel, then lifted the weapon higher, as though swearing on the cross formed by hilt, cross-guard and blade. "I so vow," he declared.

Chapter Three

Rob did not tell Mairi of the oath when she returned downstairs and again took up the vigil by her father's side. Morning would be time enough to wrest her from the only home she had ever known, and without a proper departure.

She would have a much sadder farewell to endure before that time came. He sat beside her on the bench while she leaned forward, her elbows resting upon the table where her father lay.

Suddenly, Mairi straightened and jumped as though startled out of sleep.

"What is wrong?" Rob asked her. More to the point, he should have asked her what was *not* wrong?

"Did ye hear? The cock just crowed," she muttered. He almost did not catch the words. "'Tis morn."

Laird MacInness turned his head toward where they sat and smiled his *adieu* at the both of them. "Keep her…safe," he said, and breathed his last as though well content to do so.

Noble till the end, Rob thought, admiring the man for facing death as he had done. Not with whimper or complaint. Only a smile and a demand for the safety of his daughter. Any man could be proud of such a death, and

Rob saw that pride reflected on the faces of the laird's men.

Mairi's delicate fingers trembled as she closed her father's wrinkled eyelids. Exhaustion, pain and grief had leached her features of their usual bloom, and lent her body a stiffness he wished would abate. She would do well to give way to her anguish now and be done with it.

Nay, he thought, chastising himself. She would not be done with it even if she wept for days, months. One did not relinquish a loved one to death so easily as that.

Rob could only imagine the terrible, all-pervading sadness he would feel forever did he lose the man he treasured as a father.

His real sire had been another matter altogether. Had Rob known how at the age of ten, he would have arranged a real celebration at that man's passing, for himself, his lady mother and all the others at Baincroft who had fallen under the harshness of that wicked wretch's hand. Even now, these long years later, he could never bear to call that one his father.

But then the Comte de Trouville had arrived from France to wed the widow. No finer man ever lived, Rob had decided shortly thereafter. He still believed so.

In all things, Rob struggled daily to measure up to the comte's fine example of what a noble knight should be. He called him Father from that time on, and always thought of him as such. Trouville's son, Henri, was Rob's brother in heart. And the comte's death would crush both his sons beyond bearing.

Nay, he could not expect Mairi to banish her grief in a short span of time. Mayhaps not ever, since she and the old laird obviously loved each other well.

In direct opposition to his earlier avowal concerning a show of sympathy, Rob reached out and clasped her upper arms from behind and drew her away from the body of her sire.

Though she resisted, he turned her to face him and pulled her close, surrounding her with his arms. "Weep now," he suggested.

For a moment she fought him, pushing and pounding upon his chest as powerfully as the small space between them allowed. Then, of a sudden, she collapsed against him, her small shoulders heaving as she sobbed.

"Better," he murmured into the fair, silken hair that had come loose of its plait, running his hands along her back, cradling and comforting her as he would a distraught child.

Over her head he shot dark looks at everyone around them until they moved far enough away to afford Mairi some privacy to mourn.

He waited patiently until she grew still again, wept out. Then he again took her by her shoulders and held her gently away so that he could see her tear-ravaged face. So lovely, she was, even in the throes of bereavement.

Rob raised a hand and brushed her cheeks with one finger. "We must go now," he said, hoping his words sounded as gentle as he meant them to.

"Go?" she repeated, her widened eyes searching his for meaning.

"Aye. Now. We go to Baincroft."

She pulled back from him, aghast at his words. "Nay, we *cannot!* What of Father?"

Almost desperately, she backed to the trestle where the body lay. With one hand she reached behind her and grasped the old man's bloody sleeve.

"I promised him," Rob explained, each word clear and firm, brooking no argument, knowing that she would leap upon any further display of tenderness in order to have her way.

He was uncertain whether he could deny her anything in her present state unless he braced himself against her pleas.

"We will go now," he repeated.

She flew at him then, shoving him backward with the flats of her palms. "Go then! Get out! Coward! If ye think that I will let—"

The remainder of her words were lost on him as he caught her arms and secured her wrists with the long slender tail of one flowing sleeve.

It pained him to restrain her, yet this was necessary for her own protection. Mairi would never go willingly, but she must go nonetheless. Above all, he must keep her safe as her father bade him do.

With MacInness dead and Mairi gone, there would likely be no further attacks on this keep or its inhabitants. The tanist had instigated the first invasion. Now he would simply come and assume command as the new laird. Then he would almost surely come for Mairi. What man would not?

Rob would have to kill him then, he decided. Though he'd recently found it pained him to take a life, in this instance he would not mind overmuch.

He grunted when the sharp toe of Mairi's sturdy shoe bruised his shin. She was making this much harder than need be, but he had to admire her mettle.

Fury at him for dragging her away might even set aside her sorrow for a time, he decided, justifying his necessary rudeness. Let her think him craven and heartless if it helped.

She could rant and rave all the way to Baincroft and that would be fine with him. Better so, than to have to watch her weep throughout the journey. Aye, this would serve to get her past the worst few days.

Her shouts and curses when he bent and hefted her onto his shoulder were likely startling the mounts in the stables outside, Rob mused. He could feel the harsh, angry hum of her voice where her wriggling middle made contact with his shoulder, but he was immune to the sounds of it, thank heaven.

He had discovered a few advantages to his deafness over the years. This was definitely one to add to the list.

Mairi ceased her struggles when her husband placed her in the saddle and proceeded to mount behind her. She agonized over the confusion their hasty departure was causing among the people who stood by and watched. There was nothing she could say to them to explain it and not a thing they could do to help her.

Her father's squire watched with tears in his eyes. Poor Davy.

What must he and the rest think of her husband, forcing her to abandon them to Ranald's mercies? And to leave her father to be interred in the family vault without even hearing a Mass said over him?

"Oh, please! Please stay," she begged, to no avail. MacBain simply clicked his tongue, nudged his mount and rode through the gates his man had ordered opened.

Mairi held herself as stiffly as possible, hating the feel of this man's body against her back, his arm surrounding her middle like a yoke of steel.

She raised her hands, still bound by the silken tail of her sleeve and pounded them against his forearm in one final protest. Her only reward was the bruise caused by the links of his chain mail.

Tears gathered and slid down her cheeks like a hot, sluggish waterfall. She held her breath to calm her grief and alarm. Her desire for adventure had flown away in the face of reality.

On a mount laden with their supplies as well as rider, MacBain's man rode ahead of them, leading her saddled mare. He had tied pouches stuffed with food on either side of his saddle. She could see the outline of several loaves of bread. Her mare carried two unfamiliar packs as well as one of her father's, containing what she supposed to be her gowns.

A fold of her red woolen surcoat poked out of the pack's flap like the mocking tongue of an impertinent child.

Mairi leaned sidewise and peered behind them only to see the gates of her home swing shut. Try as she might, she could not stifle a groan of purest misery.

The arm MacBain had locked around her tightened, and he had the audacity to pat her side as though to comfort her. She reached down and pinched his thigh through the heavy hose he wore and had the satisfaction of hearing his sharp intake of breath.

"I will kill ye fer this, MacBain!" she announced.

He rode on, urging his horse to a gallop as they turned sharply off the main road and cut through the forest. Then she had little breath for curses. He bent her forward beneath him to avoid low-hanging branches, all but pressing her face against his mount's sweat-pungent neck. The stiff horsehair abraded her cheek.

Add injury to indignity, why don't ye? she thought with a further burst of fury. The heat of anger dried her tears and lent her purpose.

"Ye'll pay fer this, MacBain! I *will* make ye dreadfully sorry fer this day!"

The wretch did not bother to acknowledge her threat. He rode on south by southeast at a quick and steady pace, forcing her from her duty as a Highlander's daughter toward an uncertain future as a Lowlander's wife.

And to think, she had embraced this fate of her own free will not an hour past! If only she had known MacBain would betray her this way and make her break her vow of vengeance, she would have denied him her hand and wished him to the devil. She would have held Craigmuir against Ranald and mayhaps killed that blackguard herself!

Why did she always act without proper thought aforehand? Her thoughts about MacBain had been in no way proper and just look where they had led her.

Poor Da. At least he had died believing her compliant for once in her life. Welladay, she was through being that!

Later in the day when they came upon a stream, Rob decided they were far enough away from Craigmuir to halt for a while, water the horses and allow Wee Andy a rest.

When accosted on the wall walk by the intruders, the poor fellow had taken a blow to the ribs that left him badly bruised despite his generous padding of fat. Riding in such a state must be painful, indeed, and no just reward for the man's valorous deeds. Rob felt he could stand a short rest himself.

Surely his new wife would not be foolish enough to risk returning to Craigmuir alone, but he meant to keep close watch on her. He knew she had hated leaving her father immediately on his death, and Rob greatly sympathized. However, the old man had the right of it. Mairi must be well away before the laird's successor arrived.

That cousin of hers must have been extremely impatient to have both Craigmuir and the lady to mount such a vicious attack. He would have been laird eventually anyway. Mairi's impending marriage must have led him to the act. Rob had formed an instant dislike of Ranald MacInness when introduced to him, and had not been at all surprised to hear he was behind the deed.

It greatly disturbed Rob to leave Mairi's home and people under such leadership, but there was naught he could do with only one nearly disabled man at his side and the very law of the Highlands against him.

Craigmuir, he could not hold safe from the new laird at present, but the woman, his wife, he would protect until his last breath. He would not risk having her widowed and wed to a kinsman who placed no value on the lives of his future tenants and clan. Later, once Rob had Mairi secured at Baincroft, he could return with more men and set matters to rights for them.

Telling her this would serve no purpose at present, however. She was not ready to hear it. In her need for immediate action against her cousin for his treachery, she would not welcome the necessary delay.

He dismounted and reached up to assist her down. She allowed it, glaring at him balefully as he set her on her feet.

"Untie me, ye fiend!" she ordered, presenting her hands to him.

Rob did so in a perfunctory manner and stepped back, gesturing toward the water. "Drink and wash."

He watched her regard her sleeves—the ends still covered with the dried blood of her father—and saw the effort it took for her to quell a surge of grief. How he would love to hold her again, comfort her, gentle her anger and explain more fully why he had dragged her away so swiftly.

She would not thank him for it, he decided with a shrug and turned away to lead his mount to the edge of the swiftly flowing stream they would shortly need to cross.

"Do you hurt?" he asked as he joined his friend and

lay a hand on his shoulder. Lank blond hair, darkened with sweat, clung to Wee Andy's forehead just beneath his tight-fitting leather helm. His face always looked ruddy, but pain had paled him.

"Nay." Andy shook his head, but the tightened lips and furrowed brow told the truth of it. Rob had tightly bound the injured ribs for him, but he knew that did little to prevent the pain of jostling in the saddle.

He recalled the times he had suffered the same after tourneys himself. Regretfully he made the signs to say they must ride again soon. *They will follow,* he added.

Andy nodded, glanced at Lady Mairi to show he understood why, and knelt carefully at the water's edge to scoop up a drink.

Rob also looked at his wife who was leaning over the bank to dip and scrub fitfully at the sleeves of her gown. Her face and the golden hair around it were wet where she had washed away her tears.

Aye, her anger did serve better to overcome her sorrow than his attentions would, so he would continue to let her be. He turned his regard to satisfying his own thirst and that of his horse.

Suddenly, Andy grabbed his arm and pointed. Rob leaped to his feet, his first thought of attack. Then, following Andy's frantic gesture, he spied the billow of fabric and one small boot kick out of the water.

With a roar, Rob jumped in. The strong icy current dragged unmercifully at his legs as he lunged to grasp a handful of her gown. And missed.

Throwing himself full-length into the stream, he recalled too late the weight of his mail. He sank like a stone, then struggled to the surface and kicked with all his might toward the rapidly moving tangle of skirts and flailing limbs.

At last! He wrapped his fist in the folds of her gown

and dragged her along toward the far edge of the burn.
Undecided whether to curse or pray, he did both.

Crawling out of the water himself was no mean feat,
but he managed and quickly turned to haul his burden
ashore. Flipping her onto her stomach, he lifted her at the
waist, hoping to empty some of the water that must be
filling her.

Thank the Good Lord, he immediately felt the racking
of her cough. Rob collapsed beside her, his head on one
arm, near done in himself. Next to him, she shuddered as
if thoroughly chilled. Though the late summer sun shone
mercifully and warmed the day, the water had been
damned cold.

With a heartfelt sigh of relief that she still lived, he
pulled Mairi into his arms, holding his own breath, carefully feeling the expansion of her ribs to assure himself
that her breathing was returning to normal.

She said something, for he felt the rapid movement of
her lips against his cheek. Whatever it was, he figured it
was just as well he did not understand it. It might possibly
be thanks for his saving her from death by drowning, but
more likely it was curses, blasting him for his bringing her
to this stream in the first place.

In answer to either, Rob simply held her closer and
pressed his lips to her temple. She did not fight him or
squirm away, so he hoped for the best.

He turned his head enough to see how far they had
drifted downstream. Not the leagues it had seemed, apparently. Even from here, he could see Wee Andy cautiously
making his way across to join them. He had their mounts
in tow, water splashing against their withers, threatening
to sweep the sturdy beasts off their feet.

Mairi pushed away from him and sat up, raking her hair
out of her face. Deftly ignoring him, she struggled to stand

and began wringing out the folds of heavy, sodden cloth. Her lips worked rapidly, her teeth gritted together, as if she grumbled to herself. Rob wisely hid his smile.

"Andy comes," he said. "You can change."

"Ah!" she exclaimed, throwing up her hands and shaking them at the sky, her temper more evident than ever. "He speaks! Answer me, MacBain, do ye *ever* utter more than three words in a row?"

"Not very often," he replied in three words just to vex her.

He probably should have rewarded her instead. At last she had said something that he fully understood. Difficult not to, since she flung the words at him one by one, like rocks.

Rob felt satisfied he had gotten the meaning she intended. Sarcasm was not that hard to recognize, since he often employed it himself.

She huffed with frustration, rolled her lovely blue eyes, and went back to wringing out her garments, muttering again.

He smiled to himself, glad she was holding up this well after her fright. If he were honest, he felt a bit shaken himself. However, making more of the accident and coddling her any longer only would have upset her more.

Again she took refuge in her anger, and he did not mind bearing the brunt of it. He began to see a pattern in Mairi's behavior. She would never admit to fear, but masked it immediately.

For now, he thanked providence for her bravado. Better that than for her to suffer hopelessness. That he could not bear to see and would not be able to assuage with words until he knew her better.

Rob tried to not dwell on regrets of any sort, but at the moment he did wish he had more to offer his new wife.

Once he became more accustomed to the way she spoke, he might venture into a prolonged conversation. For now, he had no time for the total attention and tremendous effort that would take on his part as well as hers. Yet he was loathe to try to explain that to her just now. She might decide he did not wish to take the trouble, ever.

He could not blame her for a lack of compassion. It must be very trying for her if she'd never before encountered anyone who lacked hearing.

As Lady of Craigmuir, she must be well used to the people around her minding her every utterance. Well, he would make up for the inconvenience as soon as he got her safely home to Baincroft. For the nonce, he must dwell solely on accomplishing that and allow no distractions.

Wee Andy plodded toward them, looking paler than ever. Rob waited patiently and helped him dismount. "Rest," he ordered, and began plundering through the pack for dry clothes for himself and Mairi.

He pushed aside a red garment and fished deeper for something of more natural color that would better blend with their surroundings.

Still dripping, Mairi stood by and waited until he handed her a grass-green gown. "Go there," he suggested, pointing to a leafy tree that would give her seclusion to change. As for himself, he needed none.

He toed off his soaked boots. Then, without any compunction at all and no thought to modesty, he shucked off his chain-mail shirt and the heavy water-logged gambeson beneath it. Next came his chausses and loincloth. Naked and still shivering a bit, Rob let the sun warm and dry his skin for a while as he tended the weary horses.

Mairi's brush with death had doused her fury and somehow made her see more clearly, past her grief. MacBain had saved her life in more ways than one, she admitted.

If they had stayed, Ranald would have arrived soon. Craigmuir's people would have had no choice but to honor that traitor as their new laird and follow his orders. He would have had MacBain killed. Then would have tried to make her his own wife. She would have died resisting that. While her death might have roused the clan enough to go against Ranald, she would still have been dead.

MacBain told her he had promised to leave, and she knew what and to whom he had given his word. In all truth, it was for the best, his taking her away from Craigmuir. But that did not absolve her from her own vow of vengeance. She would simply have to persuade MacBain to help her honor that.

Mairi peeked through the leaves that now concealed her to see whether he was brooding about her harsh words to him after the rescue.

''God's Holy Mercy!'' she whispered when she saw him. He was naked as the day he was born! Eyes wide with fascination, she watched MacBain as he checked the horses for injury and resettled the packs on their saddles. The man had no shame whatsoever!

Of course, he thought there was none to see him save his manservant who appeared to be sleeping, Mairi reminded herself. But did he not remember that she must come out of the woods soon? Did he *want* her to see him so exposed?

She shivered out of her wet gown and chemise, letting the dry one fall over her from where she had gathered it 'round her neck. Not for a moment would she bare herself to possible view as he was doing.

And yet, she did wonder what MacBain would think if he looked upon her as she now saw him. She was small and had no great attributes to boast about, but would he find her winsome?

She found him so, right enough! Her face flamed at the sight, but she could not tear her gaze away. What muscles he had, she thought, as they flexed in his arms, shoulders, and even his backside. Ah, that backside *was* something to see!

Her hands clenched, imagining the smooth feel of all that sun-kissed skin. The desire to touch him all but overcame her. Would he allow it when they stopped for the night?

A jest that was, she thought with a smirk. He would likely insist upon it! Her trepidation warred with anticipation in a battle that left her breathless and confused.

''Hoo!'' she huffed in surprise as he turned. Her eyes slammed shut, but immediately opened again for a wicked squint through her lashes.

Well made, she noted before forcing herself to face in the opposite direction. *Extremely well made.* Mairi fanned her face with her hand while she held on to a tree branch with the other. Her reaction to MacBain disturbed her more than a little.

Determined to not return to the edge of the stream until he had covered himself decently, Mairi used the time to wring out her wet clothing and remove her boots. The cold water running over her hands and arms did nothing at all to banish the persistent fever stirred by the sight of her husband.

Every few moments she would risk another peek. Finally he donned another loincloth. She watched shamelessly, highly intrigued by the unfamiliar garment.

Highland men wore nothing beneath their plaids. She had briefly caught sight of many a bared bottom and less frequently, one of the men's true pride. Not one she had glimpsed had such cause to boast as did the MacBain.

A small hum of disappointment escaped before she

could stop it when he pulled on his braies. She trudged
out of the woods a few moments later, making much noise
to announce her return. He had finished dressing by the
time she reached him.

"Your man's asleep," she whispered, pointing as she
observed the fellow who accompanied them.

MacBain nodded and prodded the fellow with his foot
until he awoke.

"Time to go," he announced to Mairi. "They follow."

"Ranald's men?" she demanded, casting an anxious
glance across the burn in the direction they'd come. "How
do you know?"

With a shrug, he took her wet clothes from her and
draped them across the back of his saddle. "He wants
you," he replied.

Mairi waited as MacBain slipped the mail hauberk back
on over his shirt and buckled on his sword belt. This time
when he reached for her, he set her upon her own mare
and handed her the reins.

She watched as he gave his man a hand up and noticed
for the first time that their companion seemed to be injured.

He was a short, stout fellow with stringy blond hair and
cheeks round as apples, though they lacked in color. She
quite appreciated his merry smile, especially since she
knew he must not feel much like smiling at the moment.

"What happened to ye?" she asked him. "Hurt in the
battle?"

"Aye. A cudgel to the ribs, my lady," he said, obviously stifling a groan. "Lord Rob wrapped 'em. They pain
me some, but I'll do."

"Verra brave of ye," she commended, pleased that he
was not a complainer. She sought Rob's agreement. "Aye,
m'laird?"

MacBain never answered or looked in her direction. He

simply rode past her and led the way into the woods from whence she'd just emerged. She followed, but not too closely.

"He's busy thinkin', my lady. Hard thinker is our Rob," the man explained as he fell in just behind her. "Thinks damned near as hard as he fights."

"Surely ye have a name," she said, sensing she might have found an ally, or at least someone who would talk to her. "No one has thought to tell me what that might be."

"I am Wee Andy," he replied, grinning when she looked over her shoulder. He went on to explain, "That's to distinguish me from Braw Andy, the miller's son. Now there's a lad with girth! Wait'll you see *him!* Rob's hard put to keep that one fed."

"Ye called yer laird by his forename?" she asked. "He allows this?"

"Nay. He just don't hear it, so I figure he won't mind now and again. No lack o' respect to him. Sometimes I forget. We've known each other since we was bairns at the breast."

"Ah, he's a good laird, then, is he?" she probed, anxious to know more about this enigma she had wed. "A fair one?"

Wee Andy sighed. "Aye, he is that. Fair in his judgment, fair in his dealings, and...muckle fair to look upon, eh, m'lady?" He chuckled wickedly and issued an almost inaudible, *"Hoo!"*

Heat swept over her face and neck. "Fair indeed," she admitted under her breath as she nudged her mare to a trot and left the portly eavesdropper several lengths behind her.

Fair, MacBain might be of face and body, but she was still not certain about the fair dealing Wee Andy had mentioned. Wise or not to do so, and all promises aside, any Highland husband would have insisted on remaining at

Craigmuir and paying Ranald MacInness in kind for his betrayal and greed.

She must believe that wisdom had led MacBain to his decision to leave. He was so different from the other men she had known, Mairi determined to not judge him unfairly.

If any justice existed, Ranald would follow and provide her the chance to exact the vengeance she had sworn. She prayed for that, and for the strength to see it done herself if her husband seemed unwilling to take her part when the time came.

Could she be a good wife to the MacBain if he did refuse to help her? The man prompted feelings in her that she could not sort out no matter how hard she tried.

He had saved her life. That should count for much, she supposed. On the other hand, he had taken her away from her father's deathbed by brute force. She misliked being forced to do anything. She much preferred a man employ simple reason. If he had taken the time to do that, she might have agreed to go quietly.

Nay, she could not ken what drove him to be so kind one moment and to act so heartless the next. But she could be absolutely certain of one thing about her husband: he was not about to explain.

Chapter Four

Rob could not say how he knew for certain they were being followed, but he did know. He could feel it in his bones. If Ranald MacInness did not come himself, he would send others, just as he had hired men to rid him of Mairi's father.

Rob knew that if anyone had deprived *him* of this woman, he would go to the very ends of the earth to retrieve her and would never trust the task to underlings. He hoped Ranald would risk himself. That would save a journey back to the Highlands to get rid of him later.

To pass the time as they traveled, Rob forced himself to think in words instead of images. Though it never came naturally for him to do so, he had made it a regular habit since he had learned to read. Early on he'd discovered that it provided good practice for forming speech, getting words in the proper order so that he would not appear unlearned.

He did that now, making lists of possible ways the eventual attack might occur if they were overtaken. Countering with exact accounts of his probable response to each and every one. In his experience, such preparedness often made a difference in dealing with any problem.

When dwelling upon Mairi, he had to make an even greater effort to prevent his mind's collective vision of her overpowering all his senses at once. He put her into words.

Rob purposely gave name to her delicate fragrance of roses that blended so enticingly with her own sweet scent. Syllable by syllable, he inwardly described her tresses, like honey-colored silk sliding over his fingers. He spelled out the tangible hum of her voice as she spoke when he was touching her, and silently narrated his joy in the act of simply looking at her.

He composed poetry of epic length to celebrate her beauty and her courage, seeing the letters unfold upon an imaginary scroll of parchment as he did so.

Separating and enumerating her charms occupied a large portion of his time, he realized. So much time that he wondered whether it helped or hindered his attempt to reduce the stunning effect she worked upon him.

His dreams of her, of course, he would not be able to control. There she would likely spring to mind in her entirety. Given the way Mairi had reacted to their first kisses, Rob could not pretend he dreaded sleep during which thinking in words was impossible.

All day they had trekked through the Highlands, moving at a steady pace, halting to rest whenever the horses seemed weary. Though they were well away from Craigmuir, Rob did not alter their pace. Her kinsmen's men could not move any more rapidly than this and hope to preserve their mounts.

He cast a brief glance behind him and noticed how proudly Mairi rode. She had her chin raised and her back straight as if she had not ridden the day long through terrain that would daunt the hardiest of travelers.

They had plodded up and down hillsides and through gorges so narrow his shoulders nearly touched each wall

as they passed. And yet Mairi continued to endure without
a protest. Or at least Wee Andy had not seen fit to pass it
on to him if she had. Rob had a feeling she would not
have waited for him to gain the news secondhand if she
meant to issue any complaint.

The small clearing they now passed through would
make as good a camp as any, he supposed. No place would
prove truly safe until they entered the gates of Baincroft,
but they could not hope to ride for four days without decent rest.

It was nearing dark and he admitted he could use a few
hours of sleep himself, having had none the night before.
The laird's deathwatch had not allowed it. His bride must
be ready to fall from the saddle, despite her determination
to show no weakness.

The decision made, Rob reined in and dismounted. "We
sleep here," he announced as he strode back the few
lengths necessary to reach Mairi's mare.

He took the reins from her hands, plucked her from the
saddle and set her on her feet. Her legs promptly buckled.
Rob caught her before she crumpled to the ground. With
a small laugh, he swung her into his arms and carried her
to the nearest tree. It was huge with giant roots that rose
above the ground. One provided a smooth seat for her.

"Make a fire," he ordered Andy, and began dragging
the packs from the horses. He unrolled a woolen blanket
and placed it over a cushion of thick grass. On the other
side of the fire Wee Andy was preparing, he placed another
coverlet.

When he indicated with a gesture that Mairi should lie
down, she frowned, shook her head and spoke. He caught
the words *sleep* and *beside you.*

No test of his reasoning here. She would not sleep with

him. Not surprising, he thought with a shrug. He had not expected her to lie willingly beneath him tonight.

Despite that, he assumed an aggrieved look and heaved a huge sigh of pretended resignation, not wanting Mairi to think he had not desired her. He certainly had…did, however, now was neither the time nor the place to relieve that. He pulled his cloak out of his pack and tossed it several feet away from the blanket meant for her.

He busied himself gathering more firewood, watching surreptitiously as she stood and tested her legs, then disappeared into the trees for a short while. When she returned, she snatched up the blanket and removed it to a place well away from where he had thrown his cloak.

Rob grinned. He would never take pleasure of his bride in such a place as this, but if it gave her peace of mind and a feeling of control to put a greater distance between them, he would allow it. Until she fell asleep.

He turned, saw the observant Andy frowning at him, and winked to assure the man he was not piqued. Wee Andy seemed to be developing protectiveness for the lady. He likely thought her sharp words might anger a new husband, but Rob did not take them amiss at all.

Mairi's ire over her forced departure from her home obviously had not abated. He believed it was that alone that drove her to deny him, not the fact that she abhorred his deafness. He had thought it might distress her, and was relieved it had not seemed to. She had kissed him willingly enough yesterday in that glade. She had wed him, had she not?

However, he wondered now if it might not have been better to have laid the matter bare between them at the outset, before the wedding. That way he would have known exactly what he faced, and so would she.

He misliked guessing what she thought of it. Not once

had she indicated that she cared one way or the other. Had she decided to ignore his lack of hearing altogether, pretend it did not exist? That would certainly not last for long.

Some people roundly feared the affliction and considered him cursed. Because of that, he had grown used to concealing it from all but his friends and family. Once he had learned to speak, that had never proved difficult with chance met acquaintances. They simply never thought to suspect such a thing.

It was a rare enough condition, so he'd been told. When it did occur, most people so stricken were also mute. His ability to speak usually prevented any suspicion of deafness.

A few did know, of course, and he imagined he was the object of some discussion behind his back. But he had never even considered withholding the knowledge from his intended bride or her father.

He had made a point of ordering Thomas to tell the laird before the betrothal contracts were drawn up, assuming that the laird would tell the daughter the problems she might encounter if she accepted the marriage.

Rob knew his deafness would affect their life together more than any other thing. Mairi would not understand that yet, but the realization must come to her one day soon.

He wondered how she would react if some fool accused him of consorting with devils, bartering his sense of sound in exchange for dark, evil powers. That had happened twice before, once with his mother's uncle and then later with Thomas and Jehannie's grandfather, Sir Simon. Even many priests believed it so.

Rob did have powers, of course. He smiled to himself, recalling the looks of awe—and sometimes fright—when he dealt with animals. Wild or tame, they loved him. He could coax them to do nearly anything he wished. Only he knew the secret was in caring about them, in showing no fear and banishing their fear of him. They sensed his respect and it calmed them, made a wild beastie as tractable as the laziest hound.

As he mulled that over, Rob unsaddled the horses and brushed them down with tufts of grass, examining their legs for scratches and their hooves for stones. All three nuzzled him in turn, thanking him for the attention.

His *familiars,* some accused. Strange word, to have such sinister meaning and yet be so descriptive of how he actually felt about most animals. He liked them more than people at times, for they were also hampered when it came to communicating what they truly needed. He made the effort to understand them and they returned the courtesy. It was that simple.

Also, his ability to see at night astounded many who knew him. For Rob, it seemed as natural as seeing in the day. God had given him that ability, he was certain. It proved quite valuable at times, and would later this night when they must rise and travel again with only the meager light of the moon. A gift.

He could sometimes divine exactly what others were thinking. This, however, was no real gift at all. He merely watched people more closely than most bothered to do. Or perhaps sounds distracted them so that they could not.

Expressions, arms closed about the chest, fists clenched, trembles of fear or rage not quite masked by a pretense of calm, shifting eyes. Those gave true thoughts away.

He could spot a liar before he opened his mouth to speak. And a plotting mind stood no chance of concealing itself. There was an air of intensity, of reckoning, so apparent as to be written in ink across the forehead.

Rob straightened from his task and looked at Mairi. She now sat upon the blanket, her elbows resting on her drawn-up knees, one finger absently twirling a strand of hair that had escaped her shining braid at the temple. Such a pensive, faraway look she wore.

Child's play to see inside that mind, Rob thought with a wry twist of his mouth. Mairi was forming a plan of some sort. She either thought to escape him and return to Craigmuir to avenge her sire, or she meant to cajole her new husband into promising he would do the deed for her.

Powerless at the moment, she obviously hadn't quite decided as yet which she would do. And so, he must watch her and keep her from acting on the first option, should she choose that one.

Mayhaps soon he would tell her he had already elected to return and set matters to rights if Ranald did not come after them and seal his fate. Rob smiled. He was not above allowing her to ply her charms first to convince him that he should accede to her wishes. He might have a bit of the devil in him, after all, to consider such a thing.

Andy soon summoned them to partake of the bread, cheese and cold meats he had packed before they left Craigmuir. They sat near the weak blaze and passed a wineskin among them.

If Mairi minded the silent meal, she did not say so. Rob suspected her exhaustion prevented her caring one way or the other.

"Sleep now," he told her when she had finished eating. Obediently, she gave them good-night and retired to her blanket. Rob wrapped himself in his cloak and sat against a nearby tree. Andy moved to the shadows beyond the fire to keep first watch, as was his duty.

Rob had not meant to sleep until he could claim a place close enough to Mairi that he might be awakened should she attempt to leave in the night. However, he awoke with a start several hours later when the pale moon had tracked high overhead.

A sense of impending threat made his skin tingle. He rose quickly and hurried toward the horses.

What is it? Andy signed as he approached from across the clearing, an arrow already nocked in his bow.

Danger, Rob indicated. *Wait here. Keep close watch.*

At Andy's obedient nod, Rob quietly saddled his horse and led him into the trees. He mounted quickly and re-traced their earlier path for nearly an hour. At intervals, he would stop, sniff the air in all directions for wood smoke. When he smelled it finally, he let the scent lead him where it would.

The enemy camp had bedded for the night. Rob counted four sleeping bodies, rolled in blankets around the glowing coals. Another man had been set to guard duty, but had fallen asleep.

Five corresponded with the number of mounts. Rob took the time to lead the horses well away from the camp and tether them near his own.

Could one of these men be the cousin, Ranald? Rob hoped so. Then it would end here.

Unthinkable to slay sleeping men, he decided. And there was the slight chance these were not sent by the new laird of Craigmuir.

"Ho, the camp!" he shouted. "MacBain is here!"

He laughed aloud at their sudden confusion. Two tangled so helplessly in their wraps, they could not gain their feet.

The wakened guard rushed him, sword drawn. Rob dispatched him cleanly and kicked him off the blade. The advantage of surprise worked quite well.

A second man managed a nearly lethal thrust before Rob cut him down. He handily caught the next one with the backswing of his blade. The fourth laggard, mouth open and eyes wide with sheer terror as he looked back, took to the woods on the opposite side of the clearing and disappeared.

Rob trapped the last of the clumsy group still fighting his way out of his blanket. The oaf smelled of strong drink. A sharp rap on the head stopped his struggles.

Ranald MacInness must have combed the Highlands for the worst trained warriors available. Rob imagined his lowliest cotters armed with sticks could have held their own against these dullards.

A pitiful excuse for a fight, Rob thought as he bound his captive. He thought about chasing down the man who had escaped, but decided not to bother. That one was on foot and would require at least two days to make Craigmuir.

Besides, Mairi's cousin needed to receive the message his minion would carry. What the MacBain claimed remained his own, and Mairi belonged to none other. Could Ranald resist such a taunt? Rob thought not. He would come after Mairi himself next time, but now would be at least three or four days behind them.

Satisfied that he had taken care of the problem for the duration of their journey to Baincroft, Rob hauled the bound man toward the horses, threw him aloft and tied him on.

He meant to have answers of this one. Rob would soon know the number and sort of men Mairi's cousin commanded and whether he would pursue her all the way to the Midlothian.

The information he would gain should assist him in eventually deposing the treacherous cousin. He hoped Mairi would feel her father partly avenged by this night's work.

* * *

"It's Lord Rob!" Wee Andy called, waving his arm and hurrying around the fire to where Mairi stood. "You see? I told you he'd be back soon!"

She pulled her blanket closer against the night's chill. "Who is that?" she asked, pointing at the body draped across the shaggy, unfamiliar mount her husband towed into camp.

"Your cousin's man," MacBain answered as he reined up before the fire. He dismounted and stretched, obviously weary.

"He only sent *one?*" she asked in disbelief.

"Five," he said calmly, and turned away to drag his captive off the horse.

"Five? Where are the others? What happened? And how did ye know they—"

"My lady, please," Wee Andy interrupted, stepping between her and MacBain. "There's naught to be worried about. Leave off a moment and let's see what we've got here, eh?"

Mairi blew out a breath of exasperation and desisted, though she could hardly contain herself.

With anxious eyes, she scanned the darkness of the tree line, wondering if at any moment the other four would emerge to wage a fight for their friend.

"Where are they?" she asked Andy. "What happened to them?"

"Dead, I expect," he said gleefully, rubbing his hands together. "Or breaking a new road straight back to where they came from."

"Rest now, Andy," her husband ordered as he returned from where he'd laid his unconscious burden against a tree. To her, he said, "Go to sleep."

"Sleep?" she all but screeched. "Ye ride in here, drag-

ging one of those devils, say there are four more out there
and expect me ta *sleep?*'' Mairi threw up her hands.
''Why, they could ride down on us at any moment! Or are
they truly dead? Five against one and ye'd have me believe
ye slew them all? If not, the least ye can do is tell me—''

He placed his fingertips to her mouth and impatiently
shook his head. ''You are safe.''

She shook off his hand. ''Safe? And that is *all* ye say?
Why do ye never answer me straightly, MacBain? Why
do ye treat me like a stray bairn unworthy of regard? Ye
might as well strike me as ignore me the way ye do. I
despise that! I would know what transpired in the woods
this night and why ye come back with only—''

''I ken *nothing!*'' he said through gritted teeth. ''Nothing you say!''

''Well I *know* that!'' she shouted, leaning toward him,
shaking one fist. ''And do not wonder at it! Ye never listen
to me! It's as if I do not exist for ye half the time, and the
other half—''

''Leave *off,* woman!'' he thundered, drawing up to his
full height, his fists clenched, causing the muscles in his
arms to bunch. The flickering light from the campfire
played over his features, lending them a menacing, other-
worldly glow.

Fear greater than any she felt for Ranald's hirelings skit-
tered up her spine. Here was true danger and all too immediate. He looked fit to strike her down.

Silently, Mairi backed away from him, gripping her
trembling hands together, sorely afraid she had tread too
far. Never before had he exhibited real anger toward her.
But she had seen the effect of his rage at Craigmuir during
that battle with Ranald's men.

Wives held no immunity from the ire of their husbands
and she had certainly courted MacBain's with her loud

demands just now. Righteous, she might be, but she should not have shouted at him.

Neither should she have refused to sleep beside him earlier, but she had not wanted to grant him forgiveness all that quickly for hauling her away from Craigmuir as roughly as he had done. To admit to him how profoundly he affected her would surely have given her husband the upper hand.

Which he certainly had now anyway.

Without another word she quickly retreated to her blanket, lay down upon the grass and turned her back to him. She would not be able to sleep, but she would pretend for all she was worth. Hopefully by morn, his surly mood would have improved. If the other four men Ranald had sent after them did not slay them all before then.

Silence reigned in the clearing behind her, which seemed odd. Why was he not telling Wee Andy what had happened? Or making plans in the event they sustained an attack? Surely he would not ride in that way and simply lie down and fall asleep! But she dared not turn over to see for herself.

Mairi closed her eyes as tightly as she could and prayed she would be alive to open them come the morn.

A pelting rain woke her soon after daybreak. Though the ground beneath her felt relatively dry, the covering above her, supported by a framework of branches, did leak a bit. She brushed the droplets off her hair and face.

How had he managed to build that thing right over her without her waking?

Mairi raised herself to her elbows and peered out into the soggy morning.

Across the clearing, Wee Andy lay beneath a makeshift

tent much like her own. She spied the hindquarters of the gray MacBain rode disappearing into the trees.

"Wait!" she cried, quickly crawling out of her cover and dashing after him. "Dinna leave us! Where is it ye go?"

Before she could get halfway to the tree line, he had disappeared.

"Gone back to bury them what he killed," Wee Andy called, "and see what he can find amongst their packs."

Mairi released a pent-up breath. For a moment she feared he had gone on without them, then realized he was headed in the wrong direction for that.

Besides, he would not have left his man behind. Now *she* was a different matter. After the way she had railed at him last night, she admitted she wouldn't much blame him.

The rain was letting up, but she was already wet. Hopefully, the sun would be out soon to dry her clothes and hair. Bedraggled and aching from her night on the hard ground, Mairi made her way to the packs that lay sheltered by a small shelf of rock.

Wee Andy joined her there, accepting the portion of bread she tore off a loaf and handed to him. "He'll be back afore noon. Said we was to stay put and guard the prisoner." Taking a bite of the bread, Andy nodded toward the unfortunate man still tied to a tree and soaked to the skin. The wretch looked miserable.

"I suppose we are taking him with us?" Mairi asked, slicing off a portion of cheese with her eating knife and offering it.

Andy thanked her with a smile and a bob of his head. "Aye. Rob—Lord Rob, that is—plans to have him questioned. Find out more about your cousin."

"To what end?"

"I did not ask," Andy admitted. "And he seldom announces his reasons. Nonetheless, they are always sound."

Mairi hesitated to talk about her husband with a man who served him, but she had to find out about him somehow. "I do wish he'd answer my questions, if not yer own! He rarely speaks to me and never seems to hear a thing I say."

Wee Andy shot her a worried frown. She realized she should never have criticized her husband's behavior to one of his men. "I do not speak ill of him," she assured. "Truly. I but wonder why he seems so stern. Is he always like that?"

"Stern?" Andy repeated with a gust of laughter. "Aye, I suppose he can be when there's a need for it." His eyes sparkled then. "But Rob loves a good jest. None of us was safe from him as lads and he's not much improved since then."

"Jests?" Mairi asked, unable to imagine the stoic MacBain playing tricks for fun.

"Oh, aye," Andy assured her, warming up to a tale. "Why just last month he smartly humbled one of his knights, Sir Belden—he's a God-cursed temper, that man. Ever one to pick a fight for no good cause."

"Go on," she encouraged. "What did the MacBain do to him?"

"Goaded the man past bearing. Did it exactly the way Sir Belden would do to another. Niggling, smirking, poking fun. Kept at him until he demanded Rob fight him."

Andy chuckled and shook his head. "The man will think twice afore he strikes up another match over some piddling words."

"MacBain defeated him soundly, did he?" she asked, ripping off another chunk of bread.

"You might say that. They was squared off, y'see."

Wee Andy demonstrated, standing with his short legs spread, stretching his arms as if about to draw his blade for attack.

"Go on, finish it!" Mairi encouraged, eager to hear the outcome.

Andy nodded and shifted his stance. "Then Robbie slides that huge sword of his out of its scabbard and holds it gleaming in the sun, evil grin on his face, looking ready to fight to the death." He narrowed his eyes at Mairi, but his lips quivered with barely contained mirth, spoiling the effect.

"Well? What then?" she demanded, leaning forward. "What happened?"

Andy grasped for a make-believe sword, yanked it from an invisible scabbard, then pretended to stare at it wide-eyed and dumbstruck. "No blade!"

He guffawed, wincing as he bent to slap his knee. "Rob secretly had replaced the dolt's weapon. The poor sod held naught but a pommel, grip and cross-guard!" Again he chortled, holding up a hand, thumb and forefinger scant inches apart. "The broken blade were this long!"

Mairi laughed with him, imagining the knight's chagrin. "Sir Belden must ha' been *furious!*"

"He was that! All of us braying about, pointing fingers. The pompous fool will pause awhile afore he makes another challenge over naught."

"Was that wise to make him look a fool? Will he not retaliate someday?"

Wee Andy sobered a little, his laughter reduced to a contented half smile. "Aye, well, Rob thought of that. When the railery was over, he praised Sir Belden for his prowess with a blade. Presented him a finely wrought sword of the best steel to be had. Made him vow he'd never use it in the heat of anger. A hot head, Rob said, like hot steel, cannot hold shape do the task it was meant to do. 'Twas understood Sir Belden would be on the road in a trice did he not agree to keep his temper cool hereafter.''

Mairi shrugged and began repacking the food for travel. So, her husband was wise in the ways of men, she reflected. Pity he was not so enlightened regarding the ways of women.

Then she recalled his sweetness toward her that day in the glade when they had kissed. And his gentle way with her when she grieved for her father. Aye, he could be curt and frustrating, barking his brief orders and ignoring her when she would have him listen.

However, it could be that he had never had much to do with women before. Mayhaps it was up to her to educate him herself as to how he should deal with them. Her, in particular.

If she was to have success in that, she definitely must go about it in a meeker way than she had been treating with him thus far. Well, if not meeker, then certainly with less antagonism and more persuasion.

When he returned, Mairi decided she would take an entirely different direction in dealing with her new husband. She was certain if she set her mind to it, she could promote a better understanding between them. Mayhaps even coax him to treat her vow of vengeance as his own.

If he needed further incentive after a day of her determined pleasantries...well, there was always the night itself for further coaxing.

She cast a glance toward the tent MacBain had constructed to keep her out of the rain. It would serve well enough for privacy if she placed it well away from the camp. Despite her childish denial of his rights last night,

Mairi knew it was past time for the consummation of their marriage.

She smiled a secret smile, supremely confident she could charm him right out of that peculiar loincloth the Lowlanders favored wearing.

Let the rogue see if he could ignore her existence then!

Chapter Five

Rob rolled the bodies of Ranald's men into a nearby ravine, climbed down and covered them with stones. After a cursory prayer for their blighted souls, he searched their supplies and belongings for any proof that might tie them to Mairi's cousin.

Each man's pack contained the same small number and kind of silver coins, indicating they had been hired for some task and received pay for it immediately on setting out. Not conclusive proof that it was the new laird of Craigmuir who had hired them, but enough to Rob's way of thinking.

The coinage looked familiar to him. If Ranald Mac-Inness had paid these men, he must have acquired his wealth the same way Rob had obtained a goodly portion of his, participating in tournaments outside Scotland. And winning, apparently. Strange that they had never met before.

He took the packs containing the men's supplies and collected the ponies that he had left tethered the night before. Rob hoped that he, Mairi and Wee Andy would be able to make the remainder of their journey in safety now.

Even should Ranald follow, he would not know he

needed to do so until the one who had gotten away with his life returned to tell his benefactor about the failure of the attack. Since that man would have to make his way back to Craigmuir afoot, it would be impossible for Ranald's men to catch up to them before they reached Baincroft.

All Rob would need to worry about now was making the journey home as comfortable and pleasant as possible for his new bride.

On the way back to his own camp, he considered his other worry about Mairi. The more he thought about her actions these past two days, the more they troubled him.

In all their time together, she had never attempted to speak so that he could understand her. When she did so, it was mere happenstance. Nor had she made mention of the fact that he could not hear, either to villify him for it or to cast it off as trivial.

The more time that passed, the more times they spoke to each other, the more peculiar that had seemed to him. He could almost believe she knew nothing of it.

Last time, he had told her that he could not ken what she had said to him. Had he not stated that as clearly as any man could do? But even then, if he were honest with himself, he'd had the feeling that she did not take his true meaning. The fact that he felt that at the time was what had begun to stir these doubts in his mind.

Could it be that her father had *not* told Mairi about him? Had the laird lied? For what purpose would he omit telling her something so important?

Possibly she knew, but was loath to speak of it to him for fear he might take offense. If that were so, mayhaps she had spoken with Andy about it.

"Ho! What have we here?" Wee Andy hurried toward him as he entered the camp. "Four more rag-tailed beasties, eh? Go, eat something. I'll tend 'em." He thumped his thick chest with his fist.

Rob tossed him the reins of the scruffy, underfed ponies and wearily slid out of his saddle.

Mairi brought him a wineskin. "Come," she said with a smile and took his hand. She said other things as well—a long string of words—but Rob could not quite make sense of any of them.

He almost told her so again, but thought better of it. Why not observe a while and try to judge what she knew? Then he would ask Andy whether she had spoken of it since they left Craigmuir.

If the old laird had left her uninformed, then Rob decided he must find a way to break the news gently.

So Rob watched her. He loved the animated way she used her graceful hands as she spoke. He liked that Mairi was so artless about her beauty and wondered why. Had the men about her never praised her loveliness? Either they had not or Mairi did not take them seriously when they did. She did not preen or fuss over her appearance as many women did. Her very naturalness intrigued him and had done so from the first. He could watch her for hours.

When she led him over to the blanket she had spread near the fire, he merely followed, hoping to give her the responses she expected until he discerned how much she knew. Rob only hoped to heaven he was in error about the extent of that knowledge.

It was entirely possible that she had as much trouble grasping his words as he did hers. This new thought did nothing whatever to banish his worries. What sort of marriage would they have if neither of them had the faintest notion what the other was saying most of the time?

His mother had taught him that accents made the mouth work very differently, even when the language was the same. Could it truly be that his words sounded so wrongly in her ear that she could not fathom what he said?

"A moment please," he said carefully, holding up one finger, adding a smile to soften his desertion when he got up to leave her. She obviously meant for him to remain there, but he could not. He had to solve this mystery now, if he could.

Wee Andy had led the captured horses and his own mount some ways distant to groom and feed them.

Rob approached him, knowing the horses would hide the movements of their hands as they used the signs. He and his mother had made up a few between them when he was very young, before he had learned enough words to get by.

Since then, Rob, the family and the others at Baincroft had devised enough signals so that words became unnecessary. He missed the silent language when forced by strange company to abandon it. Everyone who knew it found it most convenient, especially in instances where they were not close enough to speak or else did not wish to be overheard. Such as now.

Does she know? Do you think her father told her I cannot hear? Rob asked.

Andy shook his head. His mouth moved with the words as he gestured. *She does not know. I am certain of it. She asked why you do not listen. If she knew…* He shrugged, definitely concerned.

Rob nodded and traced his lips with one finger, considering what he should do next.

This would come as a shock to her now, learning that she was wed to such a one with no prior knowledge of it. She might believe her father had tricked her. Or, worse yet, that Rob had played them both false. She would feel trapped now that the marriage was a done thing.

He raised his head and looked over the back of the pony that stood between him and Mairi, shielding his hands from her view. She stood facing him, her arms folded across her chest, obviously waiting for his return.

Was their marriage a done thing? Nay, he decided, it was not. Not yet. And Mairi certainly should have a choice in whether their union became permanent. She should have a say in her future.

Rob decided his only hope was to prove to Mairi that he was a worthy husband, despite what she would soon learn of him. If he confessed it now, he might lose her forever. She would not take the time to know him. Of course, she might leave him no matter what he did, but he had this one chance to win her respect and he would take it.

Now he must keep their marriage in a state that could be undone if she should wish it so when she found out. That meant not bedding her, of course, but he had not planned to do that anyway until they reached home and he could offer her the proper comforts due an untried maid.

Wee Andy touched his sleeve to get his attention. *Do not tell her now,* he advised. *Wait until we reach Baincroft. She will see how much our people admire you. That they do not care at all.* He snapped his fingers and made a wry face to show how little it mattered. *She will not mind, once she sees that for herself.*

So Wee Andy had reached the same conclusion. Rob felt lower than the bottom of a loch to deceive his own wife. He was not entirely certain he could manage. It would not be easy to maintain the secret, traveling in such close company with her.

You must help me, he told Andy. *Keep close. Answer her queries or repeat them to me. Can you do this?*

"Aye," the man said aloud with an enthusiastic nod. "As I have done before."

Wee Andy was not as efficient in this as were Thomas and a few of the others he and his mother had taught the gestures, but Rob could not afford to be critical at present. Surely the two of them could manage the deceit for the few days necessary to reach Baincroft.

And in addition to everything else, Rob realized he must add a bit of that courting her father had suggested if he was to have any hope of keeping Mairi married to him once she learned the truth and he gave her a choice.

Together he and Andy finished with the horses and walked back to the place where Mairi had spread the meal he had missed at noon.

"This looks fine," he commented with a smile as he dropped to sit cross-legged in front of her and settled down to eat.

When she offered a wedge of cheese, he took it from her. In the doing, he captured her hand and kissed the backs of her fingers, looking into her eyes, letting her see his interest in her as a woman.

She had such an enchanting smile. He returned it full measure, feeling all the while like the sorriest knight in Christendom. But it could not be helped. This seemed the only way to win her.

"Ah, 'twas good," he assured her as he brushed the crumbs from his hands and quickly got to his feet.

Her lips moved in a totally incomprehensible question. He knew it required an answer because of her raised brows and the tilt of her head.

Glancing at Andy who was situated just behind her, he saw his lips exaggerate, "Riding soon?" The fool also added an unnecessary skipping along motion with his fingers.

Rob cleared his throat and pretended to consider while he put together an answer. Then he formed his words with care. "Aye. Make ready."

That seemed to satisfy her, for she began gathering up the remains of their meal and folding the blankets. Andy had already dismantled the makeshift tents and for the next little while, they remained busy preparing to leave.

As he had done the day before, Rob took the lead, the extra mounts behind him preventing Mairi from following closely enough to try to converse.

Occasionally he would look over his shoulder and offer her a smile of encouragement. Andy seemed to occupy her nicely enough, for often he saw a lively exchange between them.

What joy that must be, he mused, to be able to say anything to anyone without thinking so much. Not only did he have to dwell on the proper contortions of the lips and tongue, but also how much breath to push out to make the sound loud enough to be heard and yet not so loud as to make the listener wince.

Daily lessons as a child and his long years of practice had not made the chore much easier than it had been at the beginning. Still, he was grateful he could do it and spent as much time as he could spare trying to perfect the skill.

Rob glanced back at the sun now and then, judging the hours as it steadily dropped lower in the sky. They made infrequent stops to rest the horses and relieve themselves, but he kept the pauses brief. No need to tempt fate, he thought.

When they found an occasion to speak to each other, Wee Andy did remarkably well in mouthing Mairi's words behind her back or else making the signs for them. As a result, Rob had little trouble carrying off the ruse he and Andy had planned. Until night fell.

Rob hurried to make a fire once they'd dismounted. While his night vision proved helpful, it did not extend to reading lips or other features on a near moonless night.

Mairi crouched beside him as he struck flint toward the fluff of tow. The sparks refused to catch. He sensed she spoke at some length now, yet he stood no chance of catching so much as a word of it.

"Move over here," he ordered her, inclining his head to the left. "Block the wind."

She complied, and once again he noted the movement of her head as she chattered on. Rob's gut churned with frustration. Would the woman never cease this talking? Where the hell was Andy?

The blaze flared high, finally igniting the tinder. He fed dead leaves into the burgeoning fire until it wrapped its licking tongues around the sticks he had stacked.

An entirely different sort of fire shot through his veins when he felt Mairi's fingers softly touch his forearm. He faced her, at last able to see clearly the lovely features.

Her brow furrowed and she wore an expectant expression, appearing worried about what he might answer. Not half as worried as he was, however, since he had no reply.

A few feet behind her, Wee Andy waved frantically and made the signs for *sleep* and *tent*.

Rob rose to his feet, fire forgotten, except that flame within his unruly body. How he would love to crawl inside a tent with her, but he doubted there would be much sleeping going on if he did that.

"Sleep there," he said, pointing to a thick patch of new grass.

Again, Andy waved, shaking his head in a near panic.

He pointed to Mairi, to Rob and then clasped his hands together. For the word *together*. Or *married*.

Godamercy! She wanted him to join her? Wanted him to... Nay. Surely she was not suggesting that! And yet, she was smiling up at him with such a come-hither look in her eyes, he could not doubt it. Her fingers touched his sleeve again, a gentle supplication. No mistaking it.

Rob jerked his chin toward the prisoner, who lay barely visible where Andy had secured him to a huge log not far away. Then he inclined his head toward Andy himself, pointing out to her that they were not alone. "Not this night," he said to Mairi, trying to lay his rejection of her to their lack of privacy.

Her stubborn little chin rose, rosy lips pursed and eyes narrowed. Without an argument, she gathered her wounded dignity about her like a fine, protective cloak and brushed past Andy, out of the fire's light.

Andy shrugged and grimaced by way of apology for the belated and sorry attempt at relaying Mairi's meaning. Rob wanted to knock him flat. Instead, he bestowed the rudest gesture he had ever learned and stalked off toward the woods.

He had appeared an absolute idiot before her. A surly, inattentive ingrate of a husband. And a *fool,* by God.

If he had ever in his life required solitude, this was indeed the moment. Rob felt mortified and unable to do a damned thing about it.

Mairi quickly approached Wee Andy when she saw her husband disappear into the darkness.

"What is *he* angry about?" she asked. "Earlier, he seemed well enough pleased." So much so that she had risked proposing that he construct another shelter tonight and then share it with her. She was the one who should be cross. And she was.

"He's not angry, m'lady!" Andy said in a soothing voice. "Weary is all. Happens he's worried, as well." The portly squire cocked his head and regarded her thoughtfully.

Mairi sighed and rubbed her hands over her arms to dispel the chill. "I suppose I shall have to accept that he is simply a man of few words, and most of those gruff."

Andy's wry chuckle surprised her and she looked at him askance. "That seems a jest to ye?" she asked. "Do ye think I speak too much ta suit him and he, too little ta suit me? Is that the way of it?"

The rascal had the gall to snigger. "Aye," he admitted freely. "That you do." He propped one hand on his hip and adopted the very same stance the arrogant cleric who once tutored her had used.

He even went so far as to rock back on his heels and shake a finger in her direction. "See, Lord Robbie is unused to having a woman natter on and on at him about things. With the men, he can just say what's what and that's the end of it."

Mairi rolled her eyes at that. "I have not noticed him dealing any differently wi' women. At least not wi' me."

"Patience, my lady," he said kindly, almost patronizingly. "He's new at marriage. 'Tis not likely he'll change his ways in a mere few days and start rattling on constant like, now is it? In truth, he never talked much anyway. No real need."

With a considering pause and a scratch to his chin, he added, "And, of course, there's the manner of speech. 'Tis difficult to understand."

She stiffened. "Nonsense! He needn't abstain on that

account. I understand him well enough. True, Lowlanders have a peculiar way of saying things, but—"

"*Your* manner of speech," Andy declared, interrupting her. "Unlike myself who's made a few journeys North where I've got kin, our Rob's not had occasion to speak with Highland men—or women—afore."

Astounded, Mairi simply gaped at the man, unable to believe his effrontery.

"Try speaking slowly," he suggested, "and in the Lowland manner, if you can."

She crossed her arms over her chest and jerked her chin up high. "This discussion is finished. I have naught more to say to ye—*you!*"

"As you will," he answered, ticking his tongue against his teeth and shaking his head. "Only trying to help."

Mairi huffed in disgust and immediately set about unloading the packs and unwrapping enough food for the evening.

Damned if she would listen to any further suggestions from that insolent Andy. How dare he criticize her voice. Hard to understand, indeed! She slapped several stale bannocks down on the blanket and began digging for the strips of dried meat.

MacBain had certainly understood her well enough when she invited him to share her bed this night. And he'd had no problem at all in refusing the offer.

Sweetly, she had made it, too. All that praise of his ability to keep her safe? Wasted. Her assurance that she had forgiven him for binding her wrists and hauling her away from her home? Wasted.

Mairi puffed out an angry breath and shook her head vehemently. Never again. From this time forward, if he wanted her to wife—really and truly to wife—he would needs come begging on his great, knobby knees. Even then, she might have none of him. She planned to tell him just that.

And he would understand her, too! Curse it all, she could speak in proper form when she wished to. Without even a vestige of Scots. She would sound as bloody English as the damned King Edward himself. So she would, then, if that's what it took to make him ken what she said. God knew she had plenty to say!

Eagerly she awaited his return, planning a confrontation to end all. Yet, she did not see him come back to camp.

Obviously he had returned, for sometime during the meal she and Andy had shared, her husband had spirited away his horse. She noticed the great beast missing from where the others were tethered before she arranged her blankets for the night.

Restlessly she tossed and turned, trying to will herself to rest. Pulling the cover around her, she took one deep breath after another, finally calming to the point where she no longer squirmed about so.

Wee Andy had slumped to one side, asleep, propped against his saddle and the packs of foodstuffs on the far side of the fire.

The remaining logs burned down to coals as she watched through half-closed eyes. She refused to stir even when she spied the tall shadow approaching from the direction of her feet. If MacBain had changed his mind about sharing blankets at this late hour, he had definitely left it too late.

Determined to pretend sleep no matter what, she closed her eyes completely.

Next she knew there were hands around her throat, thumbs squeezing off her air. His body straddled hers, pinning her completely except for her arms. *'Twas not*

MacBain! She batted him with her fists, frantic to draw breath, unable to make a sound.

Frantic, she clawed at her waist, reaching in vain for the scabbard that held her eating knife. He was in the way. She could not tug it loose!

She could not die! Not here! Not like this!

Lights flashed and swirled behind her eyes. Her lungs burned with need. Mairi knew she had only a moment left. With one last effort, she balled her fists and slammed them hard upon his ears. He grunted, his grip slackening slightly, enough for her to draw one breath.

She struggled to gouge his eyes, but he held his head out of her reach now, his arms straight, hard hands tightening again. Still she fought, scratching at his wrists, trying to twist from under him.

The instant she surrendered to the hopelessness of it all, he seemed to fly off of her. The hands left her neck so swiftly, her natural intake of breath surprised her. She couldn't move.

Sounds of flesh striking flesh and a horrid, menacing growl mixed with high, keening cries for mercy. The overwhelming aftermath of terror held her more immobile than the attacker had done. Mairi simply could not make herself move.

She heard Wee Andy shouting, heard the horses' frightened whinnies, heard the ongoing snarls, whines and pleas of a one-sided fight.

None of it stirred her to investigate. All her efforts Mairi expended on filling lungs starved for air.

How it hurt to breathe, yet she endured it so gladly it brought tears to her eyes. She wanted to whisper thanks, shout her gladness to be alive, but no sound would come from her damaged throat. Not even the whimper escaped. She shivered, clenching her eyes shut in profound relief.

They flew open when huge arms grasped her again. Frantic with renewed terror, she fought until the deep, unchanging voice broke through her defense with constant, soothing nonsensical words.

As soon as she ceased her struggling, MacBain enfolded her, surrounded her with his body and brushed a gentle hand over her hair.

Moments later he rose, lifted her up and carried her closer to the fire. Wee Andy quickly added wood to it, making it blaze again, and squatted there, watching her with concern. MacBain crouched down and then sat, holding her on his lap.

"Turn away," he ordered. Mairi saw he meant the edict for Wee Andy instead of her when his man swiftly whirled around and gave them his back.

MacBain's reassuring caresses immediately changed into an exploration of her limbs. His long sensitive fingers felt the joint of her shoulder and quickly traced down the length of first one arm, then up the other.

He pressed lightly, then more firmly against her ribs, watching her face closely as he did so. His touch warmed her, but she shivered all the same. She tried to push his hand away when it slid under her skirts and up beyond her knees.

Though this action embarrassed Mairi, she suddenly realized what sort of damage he searched for then, so she held still for it. At the moment she was in no condition to tell him she had not suffered what he thought might have happened.

Tenderly he brushed his palm up the length of her inner thigh, his intimate touch light, caring and brief. With a grunt of obvious relief, he slowly removed his hand and held her against him, rocking slowly to and fro as a mother would a fretful bairn.

Overcome, Mairi began weeping in earnest. She shook
with it, sniffled and burrowed her face into the fine wool
of his tunic, clutched fists full of the fabric, uncaring of
the discomfort of his metal mail shirt beneath it.

Here was safety. Here was her protector who had saved
her from certain death yet again. She wanted to crawl inside him and stay there forever.

For some time he held her so, stroking his hand softly
over her arms, her hair, her back and offering his warmth
to fight off the horrid chill of her fear. Mairi had no memory of anyone ever sheltering and comforting her in such
a way.

Eventually her tears stopped and she moved her head to
look up at him.

"Do you hurt?" he asked so softly she hardly heard
him. His gaze burned into her, the heat of it intensified by
the reflection of the firelight. "Where?"

She haltingly raised a trembling hand to her throat and
shuddered at the memory of the grip that almost killed her.

He shifted closer to the fire and moved her far enough
away from him so that he could examine her neck. Frowning, he touched the skin there and then shook his head, his
eyes filled with regret.

"Can you speak?" he asked, again with almost no
sound at all, as if he thought the loudness of his voice
might frighten her more.

She shook her head and mouthed the words, "Nay. It
pains me."

He leaned toward her until his forehead touched hers.
His hand rested on the back of her neck, a gentle weight.
Then he raised his lips and tenderly kissed her brow.

The gesture brought to mind the way her father had
treated her whenever she'd suffered a childhood hurt. Not
like this. Gruffer than this man, Da had tweaked her nose,

kissed her on the head and told her to brave it out, that she would survive. Somehow Da's lesson must have stuck, for Mairi had the urge to assure MacBain that she was no wilting flower. No matter that she must look like one at the moment.

She forced herself to sit up and smile at him. "I am fine," she croaked, immediately winced, and spoiled the effect of whatever bravery she'd summoned up.

His brows drew together and he held a finger to her mouth. "Be quiet!"

Mairi nodded, holding on to her smile with determination. MacBain did care for her, she decided. He must.

She glanced around them, searching for the remains of the stinking churl who had assaulted her. No doubt her husband had dispatched him, whoever it was.

"Our captive." MacBain pointed toward the place where they had tied up the prisoner he had brought in.

So the man had worked himself free. But if that were so, why had he not run when he wriggled out of his bonds? Why had he stayed and tried to strangle her in her sleep? She did not even know him.

Unable to ask the questions, Mairi merely nodded and let her shoulders slump with fatigue.

What did it matter now? MacBain could not answer for the man and had probably killed him so that he could not speak for himself. Unlikely they would ever know why he had done what he had.

"Come lie down," he suggested, and settled her gently on the grass beside him. He stretched out behind her and pulled her against him with one strong arm. "Sleep now," he whispered. "I am here."

And so he was, she thought with a contented sigh. She felt safe now and soothed enough to close her eyes and welcome slumber.

However, a wee prickle of anger remained at his earlier refusal to sleep beside her tonight. Had he been where he should have been, no man would have dared approach her. Mairi wondered whether MacBain's guilt over that fact might be prompting all of this tenderness he offered her now.

Whatever his reasons or his faults, she would be forever grateful that he had come back in time to save her. Holding a grudge would serve no purpose, so she must let go the resentment over his denying her offer. MacBain had obviously seen the error of his ways and was now more than willing to sleep beside her.

Mairi snuggled closer, reassured by the warm, hard strength of the body lying full-length against her back. Judging by the state of that portion of him just behind her hips, she knew her husband had not refused her earlier for lack of desire.

She had made it clear that she wanted him and he quite obviously wanted her. Then why had he declined? He could have arranged for them to be alone if he had wished to, so that was not the problem.

There was no question of his ability, Mairi thought as she wriggled backward just a bit to further test her assumption.

Oh, aye. He was definitely able.

For now, however, she would do as he advised and rest. She had no right to ask more of him this night than he had already given her. Ready though he might be for it, she was too overset to attempt seduction or follow through.

Winning him to her cause could wait awhile.

Chapter Six

Mairi awakened alone later in the night. Memory of the recent attack swept over her like a repeated assault. Moving only her eyes, she located the lump against the tree where the prisoner had been tied before. So he was not yet dead. No doubt he would be unable to escape again, she thought, recalling the beating she had heard take place.

Redirecting her gaze, she saw her husband and Wee Andy crouching together on the far side of the low, flickering fire. Andy was gesturing wildly, his mouth working furiously with no sound coming out.

For a brief moment Mairi thought she had lost her hearing as well as her power of speech. But nay, there was the soft pop and crackle of the wood as it burned. Some night creature howled in the distance.

There came a scratching noise then, when MacBain drew something in the dirt with a stick. Both looked down and Andy nodded at whatever was there. Must be a map or the like, she decided.

'Twas kind of them to go to such lengths to not wake her, Mairi thought. Intrigued, she watched to see what would happen next in their silent colloquy.

Her husband propped his elbows on his knees and made

swift and unfamiliar movements of some sort with his hands and fingers. They were gracefully done gestures, for he did possess wonderful hands. She sighed softly at the recent memory of how easily they had soothed her and made her feel treasured.

Wee Andy shrugged then, waggled his head side to side and then gave answer in the same manner. Were these signals such as hunters used when silently stalking game? Or mayhaps those warriors employed when they wished to retain the element of surprise against an enemy?

She smiled to herself, wondering what other things there might be about men that women were never privy to.

Wee Andy drew a forefinger across his neck and pointed toward the man who had attacked her. Well, that was hardly a subtle question, Mairi thought. Would they slit his throat? she wondered.

MacBain shook his head, his expression regretful. He offered more of the mysterious language of the hunters. Or warriors. She watched, thoroughly fascinated, as their silent dialogue continued for some time.

Finally, MacBain rose to his feet and walked a few feet away, his back turned to his man. Andy called his name, then huffed with exasperation and got up himself.

Impatiently, it seemed to her, he stalked over and tugged on the back of her husband's sleeve.

Turning with a question in his eyes, MacBain watched Andy's hands and then responded. Clearly he had not heard the man speak to him. True, it was not a loud entreaty, yet in the quiet night, the word sounded clear enough from where she lay.

Had he been distracted by some other thing, she might credit that MacBain would ignore it, but he was idly surveying the darkness of the woods around them when Andy had spoken. Mairi felt a flutter of unease in her chest.

Memories of incidents that had occurred since the hour MacBain had arrived at Craigmuir pinched at her mind with insistent, wicked fingers.

She recalled her father exaggerating words, speaking too loudly. MacBain ignoring her. Had she spoken to his back as Wee Andy had just now?

Those damned three-word commands and answers she hated so fiercely ran through her head. Almost all of them spoken in that deliberate way, in that deep and unchanging voice.

A possible explanation for all of it hit her with the force of a sword's blow. Her breath rushed out of her.

Hot tears sprang to her eyes and she had to cover her mouth to stifle a sob. Oh, God in Heaven, he could not hear her. He could not hear anything at all.

For a time Mairi wept silently out of grief for his loss, out of fear for his safety in a dangerous world, and out of sheer disappointment that they would never be able to speak freely together. Her heart hurt for his sake and, aye, for her own.

A powerful wave of protectiveness engulfed her. Her husband would *need* her. How glad she was that, quite by chance, he had chosen her to wife and not some featherwit who might not recognize that need.

Soon, however, she began to wonder why no one had seen fit to tell her of this. Her father…had he not said something? Aye, he *had,* though Mairi had believed he spoke of his own poor hearing at the time. She clenched her eyes shut, marveling at her own lack of wits.

God's own truth, MacBain himself had told her just last night. *I ken nothing,* he had said. And she had accused him of not listening. Damn her cruelty, even though she had not meant to be unkind.

She groaned with self-disgust. It hurt her throat, but she

felt she deserved far more than that small scratch of pain. Mairi felt terrible. By all rights, he should hate her for the cruel things she had said. One consolation in that, however. At least he had not heard those awful words.

God's mercy! What was she thinking? *Consolation?* Again she groaned. The self-inflicted pain did not assuage her guilt one whit.

What could she say to him to atone for her behavior since they had met? Nothing. Wee Andy had told her quite plainly that the man could not understand her. He had lied about the reason. Or had he lied?

Thinking back, she knew that Rob had kenned what she said at times. Her manner of speech might well be the problem.

Her accent, Mairi remembered, recalling her earlier vow to mend her speech only to chastise him roundly for rejecting her advances. She would make up for those horrible thoughts of hers, she promised herself. Here on out, she must speak as a Lowlander. And slowly, too. And not so often.

Rob must have learned to see the words upon a person's mouth since he clearly grasped some of them. Not all of hers, but a few.

Mairi realized she was only now beginning to think of him by his familiar name. Her *Rob,* a dear name. *Robert* seemed too formal and *Robbie* too childlike for such a man.

She had never thought of him as Rob before, even when Wee Andy called him so. Had sympathy brought that on? Pity? Ah, nay, she must not curry either, for he would not favor that at all. No man would, even should she burst with the feelings. Any pity in her heart, she must conceal at all costs. Rob had a great deal of pride.

And she had great pride in him, Mairi thought with surprise. For a boy to reach manhood—and especially knighthood—bearing such a cross, he must be extraordinary indeed.

First thing come morn, she would assure him she stood with him in his plight and would do all within her power as a wife to...to what?

Mairi pressed her fingertips hard against her temples, trying to think more clearly.

This first reaction of hers might not play out that well over the years. At the moment she did admire him greatly for his accomplishments. That, mixed with her intense desire for him, might well have altered her good sense. She also felt tremendous gratitude for his saving her life. 'Twas all too easy to forgive him anything, considering all of that.

Just because he could not hear did not make him a saint. The fact that he had deceived her ought to be figured into her feelings, surely.

Despite what he had told her in a fit of exasperation last night, Mairi did not believe Rob truly wanted her to know he could not hear. Why else would he have troubled himself so much to reply to her as if he could understand when he usually did not? More puzzling than that, why had Wee Andy not stated the truth of it when she'd asked him about her husband?

Aye, they meant to pretend with her. Dishonesty was no way to begin a life together. However, Mairi admitted that if she had been told, not knowing of Rob's gentleness, loyalty and courage as she did now, she almost certainly would have refused the marriage.

She was not quite certain what she would have done if they had been granted time to know each other well beforehand.

What a quandary! How could she hope to deal with him now that she knew his secret and he was as yet unaware of her knowledge? They could hardly discuss it together, that being the case.

Unfortunately, he chose that particular moment to return to her side and lie down. He pulled the blankets over them and slid his arm around her waist to draw her close again.

Mairi held very still, feigning sleep, unwilling to face the problem directly before she'd had time to think it through. This assuredly required more thought than any other issue she'd ever had to deal with.

His face softly nuzzled the back of her neck and she felt his lips barely touch her there. A wild tingle of pleasure swept through her body. Not that unexpected, but not what she would have wished to happen at this moment. Desire clouded the mind and hers grew thick with it.

Mairi sighed and waited for a further caress that might lead to more intimate doings, but it never came. She knew very well it did not, because she lay awake until the dawn crept over the clearing and it was time to rise.

Her throat hurt too dreadfully to sleep, even had her mind been quiet and her body at its ease. She spent the time trying to determine what she must do about this. *If,* indeed, she was correct in all of these assumptions about him.

After long hours of mulling over all of the time they had spent together and everything that had been done and said, she was no longer as certain as she had been last night that she was right. What if her imagination had only concocted this as an excuse for the way he had behaved with her?

If her guess was accurate, Mairi had decided that she must allow Rob his pretense as long as he wished to maintain it. To admit she had recognized this flaw would make it seem as if it were apparent to everyone.

On the other hand, if she happened to be completely

wrong and he could hear perfectly well, she could only imagine what his reaction might be.

Best she say nothing about it at all, to wait and see what would follow.

"Time to wake," Rob said, shaking Mairi's shoulder gently. Without waiting for her to stir, he got up and headed for the trees.

He needed to gather his wits before dealing with her pain. She would also want explanations of how he had allowed that to happen and what he planned to do next.

Mairi had the right to know why that man had attempted to murder her. But even were he the greatest orator in Christendom, he could not question that brute this morn. If he went near him, Rob knew he would kill him.

Once they reached Baincroft, he would find out what he could when Thomas interrogated the man for him. How could he explain all of that without revealing the real reason why he could not do this himself?

When he returned to the camp, Mairi still lay upon the blanket. "Do you hurt?" he asked, concerned when he saw her still abed. She usually leaped up immediately and began preparing to travel.

He watched her fingers creep tentatively to her throat. There were tears in her eyes. The urge to kill the lout who had choked her welled up anew.

Crouching beside her, he cradled her cheek in one hand and tilted her head back. Her neck bore the bruised imprint of the attack. Robert sighed with regret and sympathy.

He called out to Andy. "Heat water." He had a few herbs in his pack. A poultice would help the swelling and a tisane, the pain she must feel.

Mairi sat up and pointed to her mouth, shaking her head.

Then she held one palm flat and made a marking gesture on it as though writing. Her brows rose in question.

Rob nodded and quickly went to his pack to withdraw foolscap and thin length of charcoal vine, tools he always carried with him since he had learned his letters as a child. In emergencies, he used them to make clear what his words could not.

Not for some time had he needed them, but he thanked heaven he had them now. Anything to ease Mairi's plight, he thought as he returned and offered her the implements. How well he knew the annoyance of having a thing to say and no way to say it.

Must we go on today? she wrote, imploring him with her eyes to allow her more rest.

Rob took the foolscap from her and brushed off the words until it was blank again. He scratched the words hastily. *By noon. Your cousin follows.*

Mairi nodded her understanding, still staring at his hasty answer. Without thought, he had written his reply instead of simply speaking to her. Where was his mind? Quickly he said, "We must go."

Again she bobbed her head and then lowered it so that he could not see her eyes. He left the writing materials by her side for later use and went to select the herbs to help her heal.

When midday arrived, she seemed to have improved. Rob rewarded her with a sympathetic smile and refused to allow her to stir until they were ready to travel.

Fortunately the day proved mild and the terrain began to level somewhat. They were leaving the Highlands behind for the gently rolling hills and dales of the Midlands.

By alternating their own mounts with those gleaned from the brigands, they made better time than Rob had expected.

Wee Andy rode up beside him. "We could reach Trouville's late the morrow's eve."

"Nay," Rob said. "On to Baincroft."

"But…"

"Home. You know why."

"I could ride ahead," Andy offered, casting a quick sly glance behind them where Mairi rode. "Tell them what to expect."

Rob considered it. Mairi must be miserable. The attack had caused her pain, upset her terribly. And her inability to eat solid food would be making her weak.

She needed a soft bed and good care. The hours more that it would take them to arrive home if they bypassed his parents' estate would surely add unnecessary discomfort.

How selfish for him to worry about his ability to deceive her when he could so easily alleviate the physical suffering she endured.

Wouldn't his parents be surprised that he had finally found a wife? How worried over him they had been when Jehannie had cried off. Now he could present them with a daughter they could surely love. He wanted them to meet Mairi and her to meet them. The more delay in that, the more his mother would be hurt by it.

He would stop for a short visit, he decided. But they must be informed of what he planned and sworn to secrecy.

"Aye, then," he said. "Noon tomorrow. Ride hard. Make certain…" He shot a meaningful look at Andy to complete the thought.

"I will see to it."

With that, Andy dropped back to ride beside Mairi and keep her company. Moments later, Rob turned in the saddle and witnessed her smile. Andy must be telling her of the comforts she soon would enjoy.

He only hoped his family would help him in this. They did not know that Thomas had arranged a marriage for him. Since his mother had so favored Jehannie as a wife for him and had been so disappointed, Rob had made the decision to not tell anyone until the deed was done. In truth, he admitted now he had feared it would not come to pass once he met the MacInness.

They would welcome Mairi because they were kind, they loved him well and wished him to be happy. Whether they would uphold his decision to withhold the truth from her, even for a day or so, was another matter altogether.

Father might, but he would certainly not agree with it privately, having been the object of just such a conspiracy for months after he had married Mother. She had been afraid her new husband would not tolerate the imperfection in a stepson and would send him away, steal his lands. He laughed now at how sorely they had misjudged Trouville. Nay, his father would not like this deception, but he would comply with Rob's wish.

Rob could only pray that his sister, Alys, was attending to business elsewhere whilst they were there.

Ah, well, he must prepare for the worst and hope for the best. Mairi had to learn the truth sooner or later. He only hoped it could be later, after she saw that he could measure up to other lords, despite the cursed deafness.

The thought shook him more than was comfortable. Never before had he truly damned his affliction. Always, he had been determined to see the good of it. The blessings of his other gifts, for one thing. The humility forced upon him at an early age, making him better prepared for knighthood than many another man. His natural compassion for faults in others. His other, keener senses. Gifts he should appreciate.

Even when Jehannie had spurned him, her grandfather citing the reason of Rob's deafness, he'd secretly felt immense relief that all but canceled the blow to his pride. Not a thing he had admitted to himself until this very moment. He had used her betrayal to avoid closeness with anyone since it happened. He'd found it so damned hard to be close, to share his heart.

Rob shook his head, amazed at the strange dark turns his mind was taking. Jehannie might have damaged his belief in himself for a while, but she had never made him curse his fate outright as he did now.

Mairi did, for he cursed it roundly at the moment, and wished to God that he could hear. More than anything he wanted the sound of her voice, to revel in it when he took her to bed, to wake to it each morning. To return her ready words with the ease most men took for granted in speaking with their women. *Their wives.*

Rob raised his head and glared heavenward, knowing his face bore defiance and accusation. Through gritted teeth he voiced the question he had always denied was there, the one that had burned quietly in his soul since he had reached the age of reason.

"Why me?"

This day added a new depth to Mairi's understanding of her taciturn husband. They stopped often because he obviously worried that the attack last night had sapped her strength. In truth, it had, but Mairi appreciated the frequent respites doubly, for they gave her the opportunity to converse with him at last.

Each time they dismounted, she brought forth the foolscap and charcoal and scratched out whatever came to mind. Then she would hand it to him and wait expectantly.

At first, he simply held the implements to one side and answered her with a word or two. When she continued to offer and pointed to the writing surface, however, he eventually shrugged and wrote out his replies.

His furrowed brow and worried look warned her that he fully expected her to remark on how much easier he seemed to find writing than speaking. Mairi never did that, of course. Two could play this game.

Likely he thought her a bit simpleminded because she seemed to not notice, but she did not care. Most men thought women were lackwits anyway. He would soon discover the truth about that as far as she was concerned, but first, she meant to find out everything she could about him. This seemed the most expedient way to do it.

He waxed rather eloquent about his family. In his descriptions, she could almost see the distinguished Trouville, his beloved stepfather, and his wise and beautiful mother, the Lady Anne. Trouville's son, Henri, had returned to his native France and Rob obviously missed his presence sorely. The sister Alys had not yet wed and he expressed concern over that.

What a proud son and brother he was. Mairi clapped her hands together and beamed at him when he told her they would visit his parents on the morrow. She already knew, of course, because Andy had told her. Rob smiled as if pleased by her reaction. But she did see that a small vestige of his worry remained.

She knew why. He feared his family might reveal his secret to her. Indeed, it could very well prove difficult for her to avoid "finding him out," but she intended to sidestep being informed of it if she possibly could. She wanted Rob to trust her enough to tell her himself.

His ready acceptance of her demand that he write his
responses to her seemed to bear out her suspicion that Rob
was indeed deaf. He certainly wrote much more volubly
than he had ever spoken. Mairi was convinced she was
right about him.

When they stopped for the night, Wee Andy went out
collecting deadwood for the fire. Rob had set about tending
the horses, tethered some distance away from the camp to
avoid the inevitable odors that accompanied their presence.

Mairi unpacked enough food for their meal. She finished
her customary chore long before the men did theirs, and
sat on her blanket to wait.

Their prisoner drew her attention. He'd been tied to a
tree, as usual, where he lay quiet save for an occasional
groan. No one had questioned him yet as to why he
thought to kill her. Mairi had already figured out that Rob
would wait until they reached Baincroft so that someone
else could make a proper job of it, but she wanted to know
now.

A quick glance across the clearing assured her that Rob
had his back turned and was busy digging a stone from
one of the horses's hooves. Andy was still in the woods.

Casually she got up and approached the man who had
threatened her life. She drew close enough to speak, yet
carefully kept a goodly space of ground between them.

He looked a fright with most of his teeth missing, lip
split and crusted with blood, one eye almost swollen shut.
Andy had trussed him up with wrists bound behind him to
his ankles so that he lay on his side, nearly unable to move.

"What's yer name?" she demanded, fondling the eating
knife that hung from a small scabbard attached to her belt.

While Mairi knew little of wielding the other weapons
men used, her father had instructed her well in how to ply
a blade for her own protection. She had never found oc-

casion to threaten anyone with it, but felt justified in doing
so now.

"I would know what ye're called ere I…take my pleasure," she informed him, injecting evil intent into her
voice. Scaring him witless seemed fair enough since he
had done more than that to her.

He turned his head—the only part of him he could manage to shift—and looked up at her, fear in his red-rimmed,
piglike eyes. "Nort. Geb Nort," he gasped. "Mercy, lady,
'twas no' my notion ye should die, I swear it!"

Mairi rolled her eyes and smirked. "Aye, well, 'tis mine
that ye should! Slowly and painfully," she added, drawing
out the words with an anticipatory gleam in her eye.

She slipped her knife out of the case and casually played
with it, testing the point with a fingertip. "I might be per-
suaded to make it quick, if ye give me a truth. Only once
will I ask, and no more," she warned. "Who or what
would tempt ye to risk a recapturing? Ye could have run."
She inclined her head toward her husband. "They'd likely
never have caught ye, had ye done so."

He swallowed hard and shot her a pleading look. "Lady,
promise me ye'll no' drag oot yer revenge? Gi' me a swift
death?"

A glance at Rob assured her he'd still not finished with
the horses and was not looking her way. She returned her
attention back to the oaf called Nort. "I vow I'll not make
ye suffer if ye tell all. Who is it wants me dead and why?"

"Ranald MacInness," he answered readily. "He offers
fifty marks to the man who brings him yer hand. One way
or t'other, he vows he means ta have it, lady."

"My *hand?*" she asked with a cough of disbelief. Had
the fool misunderstood Ranald? Surely her cousin had
meant for him to bring her back to Craigmuir so that he

could have her hand in marriage, not that he actually wanted her hand!

"Alive or dead, lady," Nort declared softly. "That's th' way of it. He made it plain he would pay either way, no matter to him. Fifty marks reward." Then he set about pleading his case, stuttering the reasons why he needed the coin badly enough to do murder.

Mairi ignored his words as she sheathed her blade and strolled idly back to the fire.

"Wait!" he cried. "Lady, ye promised me. Ye said quick like! Ye canna let them at me later…"

"Aye, I can," she answered over her shoulder. "I keep my word. I'll no' be the one to cause yer suffering. I expect *he* will," Mairi said, nodding toward her husband, who was still busy, oblivious to her brief conversation with Geb Nort.

The sound of the man's keening did not move her in any way. He should have run when he had the chance. Let him stew in his fear for the time he had left.

She would suggest to Rob that he give the man a speedy end, for she truly abhorred torture even when it was deserved. Her husband might or might not grant that, but in the end, Nort's manner of death would not be her decision to make.

The fact that Ranald wanted her dead did not surprise her all that much when she thought about it. As long as she lived, the people of Craigmuir would be slow to accept his authority, knowing he had ordered her father slain. They would be expecting her to return with a force and avenge her sire. It was the way things were done.

Yet if she were widowed and then wed to Ranald and under his power, they would be forced to kneel to him. And if she were dead, they would have no hope that she would come back and remove him from their lives. She could understand his logic.

Mairi wished that Ranald had shown what sort of man he was years ago before the clan had chosen him as her father's successor. Instead, he had gone off to foster with his mother's sire until he earned his knighthood. Then, apparently, he had traveled for a while. Two years past, he had returned, demanding that her own father place him in a position of responsibility that would prepare him to be laird. At the time, it had seemed a reasonable thing to do, so he'd been given care of one of the smaller keeps. Only later did they realize how ruthless and power hungry their cousin had become.

Mairi always avoided him, closeting herself in her chamber each time he had come to visit Craigmuir, not showing herself unless her father was near for her protection. Ranald had never disguised his intent to have her to wife and certainly had not been above forcing the issue if he found the chance.

Despite that, no one had dreamed he would dare sponsor an outright attack to remove the laird. Now she felt even more obligated to avenge her father's death and to free Craigmuir's people of her cousin's merciless rule.

Somehow she must persuade Rob to help her accomplish this. If she failed, her entire clan would suffer for it. And she would never be safe as long as Ranald lived.

Mairi saw Rob leave the place where the mounts were tethered and stride across the small meadow to join her. He wore a smile of anticipation as he approached.

His entire demeanor had changed since they had begun exchanging the written words between them. Aside from that bit of guilt she sensed in him for his deception, he seemed quite content with her for his bride.

She could only wonder what reaction she would get if

she delivered an ultimatum. Knowing him as she did now, Mairi decided she had been right all along. The MacBain would not respond well at all to demands from her or anyone else.

However, she did believe he would move heaven and earth to give aid to a friend in need. That being the case, Mairi fully intended to be the closest friend Lord Robert MacBain had ever known.

He reached her then and took her hands in his, silently smiling upon her with a sweetness that stole her breath away. Her heart seemed to skitter around inside her chest when he leaned down to brush his lips against hers in a featherlight kiss. She closed her eyes and simply enjoyed the new and wondrous sensations he created within her.

Aside from her duties to her father and her clan, Mairi felt another compelling reason to befriend her husband. He needed her even more than she needed him.

She quickly lowered her gaze so that he would not see the sympathy he would surely not welcome. It welled up inside her each time she thought of all that he must endure, living without any sounds.

If only this wildly protective feeling of hers would not get in her way whenever she tried to examine how she felt about the man himself. Was it lust or love or a need to nurture? Whatever it was, she had never experienced anything like it before and so could not define it.

In her mind, she could not properly sort her feelings for the poor lad laboring valiantly under a horrible disadvantage and the fierce, handsome warrior who had fired her blood from the moment she first saw him.

Her confusion was disconcerting, to say the least.

Chapter Seven

The next day, after their morning meal, Mairi watched as Wee Andy tied Geb Nort onto one of the stronger ponies. Their captive continued to ply her with beseeching looks, but he wisely said nothing more.

Andy took the reins from Rob. "See you afore dark," he said by way of parting, and rode on ahead to prepare Rob's parents for their arrival later in the day.

"Aye," Rob answered. "Have a care." He threw up a hand in dismissal and turned back to the fire, avoiding her eyes.

Guilt again, she realized. He had sent Andy, not only to see that they received a proper welcome, but to warn the family that they must pretend on his behalf.

A witless child could have read the looks that passed between the two men. They had even risked making quite a few of those hand signals when they thought her attention directed elsewhere.

Mairi frowned at the subterfuge, sad that he felt it necessary. Did he believe she would renounce him and return to Craigmuir? More fool he, if Rob thought that.

Her Rob, as she had begun thinking of him, would always need looking after. Since he had come all the way to the Highlands to find a wife, and then not tell her of his problem, she had to believe no other woman would have him because of it. He was hers for all and good.

Somewhere in the dark recesses of her mind, Mairi wondered if she would have done well as the wife of a strong, invincible man such as Rob if he had all his senses intact. True enough, she needed to be needed. That was her nature. But did she not also relish the fact that she would be able to outwit him? To predict his moves and mayhaps exert a bit of control over them?

Ah, 'twas an unworthy thought to have, this pride in her intellect. Yet, she admitted that pride always had been among her greatest faults. That, and being too hasty to judge. This time, she had carefully weighed the evidence, however. Mayhaps she would conquer her pride as well someday.

She sternly warned herself now to never ply her advantage over her husband. A helpmeet is what she must be to him, a guardian of his dignity and his well-being.

Rob glanced at her over his shoulder and smiled that captivating smile of his, an expression that made her feel as if she were the only woman in the world worth his attention. Mairi sighed as usual, unable to help herself. Whatever the man might be lacking, she thought with a shiver of longing, it was certainly not physical appeal. Also, he possessed a sweet innocence in his gentler moments that Mairi had only marked in children who had not yet learned how cruel the world could be. She felt she would almost willingly die to prevent his losing that innocence.

"Come, rest now," he suggested, holding out his hand to her.

Already, he had spread the blankets and rolled an extra one to pillow her head.

Was he merely being thoughtful, or did he intend to make love to her now they were alone? Mairi sidled forth and took his hand, not in the least unwilling. Ha, an understatement to end all. But he only made her comfortable upon the improvised bed and left her there while he went about clearing away all signs of their noon camp.

Finally satisfied that he only meant to while away time so that Wee Andy could reach Trouville's castle well ahead of them, Mairi took the opportunity to sleep awhile. She would likely need all her wits about her when she met his family.

Mairi did not bother to fret over whether they would accept her. If Rob had found it necessary to go so far afield to find a bride who would have him, she had no doubt they would welcome her gladly.

"He has done *what?*" Lady Anne demanded, eyes wide and mouth agape.

Wee Andy winced.

She had been crossing the bailey when he rode through the gates, and he had wasted no time in telling her the news. In fact, there *was* no time to waste. Not with some two hundred souls needing to be sworn to secrecy.

"Wed, m'lady," Wee Andy repeated, suddenly uncomfortable and growing more worried by the moment. Lady Anne looked ready to swoon.

He rushed to explain it all and be done with it. "Sir Thomas arranged the match. Searched damned near all over Scotland to find one likely to serve. Went to Craigmuir in the Highlands himself and did the betrothing."

"I see," Lady Anne said, though she did not seem to approve Thomas's actions.

Andy continued, "Lord Robbie waited the agreed-on two months to claim the bride, but Sir Thomas couldn't go back with us since he broke his leg. Soon after we arrived, the keep was attacked.''

"Rob was not injured!" she cried, grabbing his arm.

"Not a scratch," he assured her. "Though we lost three good men ourselves. Newt was among 'em, I'm sorry to say.''

Tears glazed her eyes at the news. "Poor Newton. He was a good fellow. Rob will miss him.''

As would she, Andy surmised. Her ladyship had trained Newt to Rob's service, as well, and had known him since he was born.

"The laird was slain, too," Andy told her.

"The bride's father?" Lady Anne asked, aghast.

"Aye, Laird MacInness," he confirmed. "Afore he died, he had the marriage take place so he could see his lass safe wed. Lord Rob, his bride and me, we took to the road as soon as we could. The villains gave chase, but Rob dispatched them all to hell. Save the one he took alive.'' He jerked his head toward the prisoner.

He watched, fingering the edge of his cap while the lady paced, wringing her hands.

"So the wedding is a *fait accompli.*''

"A what?"

"A done thing," she explained impatiently. "This…this is most…unfortunate," she muttered to herself, beginning to pace again, as if she could not remain still. "If only Robert had waited…"

Wee Andy had never seen her serene ladyship so upset in all the years he'd known her. "His lordship's not to home?" he asked, wishing he could impart the rest of his news on more receptive ears. Assuming Lord Trouville would react calmly.

"No!" She almost shouted the word, then hauled herself to a standstill and paused, gaze jerking from one way to the next, as if searching for solutions. "He is due home any day."

She strode toward Andy then and placed a long, slender hand on his forearm. "How long before Rob and his bride arrive, do you think?"

"Two, three hours, I'd guess," he answered. "No sooner. Longer if the lady tires and needs rest. The prisoner I brung tried to kill her night afore last. Poor lass has nigh gone mute from a strangling."

Lady Anne gasped, her hand flying to her throat. She darted a quick look toward the prisoner, slumped over and still tied to the horse, then beckoned for one of the guards who had wandered near out of curiosity.

"Lock this wretch away and set a watch. We shall deal with him later. Andy, you come with me." Without waiting for him, she set a rapid march toward the steps to the hall.

Once they entered, she sent one of the maids to fetch Andy ale and sustenance. She was thoughtful like that, even fashed as she was by this news.

Andy had grown up under Lady Anne's tutelage, learned to read and write at her knee right along with Lord Rob, Sir Thomas, Lady Jehan and many of the other bairns about the keep, like himself and Newt.

He had missed the lady sorely when Lord Trouville had built this new castle and moved her some hours away from Baincroft.

For the life of him, Andy could not see what troubled her so about Rob's marriage, but troubled she was.

"M'lady?" he dared to ask. "Why didn't Lord Robbie tell you he was to take a wife?"

She shrugged, rubbing her arms with her hands. "Last Christmas when he was here, Thomas vowed he would arrange a match for Rob. I thought it only idle talk. He felt terrible when his own sister—'' At once she halted midsentence and groaned. ''Jehan! La! We must get her away from here ere they arrive, Andy!''

''She is *here?*'' he croaked. ''God's nails, she'll queer it all! Lady Mairi does not know!''

''About Jehan?'' Lady Anne asked. ''Well, I should think not! What man with any sense would talk of his former betrothed to a new wife?''

''Nay, m'lady, she does not know about *Rob!* Lady Mairi thinks he can hear! He bade me tell the family not to let on—''

She pressed her fingers to her temples and rolled her eyes heavenward. ''Saints save us! What is he thinking? And this wife he's found! Is she simpleminded?'' She threw up her hands in dismay. ''God above us, this is all I need! A half-witted daughter-by-law!''

''The lady's not simple atall, lady, but she *does* talk overmuch. Leastwise, she did afore she was choked out of the habit. Now they write back and forth to spare her throat. Seem to get on well enough, for all that.''

''Then why…?''

Andy shrugged. ''Well, Rob wants to wait until she can see for herself that he's not made a muddle of his life. You know, observe how Baincroft fares so well at his hand? Then he'll confess it all.''

Her smile appeared crooked and her face had gone even paler. ''Ah, Andy, a faulty plan to be sure, but I employed it myself once, so I cannot throw stones at him for it.''

For a moment she said nothing, spending the time herding her thoughts and planning, Andy suspected.

Lady Anne was a thinker, for certain. She had an answer for everything. That he had learned at a very early age. She'd know exactly what to do.

In his opinion, this lady was second only to the Blessed

Mother, though not always quite so forgiving of a bairn's
misbehavior. Andy was testament to that. He worshiped
her in spite of it.

"I will caution everyone to silence. You find Jehan,"
she ordered. "Tell her she must hie to Baincroft within
the hour. Think of some—any—pretext to get her there.
You take her. Tell her Thomas requires her, or Rob is
expected there soon. *Anything* to get her gone as soon as
may be."

"Why has *she* come back?" Andy dared to ask, not
bothering to sound the least bit glad of it. Jehan, who had
been their childhood friend, who had belonged to Rob and
then betrayed him when it came time to wed, held none
of Andy's kind regard whatsoever. "Did she change her
fickle mind of a sudden?"

"No," Lady Anne said with a wry grimace. "'Twas all
her grandfather's doing, it seems. Jehan never knew he had
nullified her betrothal to Rob until he tried to wed her
elsewhere. Only last month she managed to escape Sir
Simon. A week ago she arrived at Baincroft, ready to
honor her troth to Rob."

"She left it a might late," Andy commented with a
snort.

Lady Anne nodded. "She did at that, by years. And
Thomas obviously told her nothing of these marriage plans
while she was there. He sent her straight to me and bade
her wait here. I will blister that wicked wretch when next
I see him! He could have prepared his sister for this!"

"*I'll* not be the one to tell her!" Andy announced in a
panic. "Jehan's like to kill the messenger, knowin' her
temper! I do not doubt Thomas had that in mind."

Lady Anne puffed out a beleaguered breath. "It is not
my place to explain it, for I do not know all the particulars.
You take her to Thomas, Andy. He arranged this tangle.

Tell him he is required to straighten it out.'' She paused
for effect and shook a finger. ''By *my* order, he is to have
it done ere Rob arrives there!''

''Right enough!'' Andy answered, actually anticipating
the inevitable row. Thomas and Jehan, at it again, just like
days of old. He planned to watch the brangle from behind
something thick and sturdy.

Grinning, he left it to Lady Anne to arrange the welcome
for Rob and the Lady Mairi while he went to locate the
bride who was to languish without a groom.

Mayhaps Jehan had not spurned Rob apurpose as once
thought. But if she had stayed where she belonged and not
gone off for those years to bask in the glitter of court with
her famous old English grandda, she'd never have come
to this. She'd be wed and likely a mother to a clutch of
bairns by now.

However it had happened, Jehan had broken their Rob's
gentle heart. For that act, neither Andy nor any other who
had seen how it hurt their fine young lord, would ever
forgive the wee wildcat.

Andy, for one, had never liked her much. He was might-
ily looking forward to her finding out she'd been replaced.
But he'd not tell her the tale, even if reporting the deed to
her would gain him all the gold of two kingdoms.

Mairi watched eagerly for the first sight of Trouville's
castle. Rob had written that it was the finest place in Scotland. Though not comparable in size to those castles in
Edinburgh, Stirling or Roxburgh that he had written glowing accounts of, the furnishings were more dear and its
beauty was unsurpassed, he had promised. That description
meant little to Mairi, who had seen no other keeps save
that of her father.

He had promised to travel with her now and then, show

her the world as he had seen it when he had attended tourneys for sport and gain. Mayhaps they would even venture to France one day, he'd suggested.

At last, she would have the adventures she had wished for. New places, new people and a new life. Father would be glad for her, she thought. How she wished she might write to him later and recount it all, just as he had regaled her with tales of the faraway places he had traveled in his youth.

But Da was with God now. Much as she mourned his passing, Mairi knew she must put forth all effort to make him remembered through her. The daughter of the Mac-Inness, she was, shot through with the bravery that would have graced his sons if he had sired any. Da had told her so. Therefore, she would never quail or simper when faced with a challenge.

And there the castle was as they topped a hill. Mairi's mouth gaped in shock. Never in her life had she imagined such a place existed. "By th' Rood," she whispered in awe. "'Tis grand!"

Rob made some wordless sound of satisfaction, but she could not tear her wide-eyed gaze away from that wondrous place to look at him.

White towers rose near to the clouds, it seemed. A curving wall surrounded the keep, also a glistening white that shone like snow in the sun of the late afternoon. It contrasted beautifully with the verdant slopes upon which it perched. A gracefully curved road wound uphill to the massive gates.

"How perfect!" she whispered, finally turning to Rob to judge his reaction.

"Aye," he agreed, smiling as he nudged his mount forward. "Father is gone." For some reason, that seemed to please him well.

Mairi looked more closely at the castle, noting the absence of colors. The pennons would be flying if the lord were in residence. Her father had told her of the custom, though they had not kept it at Craigmuir. Foolish to announce the laird's absence in her part of the world. It invited attack.

Their pace increased the closer they got. Mairi shored up her courage, which had begun to flag seriously. She had not worried on it before, but this family of Rob's must be as grand as their keep. Royally grand. What would they think of the simple Highland wife their son had brought home?

She brushed at her skirts and tugged her fitted sleeve points down past her wrists where they should be, knowing that no amount of straightening would make her gown acceptable. Even her finest, which had been left behind in their hurried departure, would never do for entry into this place of dreams.

The half hour it took to reach the gates gave her time to work up a galloping case of self-doubt. Only by reminding herself, time and again, who she was and what was expected of her kept her from turning about to flee like a hare before hounds. *Daughter of the MacInness. Wife of the MacBain,* she repeated.

They rode abreast up to the gates. A sharp whistle sounded and Rob's head jerked up at the sound. "Ho, Conor!" he shouted. "Ope the gates!"

Already they were swinging wide. Mairi did not miss the fact that Rob had heard that sharp whistle of the man he'd called Conor. He couldn't *hear!* Could he? All of her recent observations shriveled like parchment in flames. Wrong! She had been wrong about him.

Nay, she could not be! It had been a happenstance that

he'd looked up just then. He knew there would be a guard, she decided. Aye, he had simply raised his head to call out and saw the man there. The man had only whistled at an opportune moment, that was all. A coincidence. She released a sigh of dismay over it, nonetheless, worried that she had been too hasty in her judgment. Yet again.

"Come, come," he said, and urged his mount forward, entering the portal ahead of her. The portcullis with its wickedly sharp points slid upward with barely a creak and was fully raised before they reached it.

Never having actually seen one of the things, Mairi held her breath as they passed under, fearing it would drop by accident and impale them with its wicked-looking spikes.

A crowd of castlefolk had gathered to greet them in the bailey, surrounding their mounts as Rob slid from his saddle. Mairi, who remained mounted, felt on display. Curious eyes raked her, judging her, likely finding her lacking as a proper bride for their lord's son.

She straightened her shoulders and stared back in defiance. *Daughter of the MacInness,* she repeated in her mind. A bit of travel dirt and a simple woolen gown would not detract from her consequence. She would not let it.

Rob grasped the reins of her mare and led her through the throng of people, briefly pausing at times to exchange an arm clasp with several of the men. Before she knew it, they had reached the keep itself.

The crowd parted as Rob came around to her left and assisted her down. The moment her feet touched the paving stone, a woman's clear voice addressed them. "How well come you are, my son. Andy said you bring me a daughter!"

Rob's clasped Mairi's waist, his hand all that was holding her upright after several hours in the saddle. "My mother, Lady Anne," he said in his deep, gravelly monotone, extending his other palm toward the tall, elegant woman dressed in rich green silk. "Meet my wife." Rob inclined his head to her. "Lady Mairi."

"A glad surprise you are, my dear," the woman said, almost too brightly. "We are delighted to welcome you to our home."

"My thanks," Mairi replied with a stiff curtsy, ashamed that her voice sounded nigh as gruff as Rob's. Her throat still pained her.

Though her mother-in-law's words had been warm, Mairi imagined a glint of disappointment in the lovely gray eyes.

"Robert, please take your bride to Alys's chambers. A bath awaits."

"Where is Alys?" he asked, looking faintly disturbed by his mother's request.

"Gone to Edinburgh with your father. They will be home anon."

"Tomorrow?" he asked, his fingers digging into Mairi's waist as if seeking support himself.

"This night, I hope," she answered. "In time for the feast."

Rob's muttered curse seemed lost to all but Mairi.

His mother had turned abruptly to climb the stairs and the others crowded around them conversed amongst themselves with some excitement about the impending celebration. Mairi wondered at the occasion for it and hoped she need not attend.

Confusion reigned as they passed through the great hall. Such sumptuous fittings she had never before seen. Huge banners hung upon the walls, interspersed with formal shields and intricate tapestries. The walls themselves bore bands of painted color and a simple pattern of large golden flowers. Tables gleamed with long, white cloths. Surely even kings did not live in such splendor as this.

She stumbled upon the smooth stone steps as Rob led her up the stairs from the cavernous hall to the tower chambers. Mairi felt extremely small and insignificant at the moment and wished herself anywhere but where she was.

This had been a mistake of enormous proportion, her marriage to this man. What had her father been thinking to pledge her to such a family?

"Are you ill?" Rob asked when they had reached one of the chambers.

This warm, comfortable room looked fit for a queen, much finer than any she had ever thought to see. She had to shake herself from her disbelief to answer him. "Nay. Not ill."

"Take your bath," he ordered, nodding toward the huge wooden tub lined with white linen.

A small maid stood behind it, smiling a gap-toothed smile. Even the servant's attire appeared more costly and certainly in better repair than Mairi's own travel-stained garments.

She looked down at herself and wondered what she was to do about that. If only she had known what grandeur she would encounter after being married, she might have insisted that her father furnish her with proper clothing.

Her own things might be sufficient for life in the Highlands where comfort was the main concern, but not here. Not where the lady of the keep dressed in a style most queens must envy. With sad longing, Mairi recalled Lady Anne's green silk, cut in a manner much different from her own plain garb.

"Nonsense!" she said, shaking her head at the envious and unworthy thoughts. "It matters not at all."

"Make haste," Rob added, jerking her from one conundrum straight into another. She was not about to disrobe in his presence.

He gave a small chuckle at her obvious chagrin and squeezed her shoulder, pushing her forward gently as he did so. Then he backed out of the room and quietly closed the door.

Heaven was the word for hot water, Mairi quickly decided. She shucked off her clothes as if they were flaming and hurried into the tub.

"Ah," she rasped soulfully, sinking to her neck in the heat and floral scent. She must borrow some of this essence, Mairi noted to herself, for she had not brought her own supply of the rose oil that her father had given her. Each year on her nameday, he gifted her with it, telling her it was the same as her mother had used. Though slightly different, this scent did bring bittersweet memories of the father she would never see again.

Mairi was thankful for the subtle reminder that she must remember her sire always. And in doing so, to fulfill her promise to avenge him.

In order to gain their help to do this, she needed to make the best impression that she could upon her husband and all of his family. If they liked her well enough, they might eventually honor her wishes and lend her men to accomplish her vow of vengeance and save her clan from Ranald.

When she finally roused herself and sat up, the wee maid filled a small dipper, poured it over Mairi's hair and worked in a measure of foaming soap.

She abandoned herself to the luxury of being bathed like a weary bairn, pushing away all thoughts of what might happen when she eventually emerged from the warm and welcome haven. For now, this immediate pleasure was all she need dwell upon.

Mairi needed a respite from worry and apprehension. She would climb from the tub in a while, be dried and let to sleep in that enormous, gloriously soft-looking bed with its costly brocade hangings. The morrow would be time enough to face what devils she must.

"Your clothes," Rob announced. He tossed her pack upon the bed and jerked his chin toward the door in a silent order for the maid to leave.

The lass hastily scooped up Mairi's soiled garb and disappeared in a blink.

Mairi sat straight up, sloshing the water as she did so, holding the washing cloth to cover her chest. "Out with you!" she whispered to her husband.

"Father is home," he announced, looking none too happy about the fact. "Hurry!" With that, he grabbed up one of the large lengths of soft linen and held it out to her while he turned his head away and closed his eyes.

Caught up in his urgency, Mairi leaped at his gentlemanly grant of privacy and dried herself quickly.

In less than a moment's time Rob had divested himself and climbed into the tub. While he scrubbed and splashed, she dressed, dragging on her last clean chemise and the wrinkled red gown. It was the best one she had with her and would have to suffice.

Though the sound of Rob's bathing enticed her to watch, she refused the temptation. She had seen her husband without his clothing before, but not in such close quarters. Offering him the same courtesy he had given her, Mairi kept her back to him as he got out of the water and donned his clothes. The urge to peek nearly overcame her several times, but she held steady in her reserve.

The rattle of his sword belt signaled that it was safe to face him. There seemed little to discuss, so Mairi said nothing. She could hardly refuse to go down and meet the rest of his family.

"You meet Father. Then the feast."

She started to protest, but he pressed a finger to her lips. "Wedding feast," he explained with a comical grimace.

In all truth, Rob looked no more enthusiastic than she felt about either the introduction or the celebration to follow. Something troubled him about both events, likely that she would shame him. 'Twas the same thing that troubled her.

The best she could do was offer him comfort. It was her duty, and her wish to do so. Mairi waited until he looked her in the eye. She made certain her words were clear, pronounced as he might say them to her, one after the other and in as Lowland a manner as she could manage. "I will not disgrace you."

His expression melted from distracted to tender in two heartbeats. Mairi read complete understanding in his soft gray eyes. He stepped forward and held her face between his hands. "Nor I, you," he promised. Then he kissed her.

Oh, his mouth was soft upon hers, the touch of his tongue a bold yet restrained caress. Much more than a kiss of peace, a bit less than a prelude to seduction. It warmed her soul, calmed her fear and entreated her to trust.

When he released her, Mairi stood atremble, staring up at a smile to wring the heart. Then, slowly and formally, he took her hand and led her out.

Chapter Eight

Rob escorted Mairi down the stairs and ushered her toward the huge fireplace to await the comte and Alys.

He had watched from the east tower until he'd seen their party approaching. They had probably arrived in the bailey while he and Mairi were grooming themselves for the ordeal to come. And it would be an ordeal, he figured.

This meeting would be the most crucial of all. His whole plan could come undone. He could lose Mairi's esteem and trust before he even had a chance to acquire it.

The doors to the hall swung open and Alys dashed through, skirts in a flurry, heedless as usual with regard to propriety. He only hoped she would be too caught up in her gladness to be home again to pay much mind to their presence.

While Rob had never known his little sister to be deliberately unkind, she was not above nudging a potential calamity into motion just to view its outcome.

He released a breath of relief when their mother intercepted her, hopefully to issue firm orders that she was not to speak with her hands or to spill his secret in other ways.

The comte entered then and approached them directly.

Had he been told? Hopefully Mother had set someone outside to warn him.

The question was, would he accede to Rob's wish when he had suffered the same secret all those years ago and never guessed the truth until Rob had confessed?

"Father," Rob said by way of wary greeting, bowing and then accepting the clasp of arms.

As he squeezed the comte's strong forearms, he issued a silent plea for understanding and got only the raise of an eyebrow for his trouble. Heaven only knew what that meant. To Rob it seemed a reprimand. Well, at least someone had done their duty and spread the word.

He wondered if the Comte de Trouville had the same effect on Mairi as he did on most people at first meeting. His tall, commanding presence filled a room, even the great hall in which they stood.

Though silver strands now threaded his dark hair and a few age lines creased his once smoothly carved features, the comte's noble countenance had only grown more distinguished through the years.

From the first day the comte had arrived, Rob had seen the underlying kindness in his stepfather's heart, but he wondered if that was due to his own gift of insight. Would Mairi see it, or would Trouville terrify her?

"Robert, it is good to see you, my son!"

The sharp eyes settled immediately on Mairi in the midst of her deep curtsy. He reached for her hand to raise her up.

"Father, my wife, Lady Mairi," Rob announced. "Mairi, the Comte de Trouville." He held his breath. Gritted his teeth. Prayed a short prayer.

"Enchanté, mademoiselle," his father said kindly. *"Soyez la bienvenue?"*

Mairi glanced to Rob for help. Her face glowed red as

the coals in the fire. She had no French, Rob realized suddenly. Not even enough to understand the most common welcome in that language.

Oh, God, he knew exactly what she was feeling at this moment and wanted to embrace her, to assure her no one cared that she did not know the words. How many times had he found himself in a like situation and at such a loss for reply? He stepped closer to her and encircled her waist with his arm.

Anger almost choked his words, "A trial, Father?"

The comte's expression did not change. "Certainly not, son. 'Twas but a courtesy. You know many gentles prefer my language, even in this country," He addressed Mairi. "My apologies, daughter."

"Je regret…" Mairi began and faltered there, giving up the effort altogether. "I am sorry, *M'seiur le Comte.* My command of your language is so poor."

Nonexistent, Rob thought, exhaling sharply.

Trouville took her hands in his and smiled down on her, shaking his head. "No great matter, my dear. My attempt at Gaelic died aborning many years ago!" He laughed. "Something wrong with the back of my throat, apparently. Rob swears French is spoken mostly with the nose and refuses to attempt it."

Rob caught most of his father's apology and filled in the rest from what he knew of Trouville's phrasing. At times he still had difficulty with the accent, especially when his father spoke to Mother and did not mean for Rob to ken what he said.

Mairi returned Trouville's smile tentatively. "I am happy to meet you, my lord."

She spoke slowly and carefully for a change, likely in deference to the fact that the comte was French. Why could she not speak so to him? Rob wondered. This time he understood every word she said. However, he could see that it still pained her to speak at all.

"Her throat hurts," Rob said with full intent to spare her further unease. "Enough talk."

Alys marched up and threw her arms around Rob's neck as she usually did when he came to visit. Then she leaned back and examined his face as if checking his mood. "What of me, brother? Am I to meet her, or would you hide me away?"

Rob grinned warily and turned her around to face the rest. "Mairi, my sister, Alys," he said.

Alys embraced Mairi and kissed her cheeks. He could not see what she said, but his wife's answering smile and nod reassured him all was proceeding well enough.

Mother had obviously warned Alys to silence, as Rob had hoped. It seemed he had his sister's cooperation, after all. However, the shadow of disapproval in the comte's dark eyes remained.

Rob only hoped that was a reaction to the secret he insisted upon keeping and not on his choice of bride. He had never known Trouville to judge anyone on such short acquaintance, but there was always a first time for everything.

"A word with you, sir?"

"More than one, I promise," the comte replied clearly. "The solar?"

Rob followed dutifully, knowing this would not be an easy conversation.

The moment the door closed behind him, he received the full brunt of Trouville's fury. "You did not tell her!" he accused. *"Est-ce que tu es fou?"*

Rob sincerely hoped his words did not sound as thunderous as they looked upon his mouth.

"No, Father, I am not mad. Thomas did tell her sire.

Laird MacInness said he told her." Rob shrugged, throwing out his hands, exasperated. "I thought she *did* know! Then later I saw she did not. The marriage was done."

"Unfair, Robert! Wrong!" He made a vigorous sign for that as he said it. The fact that he gave a sign at all indicated he was beside himself. From the first, the comte refused to do it, insisting Rob increase his powers of speech instead of what he called *cheating with his hands*. In all truth, his refusal had done much to improve Rob's vocabulary over the years.

"You cannot hope to keep this from her. Tell her!"

"No, Father," Rob argued, holding up a finger to forestall a further harangue. "First, she must see that a little deafness is of no account."

"It *is* of some account! Because you lie. By omission, you lie, Rob. She could hate you for that alone."

Rob pursed his lips and shook his head before he answered. "Mayhaps she will hate me more if she cannot see past the deafness. Let her know me awhile. Then I will tell."

"She will guess, Robert. Unless she is a fool, she will soon guess."

"*You* did not. Remember?" Rob reminded him, a bit more slyly than he'd meant to do.

Trouville threw out his arms in a gesture of exasperation. "You were a child, and I newly wed to your *maman*. There were distractions! But Mairi is your *wife!*"

"Aye. And she may want free of that when she learns of this. I keep it so that she can be. We have not…" Rob could not immediately think of the polite word for bedding and so did not finish. Nor did he make the sign, but could see his father understood him right well.

Trouville ran a hand over his face and shook his head. "Then she is probably more concerned about another part of you than your ears at this point. You've been wed what...four days now?''

"Let it be, Father, please. I know what I am doing."

He hesitated a moment before asking tentatively, ''Do you like her, sir?''

"Oui," the comte confirmed with an impatient nod. ''She is beautiful, pleasant enough, well spoken if not well tutored. The question is, do *you* like her?''

Rob smiled then. ''I do. Mairi has great courage.''

"Courage? And that's *all* you noticed?'' the comte demanded with a quirk of one dark brow.

"Not all," Rob admitted with a suggestive grin. "I want her. I could love her.''

"Then you'd best start as you mean to go. Confess, and hope you have not left it too late.''

"Very soon. Not yet. Please help?'' Rob asked, knowing already by Father's expression of defeat that he had won. "Do not hinder?'' If Trouville had meant to tell Mairi the truth, he probably would have done so already.

"If you insist. She is your wife." He let the matter rest, looking deeply into Rob's eyes. "Son, there is another matter we must discuss.''

"Bad news?'' Rob guessed by the dark look.

The comte shrugged as if unsure whether or not Rob would consider it bad. "Jehan has come.''

The blow took him unawares. Rob could not quell his gasp and not a word could he form in reply.

His father continued. ''Sir William met me at the gate. He said that your *maman* sent her to Baincroft. To Thomas. Her brother has orders to return her to the English court first thing tomorrow.''

"Thank God!'' Rob murmured, unsure whether he had spoken aloud. Thomas would not dare disregard his mother's orders. Jehannie would be gone when they arrived home. Surely.

All he could think of was the disaster that might ensue if she were not. The wee cat might not have wanted him to husband, but he could only imagine her temper if she learned someone replaced her in his affections.

Again, Rob felt the relief that recently had surprised him with regard to his canceled marriage, despite the blow to his pride. He blessed his fate now that he had found Mairi.

"Why did Jehannie return?" he asked, all too afraid he could guess the reason. He would wager it was not to visit her brother.

"She did not know her *grandpère* had put aside her troth to you. Jehan was not at fault."

"A tangle," Rob admitted with a heavy sigh and a worried frown to match Trouville's. "She will ignite."

Trouville smiled at that. "Thomas's problem, not yours. Do not dwell on it. Jehan will survive. Let us go now and join the others."

"Thank you, Father," Rob said with a short, formal bow. "For everything."

He did not expect to be embraced, but the comte did so before they left the chamber. He slapped Rob's back and shook his shoulders and ruffled his hair as he had always done when they had disagreed and then come to terms. Rob felt like the errant son forgiven, just as he had so many times in the past.

Rob had never felt less than loved by this man, whom he respected above all. As a lad, he had counted very heavily on that love. He still did.

It troubled him to disappoint Trouville in any way, but Rob believed he was right in the matter of Mairi. And he was incredibly grateful to his father for setting his mind at rest about Jehannie. As he had said, she would recover.

It was not as though he and Jehannie had loved each other the way a man and wife should. Not the way he could love Mairi if she decided to remain with him. And if she did not, he would have none other. Jehannie was part of his past and would forever remain there. Mairi, he dearly hoped, was his future.

"Oh, art weary, sister?" Alys asked, all prim-lipped sympathy.

Certainly weary of the fawning attention Rob's sister showered upon her, Mairi admitted silently. The lass followed her everywhere. For the feast they now attended, she had insisted Mairi wear one of her new gowns that, while certainly less crumpled than Mairi's own, hung upon her person like a tent. And the sickly yellow of it gave her skin a deathlike pallor. Still, she supposed the girl meant well.

And girl she was, surely not more than sixteen, though she was already larger and taller than Mairi. Her dark gray eyes missed nothing and sparkled with energy, an energy focused almost entirely on Mairi for some time now. And it was wearying in its intensity.

Underlying all of Alys's apparent concern, however, Mairi thought she detected a trace of wicked humor. But what amusement could a plain Highland woman such as she provide a maid such as Lady Alys? Surely the daughter of the wealthy French count was afforded far richer amusements than entertaining her brother's wife for a few hours.

Mayhaps someone dumbstruck with awe delighted Alys, for Mairi was certain she appeared that way frequently enough since her arrival here.

And why should she not? Trouville's great hall alone could have swallowed her father's entire keep. There must be two hundred souls making merry over her marriage when she felt no merriment whatsoever at the moment. What she craved was sleep. And quiet.

The cacophony proved too great for any decent conversation, not that she'd expected to have that with Rob. Even when they had sat side by side and shared a trencher, she could hardly hear herself speak. Shouting over the noise was certainly out of the question, since her throat still ached to some extent.

The musicians seemed abnormally loud as they played during the meal, making her wonder if the entire family might be as deaf as Rob. Her head ached from it.

Finally a hoard of servants had taken away the food so the dancing could begin.

She and Alys now stood to one side of the dais and watched. Lady Anne had assembled quite a group of players for the evening. Mairi wondered, Did they live here, retained for the castlefolks' pleasure each night?

There were six altogether, with a shawm, dulcimer, psaltery, tambour, flute and *vielle*. Alys had told her the names of the instruments she had never before seen. In fact, the only ones she'd recognized were the flute and drum. This only emphasized to Mairi—and probably to Alys, as well—just how backward her life had been until now.

"Do you dance?" Alys asked. "Rob is wondrous at it. Aha! Look you there, he approaches *Maman* for the *estampie*. Watch them go to."

She laughed gleefully and clapped her hands when Rob lifted their mother high, set her back upon her feet and began the lively and intricate steps required.

Mairi's heart thudded and the very breath rushed out of her in a whoosh. She felt faint, yet could not tear her gaze away from him. God's nails! Rob danced! And danced well! He could…

He *could* hear, she thought with a sinking sensation she

knew she should not be feeling. In truth, her husband was one with the music. He and the Lady Anne appeared to enjoy themselves thoroughly, never missing a single beat in the wild rhythmic cadence provided by the musicians.

A stately carole, he might have managed, even in silence, simply by watching the others and keeping step with them. For this, however, Rob *had* to hear the music. But she had been so certain…

Mairi wished she could disappear on the instant, simply vanish as though she had never been at all. To stand here forcing a smile proved almost more than she could manage. She felt the veriest idiot, and he also must believe her so, given her behavior today. All those concessions she had made so that he could understand her now seemed so stupid.

How could she have made a such a grave error, thinking him deaf? He had heard that guard's sharp whistle this afternoon, only she had not wanted to admit it then. And tonight, he obviously heard every note the musicians played.

Once again, she had built her judgment upon supposition instead of facts. How could she have been so wrong? How could she have not minded what would have been a disastrous limitation for a knight and lord?

And, worse, why this feeling of disappointment that she was wrong, when to be so meant that her husband could hear! She was in no way worthy of him if this did not make her glad at heart.

Shame almost overcame her for all the plans she'd made to become Rob's right arm in all things, to help him through life, to be the most important person in his life.

Rob would not need her. He did not require her help because of his lack of hearing and, apparently, did not need her body for his pleasure, either. She worried that he would have no use for her at all now.

Well, it did ill become her to want to mother the man she had wed, did it not? What a fine wife she would have made to him doing that! But she had hoped she would have something of great import to offer him besides the children they might make. Now it seemed she did not. God knew her dowry accounted for little and she'd thought to make up for that in some way.

Mairi had to wonder why he had chosen her. He must have decided a Highland woman would bear him stronger sons. Highlanders were known to be fierce and like did beget like.

Now she could think of no other good reason for him to have gone so far afield for a wife. His father's hall seemed half filled with beautiful women this very night. A man as handsome as Rob could have chosen any one of them.

The music stopped and an uproar of hearty applause erupted. Then the players adopted a less rollicking tune and the dancers sought out new partners.

One particularly winsome wench grasped Rob's hands as Mairi watched, another just as lovely took hold of his elbow. He said something to them and they nodded in unison, beaming up at him as they released him. Sweet words, no doubt, to bring such smiles.

He then headed toward the place where Mairi stood beside Alys.

"Quite the ladies' man, is he not?" Mairi commented without thinking.

"Aye, he is that! Are you jealous?" Alys asked with a sly chuckle.

"Of course not!" But she was. "I merely wondered if

so many close by want to have him, why he traveled so far to find a bride.''

Alys rolled her eyes. ''La! If he'd chosen from one of these, we should have a proper riot on our hands! The poor bride would be plagued out of all bearing by the rest who fell green with envy.''

''Will they plague me?'' Mairi asked idly, distracted by the sight of her handsome husband bearing down upon them through the crowded hall.

Her sister-by-law shrugged. ''The last woman betrothed to him broke their troth. When you meet her, you must ask her if that was her reason.'' Alys grinned at Mairi as if she made a jest. ''The silly wretch must have had some good cause to end it, and I assure you, it was not for lack of love for our fine Lord Robbie.''

''Who—?'' Mairi started to ask, but Rob arrived just then and interrupted, holding out his hand to her.

''Dance?''

As badly as she wanted answers about his former intended, Mairi could think of no polite reason to refuse him. And she did not want to leave him at the mercy of those grasping females seeking partners.

''Aye,'' she announced with a firm nod. ''I would dance.''

Her husband's intense gaze never left her face as he positioned her in the inner circle the women formed around a single player. This lad was doubtless meant to sing, for she heard him clear his throat and hum a few notes. One of the ladies beside her exclaimed this was to be a chaplet, a dance Mairi had never heard of, much less performed.

Rob stepped back, opposite her in the outer ring. He bowed to her curtsy as the flute trilled the opening notes.

Mairi could think of little else save his flashing silver-gray eyes and the exciting press of his fingers upon her hand when the other instruments chimed in. He led her in the dance, pausing at the proper time to dip and sway as did the others around them.

At every third pause, the steps required that he pull her near so that their bodies almost touched. The urge to close that distance all but overwhelmed Mairi. It angered her that the urgency did not affect him, as well, but Rob seemed totally unaware of it.

However, in the final flourish of notes, instead of bowing to her curtsy, Rob cradled her cheeks and kissed her soundly on the mouth. For the duration of it, all else around them ceased to exist.

When he released her, laughter and applause erupted while he smiled down at her confusion. Before she could recover her wits, he had placed her hand on Trouville's arm and was already seeking another partner.

Had each man kissed his lady, or had Rob done that because he wished to? Or did new grooms do it routinely when they danced with their brides? She might never learn, for she certainly would not ask him. She would keep close watch, however, to see whether he kissed another of his partners.

The rest of the evening passed in a blur of activity. Mairi accepted every time Rob offered to dance with her and worried when he did not. She was much in demand herself, by Trouville and others whose names she could not recall.

The bones in her feet ached and her face hurt from constant smiling. If only the countess had not felt obliged to fete them on this first night, she thought wearily. Mairi had not yet recovered from either the attack or the journey and wanted only to rest. And hide, she wryly admitted to herself. Aye, there was the real wish.

Rob never seemed to need rest. He danced the night with all and sundry, pausing only now and again for a cup of wine or a moment of idle talk. Not with her, however. To Mairi, he said nothing, other than to ask her if she would do him the honor. Well, not even that precisely. He simply asked as he had the first time. "Dance?"

Mairi still could not believe that she had been so wrong about his ability to hear. A part of her wondered how else she could excuse his behavior toward her at Craigmuir and on the journey here.

Even now as they enjoyed a fairly quiet dance with some chance to confer, he uttered no pleasantries. Could it be he regretted his choice? Did he wish he had taken a local bride instead so that her speech would not offend him so?

"Well, ye must make do with what ye have chosen!" she declared with a decisive toss of her head when next he drew near enough to hear her.

His nod and half smile infuriated Mairi so much, she might have slapped his face had not his entire family been watching.

"No more," he announced when the last notes had sounded and he raised from his bow. "The music ends."

"Well, my thanks to you, too," she muttered angrily to herself.

"You are welcome," he replied cheerfully and tugged her toward the dais where his parents and sister were sitting.

Mairi groaned, ready to kick his shins. Instead she allowed him to usher her to their bench and take a seat beside her.

Toasts followed. Rob even made one himself. "To my bride," he announced loudly, holding his cup aloft to one side of the hall and then the other. "Bonny Lady Mairi!"

Her face heated as huzzahs rang out and everyone drank to her health. They'd do as much for the newest brood mare, she grumbled under her breath. Yet she pasted on a wide smile and acknowledged their good wishes.

What choice did she have? She was wed and might as well make what she could of it. She had wished for adventure and at least that wish had been fulfilled.

"Robert says you and he must depart for Baincroft come the morn," Trouville remarked when there came a lull in the celebratory drinking.

"Must we? He neglected to mention it to me," Mairi said, unable to keep all the bitterness from her voice.

"Robert's mother and I were very happy there for the first years of our marriage," he commented with a charming smile, motioning for a page to refill her wine cup. "Your husband's efforts have improved it tenfold since that time. He is a fine lord, if I do say so. His people adore him."

Rob's mother, who had been listening, leaned forward to speak across the comte. "Aye, you will never meet a more loyal lot than Robert commands. 'Tis because they know him so well. When you come to know him better, you will understand why. No lord in Scotland cares more than my son for those people under his protection."

Mairi thought there might be one exception to that now, however she did not speak her mind on it. "I thank you for sharing that," she said instead. "'Tis true that my lord and I are little more than strangers."

"A matter easily remedied," Trouville said, smiling, toying with the stem of his goblet.

Frustration overrode good sense. "How?" Mairi demanded.

He laughed, obviously surprised by her candor. Lady Anne bit her lips together and sat back in her chair. Mairi could not tell whether Rob's mother was aghast at her question or at a loss for an answer.

Trouville grasped Mairi's hand and leaned close, speaking so near her ear that only she could hear him. "Robert will steal your heart, my dear, and give you his if you but allow it. As one who enjoys a marriage made of love, I do heartily recommend it to you."

Mairi appreciated his good intentions. He obviously considered Rob his true son and wished him to be happy. So much so, that he would promise her what Rob would not. She sensed an innate goodness concealed inside the cloak of formality Trouville's station required. "You are fortunate, my lord," she whispered back.

"And so shall you be," he replied, releasing her hand with a comforting pat. "Trust him."

He pushed back the thronelike chair in which he sat and stood. Then he assisted Lady Anne in doing the same. Raising his voice so that all could hear, he announced, "We bid you all a good night."

That signaled the feast was over at last, Mairi thought with a grateful sigh. Rob took her arm, clasping her securely as she maneuvered her borrowed skirts around the bench. She wondered what would happen now.

Would she be expected to share Alys's chamber where she had bathed and dressed earlier? Or would she and Rob bed down on pallets in the hall as did many travelers who visited great keeps along their way?

She glanced around furtively, noting the scurry of servants clearing the tables and others carrying the benches to set them against the walls until the next meal.

All the while, Rob ushered her toward the stairs. Not hurriedly, but so that his parents and Alys ascended well ahead of them.

It seemed natural to follow his lead and forego questions. He probably would not deign to answer them, anyway. She would find out soon enough where she was to pass the night.

Not likely he would wish her to sleep with him, and for once, Mairi did not care.

She missed her poor da and the homely Craigmuir and the way things used to be. All she wanted at the moment was to lapse into tears and give way to exhaustion. The grand adventure had palled and she was sick at heart with disappointment.

For all that she was surrounded by hundreds of people in this place and unlikely to gain a moment's solitude in the near future, Mairi felt achingly alone.

Chapter Nine

Rob had thought the fete would never end. As a rule, he loved to dance, but having to witness Mairi doing so with every male in residence had certainly diminished the pleasure.

To his chagrin, he recognized his jealousy for what it was. He, who had never been envious of a soul that he could recall. Definitely humbling.

One good thing had come of the dancing, however. He had impressed his wife with how well he did it, Rob decided a bit smugly. Aye, Mairi had not even tried to hide her appraisal of that. Awed, was what she was. She had fairly gaped at him when she first saw him dancing with his mother.

Little could she know that he felt music right down to his soul. 'Twas one of the few things he could hear—at least, well enough to declare that he heard—and he adored it.

His parents permanently supported a full retinue of musicians, and had for years. Mother had hired them on when he was but a lad, as soon as Rob had told her he could hear them.

For all that it gave Mairi a chance to admire him for

something he did well, Rob wished they could have dispensed with the tiring celebration tonight. She had needed rest more than feasting or dancing. Had his mother not pointed out how important it was to Mairi's acceptance by their people, he would never have agreed to it.

Most who lived under Trouville's protection were related to those at Baincroft. Noble and commoner alike, all were considered family. Though this had been his first visit here in some months, traffic between the two estates was fairly constant.

Many here must be feeling quite confused over Jehannie's sudden appearance and then Rob arriving with another as his wife shortly afterward. Especially Jehannie's parents.

Her father was priest here and her mother, the healer. Wed for five and twenty years, they had served Rob's mother well for all that time. She had, in turn, disregarded the church's view on married clergy and provided them a living first at Baincroft, then here after she wed Trouville.

Father Michael and Lady Meg had been conspicuous by their absence since he and Mairi arrived.

Jehannie's apparent desertion of him had caused them great embarrassment just as it had Thomas. It must now seem to them as if Rob were punishing Jehannie for something that was no fault of hers, after all.

Because Rob now knew that she was not to blame, he felt he must do all he could to prevent any hard feelings among the people for his replacing her. He had attempted to explain how it had come about to those he felt certain would pass the word to the others.

The celebration had provided him the chance to assure them all that he was pleased with his new wife and yet still wished Jehannie well. The evening's efforts had proved exhausting and, he hoped, successful.

He escorted Mairi upstairs and directly to Alys's chamber where he followed her inside. "Art weary?" he asked her.

"Aye," she answered, looking around her as though searching for something. Or probably some*one*.

His sister would repair to a smaller accommodation on the upper floor for the night, as was right and proper. Since Rob was a visitor and a lord, he was due the second-best chamber. Aside from that, he had spent a number of years in this very room and considered it his whenever he came here.

Servants had removed the bath and straightened the place after their mad rush to make ready for the feast. The firelight flickered comfortably while fragrant candles added their golden glow of warmth.

A welcoming bower for lovers, if only they were. Rob heaved a sigh of resignation.

Alys had altered this room he had occupied as a lad. It bore the stamp of a female now, with its pale green brocade hangings and embroidered pillows. For the first time he was glad it was so changed. Mayhaps this would make Mairi more comfortable.

He was also glad that the huge bed remained, built to accommodate his height when he had grown too tall for the other. At least he need not sleep jowl by cheek with her in the randy state he was in.

Mairi interrupted his musings when she touched his arm and asked the question he expected. "Where is your sister?"

There, he was understanding her better, he thought. Could be that fatigue slowed her speech and made that possible. Or because she had passed the evening speaking so to his good French father and had not lost the habit yet.

How Rob wished *he* could hear her voice. Was it high-pitched or low? he wondered. Would he find her Highland accent exotic and pleasing, or exasperating?

Ah, but she awaited an answer as to where Alys might be.

"She sleeps there." Rob pointed toward the ceiling to indicate the next floor up. "We sleep here," he told her, inclining his head toward the bed. That inviting bed where he would likely spend a night in sleepless torment because he could not have her yet.

Her mouth rounded to an O and her eyes were wide. Fear? He doubted it. Surprise, more likely. She had not expected to share a chamber with him, much less a bed.

In truth, he wished other arrangements could have been made for he did not intend to claim his right to her body until she knew about him. And only then if she truly wished it so.

Not for surety of heaven would he have volunteered to sleep alone whilst biding here, however. That would have drawn too many questions since he and Mairi had been wed less than a week. They must make do.

As if they had spent every night together and this were not unusual, Rob kicked off his shoes and casually began to undress. He shrugged off his tunic and began unfastening his points.

Mairi quickly disappeared behind the screen that shielded the chamber pot and a washing basin. He smiled at how predictable she was.

When she came out of hiding, Rob had already climbed under the covers naked, though he knew that tempted fate. He reclined with one elbow propped against the handwork pillows as he watched her emerge.

She still wore her chemise, a modest piece of apparel that covered her charms almost as adequately as all of her clothing had done.

He admired modesty in a woman, yet sorely regretted that he would not be charming hers away this night. Clothed or no, the sight of her always made him ache with need, but after suffering such for several long days and nights, he had learned to bear it stoicly enough.

Rob smiled and dragged back the coverlet on her side of the bed in welcome. Would she be unwilling if he had decided to take her now?

Silently he waited, wondering, offering a small challenging smile with no intent to follow through.

She crossed the chamber with some hesitance, biting her lip and watching him warily as she slowly climbed the bed steps and eased herself upon the mattress.

Rob remained motionless until she had lain—carefully keeping as much space between them as she could—and tugged the coverlet up to her chest. Then he leaned toward her, leaving no doubt that he intended to kiss her.

Only once, he promised himself. He had thought of little else since their all-too-brief kiss after the dance tonight. One simple good-night press of lips was all he would ask now. He would not even touch her with his hands.

Rob brushed his mouth against hers, reveling in the soft, rosy fullness of hers, feeling her swift intake of breath. Unable to resist, he repeated the caress, tracing his tongue lightly along the opening caused by her wee gasp. Ah, she was sweet as marchpane.

A bit more of a taste would not hurt, he decided when she did not draw away from him. Rob angled his head more to one side and settled his mouth over hers. How perfectly they fit, he thought. Yet more delicious imaginings near wiped thoughts from his head completely.

He felt her palm slide tentatively from his chest up to his neck, her fingers flex against his nape. Hunger slashed through his body like a hot, wicked blade that carved a welcome pain. Welcome, for he knew well the sharp pleasure of alleviating such a hurt. Yet he would not. Not yet.

''Mairi...'' he whispered against her mouth, and felt the answering vibration and breath of his name upon her trembling lips.

Just a third kiss, he promised himself. Only that small torture would he take and then he would cease this madness for the night. Though even as he took it, she offered more. Another for her, he decided, so she could explore as he had done. How could he deny her that? Why on earth would he want to?

The exquisite blend of her taste and touch and scent drew a rumble of need from deep in his chest. Her hair had tumbled from its pins to cascade across the pillows. There the candlelight caught and glimmered upon it, turning some strands to purest gold.

Like blushing pearls, her skin shone the palest, near-white rose. He drank her in like a longed-for measure of honeyed mead.

Cease now, he cautioned his passion-fogged senses. And yet, she urged him on and on until he lost count of the kisses, until he lost control of his hands and where they wandered, until he did not care that she would have no *choice...*

Suddenly, Rob's honor grasped upon that word, echoed it through his brain like the beat of a bass tambour in an empty hall.

Reluctantly he withdrew his mouth from hers. His breath came in fits and starts as he looked deeply into Mairi's slumbrous eyes. Her lips beckoned again, but he closed his eyes against the temptation.

He commanded the hand he had rested upon her hip to move to her arm, to follow it up to hers, which clutched

at his shoulder. Lacing his fingers with hers, he drew them
to his lips and pressed a kiss there.

"No more," Rob whispered, breathed the words softly
to lessen the harshness of their denial, a caution as much
to himself as to her. "Not here."

Mairi cast her lambent gaze around the room as if she'd
forgotten where they were. She murmured something, for
he could see her lips barely move, tremble and then press
together.

What? What had she said? She must be asking why they
could not continue. 'Twas a certainty *he* would be asking
that now, were he Mairi.

"Tomorrow," he promised her recklessly, uncertain
what that day might bring. "We go home." Then he would
tell her everything.

Would that not be time enough for her to see all he had
accomplished? Could he not point to the wealth and condition of Baincroft castle and estate, to the folk who believed in him despite everything, and assure her he was a
good lord? A good man for a husband?

She would see. Then she would stay with him. Please
God, she would choose to stay and make their marriage
too real to undo.

"Tomorrow night," he affirmed, imploring her to understand without more explanation. "Aye?"

She retreated farther, pushing herself back to study his
face more clearly than their closeness had allowed. Her
sharpening gaze then traveled down his body, which now
lay uncovered to just below his waist. The rigid shape
beneath the coverlet made clear his desire for her.

When her eyes met his again, he smiled wryly. "Not
here," he repeated, hoping she would assume that he did
not want to do this in his sister's chamber.

She blew out the breath she had been holding, causing

her lovely shoulders to relax. Rob noticed that in his fervor, he had loosened the ties of her chemise so that it fell open, revealing the inner half of her breasts and the enticing valley between them. He had touched her there all too briefly, but the texture of that skin remained an erotic imprint on his mind.

Rob thought at that moment he would give everything he owned or could hope to have if he could but press his lips to that treasured place his eyes adored. Instead he dragged his gaze back to her puzzled one and smiled full-out, cocking both brows in rueful, silent apology.

''Tomorrow,'' she said with a slow, hesitant nod, her word as clear to him as the fact that she did not appreciate the wait any more than he.

Heartening, to say the least. Mairi wanted him as he wanted her.

If only she would still want him after he confessed, Rob would move heaven and earth to not disappoint her in any way, in any thing. Ever.

She did not look at him again. After retying her chemise with less than her usual nimbleness, she turned her back to him and pulled the covers up around her neck.

Rob found it impossible to not touch her one last time. He placed his hand upon her shoulder and smoothed the soft wool over it, knowing full well how silken the skin there would feel beneath his fingers if the fabric disappeared. Then he slid the one remaining pin from her hair and placed it on the table beside the bed.

The candles there needed pinching out and so he did, eliminating the visual temptation. In the darkness her woman's scent teased him even more. The memories of her delectable mouth and the creamy surface of her skin seemed to intensify without the benefit of light. He found his erotic image of Mairi in no way depended upon seeing her.

Deprived of both his sight and sound, Rob battled the overcompensation of his other senses until an exhausted sleep finally provided him mercy.

Tomorrow was his last thought, his fervent prayer, even as consciousness stole away.

The next morn Rob allowed Mairi to sleep as long as she would. He awoke early as he always did. When the sun rose enough to light the chamber, he watched her as she lay lost in slumber. She slept like a child, fists folded beneath her chin, her knees drawn up.

How young she appeared, even aside from the pose. How fortunate that the old laird had not wed her years ago to that wretched cousin of hers, or to some other Highland man. Now she belonged to him, for a while anyway. Forever, if he could keep her.

I am half in love with you even now. Rob reached out and plucked a wild lock of gold from her cheek and gently moved it off her face. Nay, more than half. More like heels over noggin, he thought with a rueful grimace.

She stirred and he leaned back, watching her stretch like a waking kitten. Suddenly her eyes flew open and her gaze locked with his.

"Good morn, Mairi," he said with a smile.

Her reply was lost to him behind the hand that covered her mouth, but he read apprehension and uncertainty in her wide eyes and worried frown.

"Never fear," he said calmly. "No need."

She laughed a little, shook her head and fisted her hand in the covers to throw them back so she could get up. He rose, as well, but kept the bed between them as he pulled on his braies.

After she crossed the room, Mairi turned to face him. He could see her lips now, but a jumble of words slid past before he caught on one. *Baincroft*. That gave him little clue as to what her worry was, but as luck would have it, she glared balefully at her pack of clothing.

Aha, a typically female problem. *What to wear.* Rob had found out early on in life that decisions of that nature plagued women sorely. He could help here.

"The red one," he said, enforcing his decision with a curt nod and a grin. "I like red."

She pursed her lips, pulled out the folded garment and heaved a great and obviously doubtful sigh.

"Trust me," he ventured, experiencing a sharp stab of guilt for the suggestion when he had been living a lie in her company for four, nearly five, long days.

He dressed hurriedly and stepped outside to allow her privacy to complete her morning ablutions.

They attended Mass together, a first for them as man and wife. Father Michael offered them a special blessing, though he did so with such an attitude of sadness and regret, it might have been a eulogy he performed.

The priest was Jehannie's sire, after all, and loved his daughter well. Lady Meg, Jehannie's mother, also attended the Mass, but neither her nor Father Michael offered him and Mairi any private good wishes after the service.

Rob hoped this turn of events had not caused him to lose the couple's friendship. They had been a mainstay in Rob's life since birth, an extra set of parents, which they would have been in truth if he had wed Jehannie.

Had the saucy little wench not insisted on accompanying her grandfather to the English court when he'd come to visit, and remaining there overlong, Rob would now be wed to her.

Fate had been kind in preventing that, he thought with but a brief twinge of guilt. If they had married as planned, he would never have met Mairi.

Mother had trained Jehannie from childhood to be the baroness, believing Rob would need the assistance of a canny young wife to help deal with the problems he would encounter as Lord of Baincroft.

She had also instructed Jehannie's brother, Thomas, whom Trouville had knighted, in the things he must know in order to act as Rob's steward and factor. Rob consoled himself that, at least, he would not lose Thomas's kind regard over this, since the marriage to Mairi was Thomas's idea and he had arranged it.

Do they hate me now? Rob asked his mother in signs when Mairi was not looking. He nodded toward Father Michael and Lady Meg.

No! She answered emphatically. *Give them time. They hurt.*

Rob nodded thoughtfully as he took Mairi's arm and escorted her from the chapel back into the hall.

How serene she appeared, and how beautiful even in her creased red surcoat and simple linen headrail. She was one woman who needed no jewels to add sparkle to her radiance, but he would enjoy indulging her in them all the same.

Rob cursed himself for not having thought to take a few as gifts when he'd gone to fetch her. He did have a perfect emerald brooch at Baincroft that would serve nicely as a morning gift after they had consummated their marriage.

If that happened, he reminded himself.

But he would not dwell on that at the moment. Pride swelled his chest each time he looked at her. His feelings had already progressed well beyond lust and the need to protect, tenfold and more above anything he had felt toward Jehannie, though he had known her all his life.

'Twas unfortunate for her family that Sir Simon had played his granddaughter false and hurt them in the process. And yet, how fortunate for Rob. He was so incredibly glad to have Mairi instead of Jehannie, and he adamantly resolved to feel no further guilt about that. At least, that particular deceit was none of his doing.

After they broke fast with the family, Rob allowed his mother to cajole them into staying awhile. Baincroft was only two hours' ride and he wanted to give Jehannie time aplenty to be well on her way back to the court and her grandfather before they arrived home.

One day soon he would meet with her and make peace between them, but he much doubted that could be accomplished with a beautiful new wife by his side.

Also, Mairi might be piqued enough that she had been his second choice without having to deal with his temperamental first.

They passed an hour or so visiting in his mother's solar. Rob watched Mother and Alys chat happily with Mairi. They were making her welcome, bless them both. Until now, Mairi had seemed ill at ease.

The women seemed to get on quite well, for which he silently gave thanks. Considering how his mother felt about Jehannie, matters easily could have taken a different path.

Alys had never liked his former betrothed. Though his sister had never been neglected, she might have harbored a bit of envy because of the attention Jehannie always received from his mother as Rob's future baroness.

Thus far with Mairi, Alys was behaving herself. He prayed that would continue.

While the ladies talked together, Rob sat before the fire

with Father, suffering surreptitious advice on honesty. Their conversation—half words and half signs disguised as emphatic gestures—might have proved humorous had not Rob worried that Mairi would guess the secret from that alone.

"I will tell her today, Father!" Rob declared finally, devoutly hoping to end the discussion once and for all.

Out of the corner of his eye, Rob saw the women's heads turn with a collective start.

Damn his eyes! Impatience had overcome him and he had forgotten to keep his voice low. The women had been busily discussing a tapestry in progress on a large frame by the window. Now all three were studying him, Mairi most especially.

"Time to leave," he declared, rising quickly to forestall any of her questions that could not be answered at this point. He held out his hand to her. "Come, Mairi."

No one objected, he noticed. Obviously they were eager for him to get on with the business of introducing Mairi to Baincroft so that he would tell her the truth about himself. He was not all that eager himself, but he knew it must be done. And done this very day.

Was it possible his parents entertained some small hope that Mairi would want out of the marriage contract when he told her what he must? He sincerely hoped not. And yet, they might be thinking if that happened, it certainly would smooth the path for Jehannie.

What they could not know was that Rob would never have her to wife now. Not after meeting and wedding Mairi.

Somehow he had to make her want to stay. And to love him in return.

Alys volunteered to help Mairi ready their travel packs

while Rob and his father went out to order the horses saddled.

As soon as the women had left, the comte gave him news of the prisoner Wee Andy had brought. "The man who attacked your wife is dead," the comte informed him.

"You killed him?" Rob demanded, unwilling to believe Trouville would slay a prisoner outright.

One dark brow arched as if to indicate he'd been tempted. "I conveniently left him a blade. He feared torture."

"I wanted answers," Rob muttered in disappointment. "Information."

The comte shrugged as if it mattered not. "I have from him what you would know."

"Well?" Rob turned, giving full attention.

"Ranald MacInness leads a band of rough hirelings, a score of outcasts from other clans who would serve any master with coin."

"A full score," Rob repeated to himself.

"He wants your bride. Alive or dead," his father warned.

"Why dead?" Rob asked. Why Ranald might want to kill Mairi escaped him. He'd thought surely the man who attacked her must have gone mad or misunderstood Ranald.

"Her people will not serve him as laird while Mairi still lives," Trouville explained. "Unless he holds her hostage as his wife."

"He will come," Rob said. He needed no one to answer that, for he had never questioned it. Only now he understood that neither love nor desire for Mairi played any part in his enemy's pursuit. Her life would be forfeit or made hell to bear if Ranald had his way.

Though willing and eager to avenge Mairi's father and

also rid her of any future threat, Rob had hoped for time to resolve things between Mairi and himself first. Here was another reason he must not delay on that issue.

"Two, three days, at most," Rob said. "He will arrive."

Rob felt a steady and comforting hand upon his shoulder and turned again to watch Trouville speak. "I will station a watch. He will never reach Baincroft."

"Nay. Let him come," Rob declared angrily.

"You will not like killing, Robert," Trouville said, his piercing dark eyes gone gentle with regret. "It is no easy thing."

Rob then realized he had never described the Craigmuir battle when he had slain men past the counting. Apparently, neither had Wee Andy, who must not have had the time to recount it, other than announcing Mairi's father had been killed.

The comte had trained Rob well since boyhood, then looked on proudly as the boy he'd knighted performed and won at tourneys throughout the Continent against seasoned opponents. Yet he thought him still a tenderhearted fledgling to be warned against engaging against a real threat.

"I have been blooded, Father," he admitted sadly. "True, I do not like it. But this man must die by my sword."

"So be it," said Trouville, removing the fatherly hand and lapsing back into his customary formality. "Then I wish you Godspeed."

Chapter Ten

"Where is Wee Andy?" Mairi asked Rob as they rode side by side on their way to Baincroft.

Though she had seen Rob place fresh parchment and several thin lengths of charcoal just under the flaps of her pack and his own, she chose not to fish hers out.

Her throat felt only a bit tender today. Also, she now knew Rob could hear her perfectly well and writing was pointless. She had only kept to that because she thought it easier for him.

He attended her, yet he seemed preoccupied. "Hmm? Andy?"

She nodded.

"At Baincroft," he explained in his deep, resonant voice. The unchanging timbre of it sent tremors of longing through her. How could she ever have wondered whether she liked it? None other sounded as did he, mayhaps that was why. It was so much a part of him, she had grown fond of it.

Mairi recalled how his urgent growl of desire had moved her last night. And also his promise that today he would make her his in every way. Her anticipation increased with every step their mounts took.

Rob had awakened needs in her and made her want to be a wife. *His* wife. She wanted him, certainly, but even more than the pleasure he would offer in the bedding, Mairi wished to know Rob. Really know him, in every way she did not already.

No question, he was kind and brave and honorable. Yet she needed to share his thoughts and his dreams and tell him hers. It seemed that, thus far, they had spent an inordinate amount of their time together avoiding intimacy.

He had been determined to delay it, though she knew he desired her as urgently as she desired him. He could hardly hide that fact when the evidence presented itself with astounding regularity. She noticed and he knew she did.

Mairi understood why he had not wanted to lie with her for the first time upon the ground during their journey, or later in his own sister's chamber. Home—Baincroft—must represent something very precious to this man. He would want to begin their marriage in the place where they would live and grow old together, where their children would be born and where she and Rob would rest together in eternity when their time was over.

Alys had told her Rob became lord there at the age of ten when his real father had perished from a fever. No wonder he was proud of it, having ruled it for so long.

He rode a length ahead of her now in his eagerness to reach his home. Mairi wondered what awaited them there.

Wee Andy had preceded them to make ready for their arrival, just as he had on the way to Trouville's castle. She had not seen him since he'd left them at noon the day before with their prisoner and the captured horses in tow. At least she could expect one friendly face to greet her at Baincroft.

"Will they arrange another feast for us?" she asked.

"Look there," he ordered, ignoring her question to point out a series of low rolling hills interspersed with copses of trees. He had slowed his mount so that she caught up to him. Together they silently shared the view.

In the distance a winding burn wove its way through the landscape and flowed into a huge blue loch. The afternoon sun twinkled on the wavelets like jewels.

"Beyond the water," Rob announced with a sweep of his arm, "That is mine."

Ours, Mairi thought to herself, for she had no other place to call her own. Not anymore.

It seemed to her they had quite a way to go yet, but the countryside hereabout offered much beauty and the afternoon bode fair for the ride. The weather was deliciously warm, even for summer, and the scent of wildflowers surrounded them like a welcoming mantle. Never mind that her backside felt as if it had sat a saddle for a fortnight without pause or comfort.

"How far?" she asked, noting the questioning look he had fastened upon her.

"A few leagues," he answered curtly, appearing disappointed by her reaction. He turned away and clicked his tongue to hasten his mount.

"Your lands look lovely, what little I can see of them yet," she said, urging her mare, trying to catch up. "I can hardly wait to arrive there. Rob? *Rob!*"

Too late to placate him now, she supposed, for he had ridden well ahead, guiding his mount through the fragrant heather and gray gorse that covered the ground around them.

She must remember to respond more quickly with her compliments when he made his boasts. Proud as he was of all he owned, naturally he would expect her to feel the same and be disgruntled if she did not.

"This must be fertile soil," she called, hoping to make amends. "The heather grows in such abundance! Your trees and grasses so verdant."

He said nothing, merely continued on his way. So temperamental was this husband of hers! She'd try again. Riding just behind him now, she asked eagerly, "Tell me, the kine hereabout, are they similar to the Highland beasts? Do they grow larger?"

Nothing. Hmm. She must have angered him sorely.

Then suddenly he turned to look over his shoulder at her and he wore a smile, that heart-stunning one that he was so miserly with. "You swim?"

Taken aback by the question, Mairi shook her head.

"You will learn."

"Not likely," she muttered. Cold Highland lochs and burns with their runoff from melting spring snows did not encourage swimming. No one swam apurpose there, only to save themselves when they fell in by accident. Did he not recall their adventure near Craigmuir? Swim, indeed!

"Will there be danger crossing over?" she demanded, thinking surely they could ford where the burn was shallow and not risk themselves in swift currents.

After a moment's hesitation he turned again in the saddle, his happy expression unaltered. "Two hundred cottars."

What did his number of villeins have to do with accidental drowning? Joy at returning home must have addled his brain. Oh, well. She nodded, smiling brightly as he waited, watching her, gauging her response as she made it. "So many!"

"Aye, two hundred," he repeated with a satisfied sigh and again faced the land across the loch. "And they prosper."

She quickly cast about for something to ask that might

please him since she'd got him talking for a change. "And the crops? What do you grow hereabout?"

"The children," he said, still gazing with pride upon the small part of his estate they could see. "They are healthy."

Mairi laughed aloud. "Bounty indeed! Crops of bairns." An intentional jest from him? Here was some progress! "Do they bloom fair, my lord?"

He finally turned and faced her once more, looking very serious now. "Three trained knights," he said. "Five squires. Two pages. Good lads, all."

"Mmm-hmm!" she exclaimed, uncertain what else he might want her to say about this proclamation. The men in his retinue were his business and had little to do with her.

Why did he keep casting topics about like seeds in the wind? No sooner did he introduce one than he abandoned it for another. And he did not answer her questions unless he was facing her when she asked them.

A former suspicion niggled at her, worried her for nigh a quarter league as they rode on.

Mairi waited until his attention completely focused upon their direction again. She dropped a half length behind him so that he could not see her face, even from the corner of his eye.

Then she said clearly, "Could we halt a moment? I believe my mare is limping."

He made no reply, nor did he slow his pace one whit. Now *her,* he might ignore, but Rob would never risk laming a valuable animal just to spite her.

Again Mairi tested him. "Nature calls, my lord. Please, might we bide here a wee while?" she said rather loudly.

He rode on as though she had said nothing.

Mairi's heart pounded. Her hands clenched upon her

reins and her breath caught on a small sob of sorrow. "I will curse you to perdition if you do not stop this very instant!" she shouted, willing him to turn around, to answer. "Look at me, Robert MacBain!"

He did not.

A short while later Rob did rein up and await her. He looked aghast at the tears streaming down her face. Tears she could neither halt nor hide.

"You miss home," he said sadly with much gentleness and concern, "and the laird."

All she could do was nod while he lifted her hand and held it to his face, then placed a comforting kiss inside her palm.

The sympathy in his eyes was almost more than she could bear when hers for him was breaking her heart. Yet again.

She could not explain how he had danced so well to the music, nor how he'd seemed to answer the whistle at the castle gate. But Rob had not understood a single word she had uttered to him this day. That, she would swear to.

Though she could not see how, mayhaps he heard those other things, but Mairi was absolutely certain now that he could not hear her. Somehow he saw the words upon her lips when he was watching her speak, but when he was not, she might as well speak to the wind.

"Do not weep," he beseeched, looking deeply into her eyes.

Mairi forced a tight-lipped smile and wiped her face with her sleeve. With a fortifying sniff, she pointed toward their destination. "*You* are my laird now," she declared, carefully forming each word upon her mouth so he could not mistake them. "And home is Baincroft."

The somber relief in his eyes rewarded her effort, but Mairi had to wonder what trials she would face in the future because of this. Only since last evening when she thought that he *could* hear, had she allowed herself to ponder the problems of a husband and lord who could not. They'd seemed manifold and she had given thanks that she would not have to face them. Only then had she realized how much his deafness could have affected her own life.

When she had first thought him deaf, she'd not considered at length the far-reaching effects of it, only the immediate tragedy of it for Rob's sake. Many souls depended upon him as lord. They must look to him for their protection and well-being.

How ever had he managed thus far? Who had looked after his affairs, seen that he was not cheated of his due or made jest of behind his back? And why had that person not accompanied him on his journey to Craigmuir?

Rob had no protector among those who'd traveled with him, she knew, for they were not even knighted men and had not attended him when he entered her father's hall to make final the arrangements. It must be that Sir Thomas, the one responsible for their betrothal, had let Rob go alone.

How angry it made her that no one had seen fit to assist him! Could she fill that position at Baincroft if his protector had deserted him? She would need to figure out how. No small task since hardly anyone gave any credence to a woman.

Mairi slumped under the weight of the responsibility she had assumed all unknowing. She must brace herself for this task and make a plan. A MacInness did not give up when pressed with a challenge.

Apparently neither did a MacBain. Her Rob was no faintheart, that was certain. He had faced his duty and made his way as best he could. This knowledge of him heartened her flagging spirit.

First of all, she would have to gain his trust. Obviously she did not have it yet since he still feared to tell her what she must face.

Next, she would have to make certain she always spoke so that he could understand her. She'd already begun doing that and it seemed to work just now.

Last of all, Mairi knew she had to win the respect of those who lived at Baincroft. For a lady to share her lord's rule of them might not sit kindly upon men used to governing themselves for so long.

Rob was no feckless child, however. And definitely not simple of thought, for a bright intelligence gleamed in those watchful gray eyes. Quick of mind, aye, and quick on his feet for such a large man. He had proved himself an able warrior. Yet to manage an entire barony without an ear to what went on around him would surely be impossible for any man.

Mairi determined she would win his love before the next sunrise, and then he'd grant her his trust. He would confess his plight to her and seek her help. If he did not, she would ask him outright and then offer it. That would be the first order of business. All else would follow as day followed night. She would see to it.

For the moment she must delay avenging her father. Though postponing that made her feel disloyal and disappointed her greatly, there would be too much to set right here. She could not expect her husband and his men to mount a war upon her cousin halfway across Scotland. At least, not yet.

Ranald might follow them here, of course. Rob obviously believed he would. If that happened, Mairi only hoped Rob and his folk knew how to conduct a defense.

Though she had seen many a raid upon Craigmuir, she
knew little of how to organize men for such an event.

Her husband certainly could hold his own in a hand-to-
hand battle, but she wondered if he was capable of command. In a place such as this, where it seemed war had
not touched, he might never have had the need to learn.

Lord's mercy, she hoped he would confide in her soon.
Today. They sorely needed to speak of how profoundly
his deafness affected his abilities, so she could decide what
she must do next.

Rob worried that Mairi would arrive at home exhausted
and in tears. He should have allowed her another day to
rest before traveling on, but he needed to be at Baincroft.

He felt certain that her cousin Ranald would arrive
within a few days. Rob needed his defenses in perfect order before that happened.

Also, the pretense that he could hear grew wearying and
he was not certain how long he could maintain it. Nor did
he wish to keep it up. Mairi should know. She had the
right. If only he could find a way to tell her gently.

Never since he was ten—and living the lie with Trouville for those few months—had he given more than a
minimal effort to concealing the deafness. He never denied
it, but neither did he volunteer the information. 'Twas no
one else's business, after all.

Henri or Thomas, and often the comte himself, were
usually with him at tournaments, taking up the burden of
conversing when other knights joined them in any social
discourse.

His squire had served to keep him informed when they
did not, but Gareth was knighted himself now and gone
on to win his own rewards. Henri had assumed his duties
in France on Trouville's estates, which he would inherit

one day. And Thomas, of course, languished about with that broken leg.

This venture Rob had attempted alone had been more difficult than he'd ever imagined, but not impossible, thank God. He had managed on his own for once. Now, however, he badly needed a rest from it all. He longed to be himself again.

He needed Mairi. And, worst of all, he needed truth between them. That could not come before she believed in him. She must see how he had succeeded at Baincroft and know that the bargain her father had made would prove to her benefit.

Mairi had to *want* to be his before his passion for her ruled, and he made it so. And, because of his promise last night, he had only this day to convince her.

They came to the crossing place at the burn. His men and Trouville's had erected a bridge there made of timber anchored in stones. He dismounted and helped Mairi to alight, allowing her body to slide down the front of his until her feet touched the grass. Sweet torture, and welcome.

She smiled at him, her tears all dry and the pink blossoming on her cheeks like delicate rose petals. He loved her skin, so fine and fair, so soft.

Rob's heartbeat quickened as he moved his hands from her waist. "Here we are," he said, gesturing toward the other side of the bridge.

"Aye," she replied.

He marked the trepidation she tried to conceal. She worried that those at Baincroft would look awry at her, he supposed. And well some might, for she was not of their people, but a Highland woman.

Thomas better have seen to that possibility or Rob meant to have his hide, bad leg or no. And if the rascal had not packed that sister of his off by the time they arrived, Rob would set them both on the road for good and all. Mairi needed no distress after all she had suffered on the journey here, and he meant to see she had none.

He took her hand in his and they walked across the burn leading the mounts. There, he pulled his cloak from his pack and spread it upon the ground beside the burn.

"Rest," he offered, then led the beasts to drink at the edge of the flowing water.

Rob knelt a few feet upstream, washed his face and scooped up a drink. When he blinked away the droplets, he saw Mairi had followed him to likewise refresh herself.

On impulse, he dipped his hand and flicked the moisture at her with a teasing grin.

She winced and laughed, trailed her own fingers at the edge and flung enough at him to sprinkle his face.

"Bad lass!" he scolded, then looked longingly at the water. The current ran swiftly here, but was shallow enough that it would not be a danger. He gestured toward it with a questioning look.

"Ach, *nay!*" she exclaimed, "…home wet?"

He shrugged, conceding she was right. Unlikely she would agree to gamboling about naked and certainly could not swim in her clothes.

One day soon he would bring her back, farther downstream where there lay a quiet pool. It was much like the peaceful place near Craigmuir where they had first kissed.

Thinking of that, Rob reached behind him and broke off several stalks of heather. "For you," he said, holding his voice soft as he handed them to her.

He stretched his arm wide in a gesture encompassing all that lay within his domain. "All for you."

She swallowed hard, then inclined her head in acceptance and touched the heather to her nose.

Rob wanted so to reassure her, to promise on his life and honor that she would remain happy and protected and loved here for the rest of her days. He wanted her to know that, to depend on it and be comforted by it.

But the words tumbled over themselves in his mind until he feared they would emerge in the wrong order, or that his tone of voice would sound too harsh and give lie to the tenderness behind it.

Instead, he leaned toward her and placed a gentle kiss of peace upon her lips. And yet, that did not seem enough to seal the unspoken, heartfelt promises he wished to make. Not for him, and apparently not for her.

When Mairi's lips opened beneath his in sweet invitation, Rob felt all his good intentions flow south.

Chapter Eleven

Mairi slid her fingers through his sun-streaked hair and gloried in the feel of his mouth, the taste of him, and the pressure of his body flush against hers as they lay back upon the soft, sweet grass. A terrible hunger for him swept through her, an urgent need to offer him all that she had to give.

The musical tumble of water over rocks and the trill of the meadowlark in the distance would be lost to her Rob, Mairi thought sadly. As would the words she would give him in the heat of their loving. With that thought, she increased the fervor of their kiss, poured everything she felt for him into it.

For an endless yet all-too-brief interlude, Mairi abandoned herself to passion, trusting that Rob would either halt their lovemaking or not, as he wished. In truth she did not want him to stop, but realized somewhere in the back of her mind that he probably would.

Finally he released her mouth, yet kept her close, running his strong and nimble hands over her as if to soothe away any distress he had caused by arousing her.

"It will take more than that," she murmured to herself.

He drew back then, likely because he had felt her breath

rush out just beside his ear. "Hmm?" he asked, smiling as though she had spoken a jest.

Mairi decided to be direct. "I want you," she whispered the individual words as though his heeding them were a matter of life and death.

"I know," he answered, those wicked gray eyes filled with blatant desire and rueful understanding.

He brushed her hair away from her brow and picked up the modest headrail that he had recently tugged from her. She did not want gentleness at the moment. 'Twas not enough.

Mairi snatched the length of linen from his hand and pushed herself to a sitting position, keeping her back to him. How well she knew the state of his body, and was struggling with all her might not to look at it and point out how simple it would be to remedy his discomfort. And hers.

Not now, she cautioned herself. Rob was impatient to get home. And certainly eager enough to bed her that she need not worry that he wouldn't once they got there.

If only she could dismiss the raging fever that flared within her now, she might find some amusement in the episode. It angered her that he saw humor in it, but she supposed that was better than grumbling as she felt inclined to do.

After all, there they were, sprawled upon the bank of the burn in broad daylight, well within sight of the bridge. Anyone could come along and see them. She could only imagine what a sight they would present if they continued.

Fumble fingers! Mairi cursed her trembling hands. She shoved her untidy braid back beneath the headpiece and forced a smile upon her face before she turned. He was already standing and holding out his hand to help her rise.

"You are sweet," he said with a teasing grin.

"And you are cruel," she replied with a mock frown.

Too seldom had she heard his unrestrained laughter, only once before. Now, as then, 'twas deep-throated, as his voice, and genuine as a child's. Contagious, too.

She had to laugh with him, at herself for such outrageously improper acts and thoughts. And at him, too, simply because he'd denied himself and could stand there heavily aroused and jest about it.

Still chuckling, he led her to her mare and lifted her to the saddle. Once she had her seat, he patted her thigh and squeezed gently.

"My merry Rob," she said dryly, shaking her head at him.

He handed her the reins and closed her hands around them. "My lusty Mairi," he returned in a suggestive growl, accompanied by a lift of his brow.

Well, she wasn't certain she liked that observation! *Lusty* was not a word she would ever have used to describe herself before, yet she had to admit, it was true enough where Rob was concerned.

Too many times now had they come together and backed away. No more, she decided. If he kissed her again, unless 'twas in the midst of the hall during mealtime with all his people in attendance, she meant to follow through!

Be warned, my fine Lord Robbie. The pictures forming in her mind of what could happen if he did not heed her silent admonition kept her smiling all the way to Baincroft.

Rob picked up their pace the closer they got and soon, the castle loomed near.

"'Tis beautiful!" she said. Then she realized that her husband's eyes were not upon her, rode up beside him and repeated what she had said. She must remember, Mairi chastised herself. He must *see* the words.

"Aye," he said, his quick gray eyes shining with emo-

tion, thanking her, praising her for echoing what he surely
felt. "A fine home."

Alys had warned Mairi to not expect Baincroft to equal
Trouville's castle and it did not. At least not in its size,
which appeared to be only about half again as large as
Craigmuir, yet smaller by far than Rob's parents' castle.

Unlike her father's Highland keep and stout wall, these
had been whitewashed and lacked any marks of siege or
neglect.

The laird had never attached much importance to appearance, only to defense. Surely this was a much more
peaceful place than her Highland home had been.

A fair trade, Mairi reckoned. The rugged magnificence
of the land from whence she had hailed for the peace and
beauty of this resplendent estate.

She heard the welcome horn sound upon the battlements. Then, as they approached the gate, there came a
shrill whistle much like the one that had greeted them
when they'd arrived at Trouville's.

Rob immediately looked up and waved a perfunctory
greeting at the man standing upon the wall. The fellow did
not smile in welcome, however, and even appeared somewhat distraught at seeing them there.

The gates already stood open and Rob rode through,
leading the way. The bailey teemed with folk who had
been about their daily activities, though they seemed to
have frozen in place at the sight of their lord.

Or mayhaps it was *her* they cast their worried frowns
upon. Some of them exchanged looks of apprehension with
each other and began to whisper amongst themselves.

Rob noted this, too, she decided from the tense set of
his shoulders and his white-knuckled grip upon his reins.
With an occasional nod to one or another of those who

stood about marking their progress, he continued riding right up to the keep's wooden steps.

A slender, handsome man awaited them at the top in front of the doors. He leaned upon two canes. Mairi recognized him as the dark-haired knight, Sir Thomas, who had come to Craigmuir in his lord's stead to arrange her betrothal to Rob.

So, he had been somehow injured, Mairi noted. That would explain why he had not been able to return to Craigmuir and assist Rob as he should have done. Seeing him here was a great relief. Hopefully, he was still able to perform his duties as factor for Rob, at the very least.

Mairi smiled up at him, but he merely chewed upon his bottom lip and frowned at her husband.

Were his people afraid of him? Had they dreaded his arrival? Wee Andy had seemed to like Rob well enough, and fear him so little as to wax impertinent at times. Mairi now worried there might be a darker side to the MacBain that she had not yet encountered.

Rob dismounted and came to assist her down. With one hand at her waist, he ushered her up the steps while servants rushed forward and began unloading their packs from the mounts.

Halfway up, Sir Thomas nodded frantically. Mairi surmised that Rob had made a question with his hands that she could not see, for he mumbled a truly vivid curse at his man's answering gesture.

"You know Thomas?" he asked her when they reached his man, his impatience with the introduction evident.

"Aye," she answered. "Good greetings, sir."

The knight bowed as well as he could while balanced upon one leg and his canes. "Welcome, my lady."

Rob hardly gave him time to right himself before pushing past him to the door.

The moment they entered the great hall, Rob rushed her toward the stairs. So urgently he moved, he had not bothered to close the door behind them.

Somehow, Mairi did not believe he did this due to any powerful need to be alone with her. It was as if he wanted her secluded, out of the way, and with a great hurry.

Something strange was going on here or about to happen. Something everyone was aware of but her.

"So! It is *true!*" came a shrill, angry shout.

The outburst jerked Mairi's attention from her passing appraisal of her new surroundings back to the stairway they were approaching.

A small, dark-haired virago stood, hands on hips, having just rounded the final curve within the winding stairs. She looked to be near the same age as Mairi, though even shorter in stature than Mairi's meager height. The beauty appeared very delicately made and was beautifully dressed in embroidered linen. And absolutely furious.

She met them three steps up from where they would have entered had she not appeared.

Rob halted, blew out a harsh breath and raised his eyes toward the high, vaulted ceiling. "Shite," he hissed, low enough that only she could hear.

The woman's hands suddenly flew into motion as though weaving some virulent curse upon them. Mairi watched in fascination.

Then, swift as the dive of a hawk, the woman marched down those last three steps, straight up to Rob and slapped him full across the face. Hard. The crack of it echoed off the walls, punctuated with the loud gasps of a number of servants who had witnessed it.

Rob withstood the blow without flinching, but he made no answer to it, either by word, deed or expression. Mairi suspected he was too shocked.

She certainly was. Had any person, male or female, ever struck her father that way in anger, the fool's head would be bouncing on the floor beside the feet by this time.

At that moment the infuriated lady marched swiftly around them, straight across the hall and out the open door. Rob did stir himself to turn and watch her departure, but that was the only move he made.

"Who in heaven's name was *that?*" Mairi dared to ask.

Rob did not answer. The left side of his face bore a dull crimson hand print. His usually expressive mouth had drawn into a firm line that tilted neither up nor down, and a muscle ticked in his jaw.

The servants in the hall still gaped, their eyes darting collectively from the portal where the woman had exited to Rob and back again. They, like Mairi, clearly awaited his reaction. One certainly seemed called for, in her opinion.

After standing silently for a good long while, he casually retraced their steps to the hall door and met Sir Thomas coming back inside.

The knight moved somewhat clumsily, wincing with pain as he stopped and leaned against the oaken jamb.

"She is gone," he gasped.

"Where?" Rob asked.

Sir Thomas shook his head and shrugged. "Rode out," he said, hesitating only a heartbeat before adding, "On *your* horse."

Again the muscle ticked as Rob clenched his teeth. A tense few moments of silence ensued.

The woman had struck her lord, embarrassed him before his people, and stolen a valuable steed. Mairi dreaded hearing what penalty would be levied against the offender, even though punishment was obviously warranted for such monumental acts of idiocy.

"Show Mairi Baincroft," Rob ordered curtly, leveling Sir Thomas with a look that promised severe retribution if he did not comply immediately.

That expression frightened her, for she had not seen such fury upon his face except during the battle at Craigmuir and later after she'd been attacked.

Even fearing his present mood, she had to ask him the question that plagued her. Grasping his sleeve to gain his attention, she demanded, "Will you go after her?"

"No." He gripped her shoulder, then let his hand slide down her arm, his hold gentling as it reached her hand. "Go with Thomas." He tried a smile, but it proved merely a stretch of his lips. An ordeal. "Please."

Mairi acquiesced, not unwilling at this juncture to part company with him, given his foul mood. He had good reason for it, she admitted, though it troubled her to see him so. There was naught she could do to help resolve matters for him in this instance, so she would leave him to it.

If she knew aught of her husband, his good humor would return soon enough. He did not seem one to hold to anger overlong. For that poor woman's sake, Mairi hoped she was right about that.

Sir Thomas offered his elbow and she placed her hand upon it. The formality seemed ridiculous since he had to use that hand to ply his second cane in order to walk. She felt as if she should be supporting *him*.

The poor man looked fit to collapse, either due to the current happenings—whatever they might be, aside from the woman's attack—or from the pain of his leg injury. Rob had already left them.

"What happened to you?" she asked the knight.

He managed a sheepish grin that turned his pale face boyish. "I fell and broke my leg a fortnight past."

"Then you should be abed," she commented. "Or sitting with it propped on a stool. It will not mend with you hopping about so on it."

Mairi thought to win his confidence with her concern, and hopefully get him to tell the true tale of what was taking place here and the reasons for it.

"Not to worry, my lady," he assured her as he limped along toward the back of the hall. "Allow me to summon Mistress Morgan and make her known to you. She will give you a tour of the tower rooms and get you settled in the lord's chamber. 'Tis difficult for me to take the stairs."

She patted his arm. "I'm certain Lord MacBain did not mean for you to try!"

He scoffed and clicked his tongue. "Do not be fooled, my lady. Rob could cheerfully have broken my remaining leg and my head, as well, just now."

"You call him rather familiar, sir," she admonished. Did all his vassals treat him with such disrespect? Even Wee Andy had done so. This use of Rob's forename with no title at all was unheard of in her experience. She even felt remiss in using it herself, though the only time she'd done so aloud was during their near intimate encounters. For his men to do this did not seem proper at all.

Matters here might be even worse than she had suspected. Aye, he would need her help to right them.

"My sincere apologies," Thomas muttered, obviously rankled by the rebuke. "Rob and I were lads together, and betimes I forget my place. I am but the humble steward, after all, and likely to be less than that after this day's work."

"I wish ye...*you* would tell me what's amiss, Sir Thomas. The folk here tremble with dread, as if our arrival bodes ill. That angry shrew who struck my husband has something to do with this, eh?"

"Obviously," he admitted with a puff of resignation. "However, I am not at liberty to say what."

Mairi considered that and decided the lass must be Rob's leman. "Well, she is no relative, I'll wager. Nor is she a mere servant, judging by her daring."

The steward's pained expression grew darker. He opened his mouth to speak, clamped it shut, then began again, "I should say nothing of her to you, my lady. She is not your concern."

Mairi took her hand from his arm. "Never mind. I believe you have already said sufficient."

What other reason could her husband possibly have had to order his people not to talk of that female unless she was his paramour?

Rob had not been the only one to suffer the glare of the woman's hatred, so Mairi knew that she, as Rob's new wife, somehow played a part in bringing on the assault. And the lord's introducing his lady to Baincroft hardly would have prompted that sort of tirade from anyone other than a lover.

Thomas led Mairi through the back of the hall and into the kitchens where he placed her in care of Mistress Morgan. That one proved a dour-faced woman of considerable girth who would likely offer fewer words on the matter than did Rob's steward. Mairi did not even bother to ask.

Well, so much for the new bride's welcome to Baincroft, Mairi thought with a woeful shake of her head. 'Twas a fair and comfortable keep she had come to, full of unfair and uncomfortable secrets.

It seemed that her husband had his vassals' fear, yet not their respect. Added to that, Mairi must deal with Rob's leman, who was all harsh temper and no common sense. That woman would be back, she had no doubt.

His mistress's living here could no longer be countenanced, of course. After Rob had exacted punishment for the blow and the theft, Mairi must see the woman settled with a husband of some sort in the very near future. Turning out any female—even one of easy virtue—would be unconscionable, and 'twas the lady of the keep's responsibility to see such matters concluded.

Thank heaven Rob had chosen a MacInness to wife. A lesser woman might have quailed at such an odious task. But she relished the challenge, Mairi told herself firmly.

No feast tonight, Rob declared with his signs, then crossed his arms over his chest, frowning.

"Good!" Thomas replied aloud, obviously relieved. *I am sorry about Jehannie,* he added, rubbing a palm over his heart and raking a thumb along his face for his sister's name sign. He continued, his motions harsh and emphatic. *I tried to make her go. I tried!*

No doubt Thomas had. Rob knew exactly how fractious and unmanageable Jehannie could be.

Thomas caught Rob's eye again, but his hands were hesitant now. *Your wife thinks my sister is your whore.*

Rob rolled his eyes and with a gesture of defeat, collapsed upon the chair that sat beside the fire in the solar. He sighed, shook his head and signed. *I will explain to her. Later.*

Thomas nodded, his face tight with worry. "Jehannie's overset."

"Jehannie will go to Mother," Rob assured him verbally, since Thomas had turned away. "That is best."

He then changed the subject, for there was nothing more either of them could do at the moment about his former betrothed. "We must prepare. Fight my wife's cousin," he said, slurring his words and not bothering to correct himself. With Thomas he did not have to take such care in speaking, for they understood each other well.

Thomas faced him again and signed. *Andy said the new laird's men followed, and you dispatched them.*

Rob fell to using hand language yet again to speed the telling, and related to Thomas all that had transpired. He suspected Andy had told him much of it after he arrived at Baincroft with Jehannie the day before.

You questioned the prisoner you took? Thomas asked.

Trouville did so. Ranald MacInness wants Mairi to die if he cannot have her. He then explained to Thomas that he had learned how many men and what kind of force Mairi's cousin might bring against them when he came. Unless more had been hired to replace those Rob had slain.

Thomas admitted that could be a problem, since Baincroft retained few men who were accustomed to battle.

Rob rose and started for the solar door, intent on doing at least one thing productive this day. "I see to defense," he announced.

Thomas caught his arm as he passed. Rob looked down at his friend, who was still seated. "Aye?"

"What of Jehannie, Rob? I agree she will go to Lady Anne and Lord Edouard, but what then? What might she do? You have to think of something."

There was a plea in Thomas's eyes that had naught to do with supplication of steward to lord. 'Twas friend to friend, for Thomas loved Jehannie.

Rob realized that he loved her, too. Much like Thomas did, as a sister. It was not right that she should suffer for something that was no fault of hers, the broken betrothal. Though she had reacted badly and embarrassed both him and herself before their people today, he had no wish to punish her.

It might do her good, however. She needed to learn

control. How many times had he and Thomas found it necessary to save Jehannie from herself? To ward off foolery that might well have landed all three of them in more trouble than they could handle? Too many times. 'Twas a wonder that they had reached adulthood unscathed. Even now, Rob knew he would do anything within his power to prevent her suffering.

"I will put all to rights, Tom," he reassured his best friend with a smile that he hoped showed no doubt. For good measure, he affectionately cuffed Thomas on the arm and gave him a firm nod and a wink.

"You should speak with her," Thomas said. "Will you not?"

"Aye, after I deal with Ranald MacInness."

As Thomas's shoulders relaxed, his whole demeanor changed and worry seemed to flee, leaving him at ease.

Thomas probably knew him better than any other man alive, and yet still believed that Rob could solve any problem set before him.

Even though he had courted it assiduously long before he became a man and assumed his rightful place as their lord, the absolute confidence his people placed in him always daunted Rob a bit.

Not for the first time did he wonder whether he could deliver a solution to what seemed unsolvable. But somehow, he would manage it.

Responsibility weighed upon him like a heavy mantle, but one he had donned readily enough, for all that. That mantle had settled upon him by right of birth and he had held it only by virtue of his family's hard work in preparing him properly. He could never willingly cast it off.

If only Mairi would take a page from Thomas's book, Rob thought with an inner scoff. *Trust.* A precious commodity he did not warrant from his bride, but must gain before he could call her his. Unfair, mayhaps, but he had found that life seldom was fair.

With that, he drew in a deep breath and went out to summon his guard. 'Twould be a long afternoon and an even longer night, he suspected.

There was the armory to be inspected first, to determine if all there was in order. Weapons must be inspected and allocated, then each man assigned his position to defend in case of attack.

Thank God, there had been monthly drills and his men kept fit, even though he had not many to instruct. Until now, there had been little need for hiring more. It would have been an unnecessary expense to feed and house them. Who could have guessed he would ever require such a force?

The night would require more effort than preparing for a battle. As much as he desired Mairi, Rob now realized that he'd been rash in promising her what he had promised.

If he delivered upon that and took her to his bed, he must reveal his secret first, so that she could choose whether to stay with him or to dissolve their marriage. And there was not time enough before they would retire to evaluate her reaction to his worthiness. He would be too busy preparing for attack.

Rob ran a hand over his face, pausing over the cheek that still smarted from Jehannie's slap. As matters stood, Mairi suspected that he had a mistress, one with the audacity to make free with her anger and his horse.

The devotion of his people had certainly not been apparent in their faces today. Only sharp curiosity as to what would happen once Jehannie let fly with her fury.

What must his wife be thinking of him at this moment? And how the devil could he repair her thoughts to his advantage in but a few hours' time?

As the day wore on, Rob put aside his concerns as best he could and concentrated on his preparations. He figured that MacInness would not expect him to be ready. He hoped that the men hired by Ranald would be no more experienced in fighting than those Rob had encountered at Craigmuir and on the way home. If so, the numbers would not matter so much.

The horn sounded late in the afternoon as Rob was coming out of the armory with his newly sharpened sword. He waited for a sign from the battlements that the Highlanders were approaching.

Instead, one of the gates swung open just widely enough for Wee Andy to ride through. Rob knew immediately something was wrong. He had ordered Andy to follow Jehannie and see her safe.

Rob threw up his hand and beckoned. Andy galloped across the bailey and quickly dismounted, tossing his reins to young Elfled who had been assisting Rob with the weaponry.

"She's gone!" Andy announced, red in the face and huffing from his hard ride. He made the sign for lost.

Not with my mother? Rob asked.

Andy raked off his cap and shook his head, motioning with one hand as he spoke. "Nay. Nowhere along the way. Just *gone!* You must *find* her!"

For a moment Rob's heart nearly stopped. If Jehannie had happened upon MacInness and his men... Then he remembered her disappearances as a child when something did not go her way. It would not be at all unlike her to use such a trick now. She had been as upset and angry as he had ever seen her.

Even so, Jehannie knew better than to approach a party of strange men and also how to elude such a group if she heard them coming. It was not as if MacInness and that many followers could travel unnoticed.

If by some quirk of fate, the men should have spotted her, Rob knew the mount Jehannie had taken could outrun a Highland pony any day. She was an excellent horse-woman and the gelding was as fast as the wind. Given MacInness's quest, he would have no reason to give chase to her.

Rob wondered where she had decided to seclude herself this time, the crumbling old peel tower or some vacant herder's hut. He had no doubt she'd remain wherever that was until the entire population of both castles had exhausted every effort to find her.

Not this time, Rob decided. He had not the men to spare for a useless search, and none to ride to his father and request him to do it. If she were still vain enough to think everyone would drop their tasks and run about like puzzled hounds seeking her tracks, she was sadly mistaken.

She's hiding, he told Andy. *Let her be.*

"Thomas won't like it!"

Rob quirked a brow at that. Andy had never cared very much what Thomas thought. Though the two usually got on well enough, Thomas never let Andy forget which one of them wore spurs and had the greater rank. Wee Andy usually thumbed his nose at that, saying he could have gained a knighthood, also, if he had preened before Trouville for years as Tom had.

Now he seemed truly concerned that Jehannie's brother might worry about her. Either that, or Wee Andy still worshiped the lass as he had when they were children.

I will tell Thomas, Rob assured him.

Andy nodded reluctantly. He then looked around them and remarked on the unusual scurry of activity within the bailey. "MacInness?"

"Likely. In another day or two." Absently Rob ran his fingers along the flat of the blade as he spoke, pleased with the smoothness of the fine-tempered steel.

"Orders?" Andy asked, gamely squaring his shoulders and leaving the concern about Jehannie to Rob.

"See to your weapons. Rest. Take watch at midnight."

"Right you are," Andy agreed, then stalled for a moment before heading for the barracks across the way. "Lady Mairi, she fares well?"

"Well enough," Rob replied, glad that she had at least gained the kind regard of one of his friends.

"Did you tell her yet?" Andy asked pointedly, wearing a meaningful look.

Rob exhaled sharply, unwilling to dwell on that when he had too much else to think about. "*No* advice, Andy!"

The man had the grace to leave without another comment by sign or by speech. For a change.

If one more person sought to tell him what he should do this day, Rob thought he might treat them to a true Jehannie sort of fit.

Chapter Twelve

Mairi soon realized if she meant to gain a foothold at Baincroft, she needed to act quickly. Thus far, both Sir Thomas and the redoubtable Mistress Morgan had shuffled her off like some poor relation come to impose.

Her tour of Baincroft included a brief look around the kitchens and the interior of the one stairwell that led up to the master chamber.

There was the chamber itself, of course, which offered an enormous bed, Rob's chest of clothing, a small table and two chairs before the fireplace. He had a few weapons hung upon the wall from hooks and a sturdy wooden frame to support his mail hauberk.

'Twas a bachelor cell, not embellished with costly hangings or any other frivolous trappings, but admittedly larger than most knights enjoyed. And it was spotlessly clean. That heartened her. She would not need to train the maids in their proper housekeeping tasks.

It would not hurt to add her own touches eventually, if her husband did not object. Mairi wondered if Rob disliked tapestries and rich fabrics in the bedchamber. She had much to learn of him. Could he be miserly? He did not seem so in other respects.

At least he favored beeswax candles instead of the noisome tallow, she thought as she picked up an unlighted one and sniffed the pleasant scent.

How little she knew about Rob and what he preferred. He must like furs, for there were those aplenty upon the bed. The hangings he did have were plain, saffron-colored linen, devoid of any embroidery. They begged for it. She imagined a pattern.

The trunk beside the window bore no fancy carving. 'Twas plain oak with simple, unadorned hasp and hinges, like her father's had been. Mairi suffered a pang of homesickness.

The window was glazed, a welcome concession to warmth and draft prevention. Also, much to her delight, there was the large fireplace set into the wall instead of the open braziers they had used at Craigmuir.

No blaze warmed the room now, however, and Mistress Morgan had offered none. She had simply deposited Mairi there in the chamber, and promptly set off as if she had more important business to attend.

That being the case, Mairi decided she would not stay where she was put. After all, *she* was the lady here now, and could go where she pleased.

With that thought, she marched directly to the door and back down the stairs to explore.

If no one saw fit to introduce her about and make the place known to her, she would see Baincroft on her own. This was to be her home, after all.

Her determined step brought her back into the hall. The bustle of confusion and so many people rushing about the huge chamber had her backing into a niche in the wall and watching from the shadows.

Men were busily dragging the trestles into a U-shape and maids were shooing them away as soon as the tables were set up. Flutters of white cloth billowed up and landed on the planks.

She much feared they were readying the place for another feast, and Mairi had already had one too many of those. If Rob were about, she would have protested.

Yet even as she supposed that was so, she saw men enter wearing mail and settling their weapons about them. The noise and general excitement increased with the number of people.

Since many of the men were armed and posturing about as though readying for war, Mairi realized their cause. A pity no one saw fit to include the lady of the house in the planning for it all. Mayhaps most of them did not realize they had a lady now. Andy might not have announced it with that woman in residence.

Mairi moved out of the alcove and walked among them. Now and then, one of the folk would cast a curious glance her way, but none spoke to her directly or paid her much mind.

Small wonder, since she had not been made known to them as yet. Considering her simple raiment, they might think her a poor maid their lord had plucked up on his travels.

The thought rankled, doing nothing to improve her mood. 'Twas obvious Rob had not warned them aforehand that he was to wed. None had expected it, most especially that woman who had slapped him.

"Lady Mairi, what do you here?" Sir Thomas said from behind her. He had the effrontery to sound impatient.

She rounded on him, hands on hips. "Have you forgotten, sir? This is my home. Can I not roam where I will? What is all of this? What are they doing?"

Now that she noted baskets of simples the women were stacking and the folds of linen being torn into strips, Mairi knew exactly what they were doing. Collecting their medicaments and readying bandages. She had done it herself many times.

Sir Thomas hobbled forth to stand closer and seemed at a loss for words. "Rob...Lord Robert merely wished us to...uh...to put all in order for...uh—"

"He is expecting Ranald, is he not? My cousin?"

Thomas blew out a breath of defeat. "Aye, he is." With the sweep of a hand, he indicated the tables. "We will leave them set up in the event there are wounded to tend. You were not to know of this, or to worry on it."

She raised a brow, much as Rob sometimes did, hoping to look as imperious as a baroness should. "I will not be treated as a child, Sir Thomas. Just as Lord Robert should direct our defense and a possible battle, 'tis my place to arrange for the results of one."

"As you will, my lady," he agreed reluctantly. "But you need not."

Mairi glanced toward the kitchens, and in so doing, saw that their conversation had gained them audience. The noise level within the hall had decreased, and so had the work, as people stopped to listen. Just as well, Mairi thought. Now was as good a time as any to establish her authority.

"How are we set for supplies should there be a siege?" she demanded of the steward. Mairi spoke carefully, mindful to sound as much like these people as she could manage. If they did not accept her, if she were too different, she would have no say here even if she was the lord's wife.

"The storerooms are nigh half filled," he answered proudly, as if he had gathered the stuff himself. "Meat aplenty, dried and freshly hung. We are somewhat short on grains since we are so long from harvest, this being summer—"

"Aye, I ken," she said, waving off his words, so he would elaborate no further. There were other matters more urgent than bread. "Water? Where are the wells?"

He straightened, looking about him at those who were now hanging on his every word and hers. "Two, my lady. Well protected and accessible."

"Have enough water drawn and kept heated for tending wounded. I see we have the baskets within easy reach, as well as bindings. Also, we shall need plenty of linen thread and the sharpest needles."

She paused only an instant. "Aye, and send several people to the least used storerooms and chambers to collect all the spiders' webs they may find." She paused to think what else, tapping her lips with a finger.

"Webs, my lady?"

"To staunch bleeding," she answered absently, still lost in thought.

"Mayhaps you would also like to order the drill for the men," he suggested smugly.

"Nay, never that," she said, choosing to ignore his sarcasm. "However, do inform the guards at the main gates and also at the postern, that no person unknown to them may enter our walls. Heed me, if this man come here, you may be certain he will attempt to conquer by subterfuge first. 'Ware of any stranger seeking entrance or we could find our walls breached from within before we know it."

He almost sneered. "I suppose you are the voice of experience in warfare, eh?"

She met him glare for glare. "How many attacks have you had upon Baincroft, Sir Thomas?"

The skin of his cheeks turned bright red. He shifted a bit on his canes and looked away. "Only one in my memory,'' he admitted in an almost inaudible voice. "But that one was not really—"

"How *many,* sir?" she prompted. "I did not hear you."

"One!" he all but shouted. "And it was not by an enemy. It was a misunderstanding. This is a peaceful place. We do not war against each other hereabout."

She inclined her head in thanks for his cooperation. "Well, sir, we suffer attack regularly where I am from. And by just such a reiver as my lord expects to arrive here soon."

A rumble of whispers broke the silence. Mairi had not meant to undermine any of the steward's orders, or to give him such a set-down. He looked fit to kill.

"My lord values you so highly, Sir Thomas. I felt compelled to seek your assistance in what I believe needs doing. If I have overstepped my venue as lady of this house, I beg you to forgive me. Lord MacBain's people are my people now, and I would see to their welfare as best I may. Will you help me?"

"Aye, I will," he agreed, his pride still dented, she could see. Yet he proved gracious enough now that she had relented a little in her demands.

"Then I thank you from my heart." She looked around them at the searching eyes and tensely held postures. "Each of you mind what task Sir Thomas has assigned you now. We have no time to loll about. Set to!"

The crowd that had gathered around them dispersed immediately and the hall soon teemed again with activity.

Only then did she see her husband leaning against the hall door, his great arms crossed over his chest, watching her with that hawklike intensity only he possessed.

Not knowing what else to do, Mairi smiled her innocent smile.

He did not smile back.

Beside her, she heard Sir Thomas clear his throat. When he spoke, his voice betrayed a hint of humor. "I do wonder how Rob will take to sharing his rule with you."

"You forget and use the familiar again to speak of your lord, sir."

His chuckle unnerved her. "I did not forget. I use his forename because we *are* familiar, lady. We are as brothers in every way. Think you he will abandon our lifelong friendship for the regard of a Highland stranger?"

"Nay," she replied sweetly. "But if it comes to his choosing one or the other of us—which I never intended to demand of him—you must consider what weapons you possess that might counter what *I* have to offer, sir."

"Your weapons, as you call them, do not hold a candle to mine, lady. The beautiful woman he has loved forever and truly wished to wed is my sister. Your precious lord loves her still and always shall. What think you of that!"

Stunned, Mairi had to force herself to not tremble in the face of that news. But she would not give the odious steward that satisfaction. Instead she stretched her lips into a smile of what she dearly hoped looked like victory. "Aye, well, I think 'twas not that canny of ye to ha' betrothed him to me, then, was it?"

"A mistake, I admit, and one circumstance forced me to make," he said with a haughty jerk of his chin. "A circumstance that recently has changed, I might add."

The pregnant silence after that pronouncement prompted her to pry her gaze from Rob and fasten it upon him, assuming her most formal pose. A stance she hoped made her appear the lady she was supposed to be. "I know not where she bides at present, but you keep your sister from this place, Sir Thomas, or rue the day we met! You do not wish to make of me your enemy. Trust that as a truth!"

"I fear it may be too late to consider an alternative,"

he replied silkily. "Soon Rob will see, as I have, what an ill choice you are. Unfortunately, I have made you baroness here, Mairi MacInness, but believe me, I can just as easily unmake you."

"And your lord will have no say in this? I care not how well you say you know him, you sorely underestimate Robert MacBain. He is no puppet to dance on strings you hold!"

"Tell him, then," Sir Thomas challenged, gesturing toward Rob, who still stood watching their exchange from a distance. "Go now and repeat all I have said to you, word for word. See what he has to say to it."

Mairi fastened a sultry look upon her husband. "I believe I shall wait until the night to do my speaking, sir. I might not know the motions of your secret language with my lord as yet, but I do believe I may invent a few that surpass what you have invented."

His shock at her discovery gratified her no end. Mairi cast him one more glance, a gauntlet tossed at his feet, and whisked away to see to her newly assumed role as Lady MacBain.

Rob had no desire to confront either his steward or his wife about the scene that had just taken place between them. Their false smiles and bitter words for each other did not bode well for peace in his household, and he had enough to worry on as it was.

However, he supposed he must get to the heart of the matter and try to settle their differences at the outset. Since Mairi had stalked away to the kitchens, he beckoned to Thomas and then stepped back outside the hall onto the steps to await him.

It was nearly as busy around the bailey as inside the keep so he stopped on the landing just outside the door.

The traffic in and out had stopped for the present. Short of closeting themselves within the solar, this appeared to be the only place he and Thomas might find a bit of privacy without going abovestairs.

His men were no slackards, he noted with pride, even though one might think they were preparing for a tournament instead of a probable battle. They appeared to look forward to it. They would be sorely disappointed now if MacInness did not come.

Only a few were seasoned soldiers, having fought in France against the English, but most were as he had been before that attack on Craigmuir. They were young and untried in a real confrontation with an enemy and only used to the rules of the melee, mock battle governed by the grand marshal of the tournaments. *Games.*

In view of that, Rob supposed he should be hoping he was wrong in his assessment of Ranald MacInness, that the man would be satisfied to remain in the Highlands until Rob could collect a force to go and unseat him as laird. Not much chance of that, however, when Mairi's cousin would be expecting retaliation on her part for the death of her father. Ranald would come.

Baincroft had no more than one or two days yet to make ready for an attack. Therefore, any squabbles within could not be tolerated. One war at a time was quite enough.

As soon as Thomas appeared, Rob extended his hand, palm up with a short shoving motion. *Explain yourself.*

A head shake. A look of feigned innocence. Guilt in the dark eyes that would not meet his.

Rob simply held his position, demanding an answer, knowing full well this would be no pleasant conversation.

"She has a sharp tongue, Rob!" Thomas exclaimed, exasperated. His grip on the canes looked fit to break off the carved handles and prevented his use of signs.

"You chose her," Rob reminded him curtly.

"My mistake." Thomas sighed and shook his head.

The next words were a plea and entirely expected. Rob had known Thomas would get around to this sooner or later.

"Set her aside, Robbie. Take Jehannie in her stead." He lifted one of his canes, pressing the fisted hand that held it to his chest. A small concession to convenience, a half sign, indicating his willingness to forego speech if Rob wished it.

He did not.

"Go on," Rob instructed. "Speak your mind."

"Had I but waited..." Thomas's words drifted off, looking sad, leaving Rob to imagine the rest.

He understood how Thomas felt, of course, but he could not allow that to continue. He placed a hand upon his friend's shoulder and looked him in the eye as he spoke. "I wed this woman, Tom. 'Tis done."

"But you love *Jehannie!*" Thomas insisted. "Your heart broke when we thought she would not wed you. Remember? Now, you are just angry because she struck you. But that haughty Highland wench will do you worse!"

Rob tightened his grip for emphasis and felt Thomas tense with the pain of it. "Mairi is my lady, Thomas, for all and good," he said, holding his voice low, injecting a warning. "Accept this. No matter what should happen, I shall never wed your sister."

"This woman will seek to set you against me," Thomas warned him, shaking off his hand and shifting away the instant Rob loosened his grip.

"As you seek to set me against her?" Rob asked. "I cannot have this, Thomas. Make peace."

"But—"

Rob turned away to emphasize that he would brook no argument, tolerate no further protest.

He folded his arms across his chest, figuring it was time to play the liege lord. Not that he enjoyed blandishing his rank overmuch, but sometimes that was the only way to end an argument with Thomas. "I command it!"

A moment later he sensed that Thomas was gone. He also discerned that he had made little progress in repairing the breach between his steward and his wife.

Whatever had passed between them in the hall had naught to do with dislike between the two. They did not know one another well enough yet for that.

'Twas born of Thomas's longing to have things the way everyone always thought they would be. Thomas was to have seen to Rob's lands, and Jehannie to the household and his personal needs.

Mother had planned out his life like a sectioned estate, planting whatever she thought necessary to ensure his survival. He could not fault her for that. But the best laid plans often went awry.

In the instance of his marriage, Rob could not help being glad of that. But he would hate to lose his friend.

Much as he loved Thomas, however, he would replace him if the man could not accept Mairi and give her the respect due as Lady of Baincroft. That would pain Rob far more than when he thought he had lost Jehannie, for he could not think what Thomas might do with himself if that happened.

Jehannie could always wed another and have a happy life, but Thomas knew nothing else but how to manage this place. No other lord would give him such free rein and such trust. Tom had been born to this, trained for it exclusively and was good at it. Rob owed much of his success as baron to Thomas de Brus.

Somehow, Rob had to convince him that he need not abandon either his loyalty to his sister or to his lord and friend. Unfortunately, this confrontation had not accomplished that.

The poor fellow felt pulled both ways. Rob would give him time to assess things in his own mind and they would speak on it again.

Mairi would not understand what was happening here. She would assume that Thomas's dislike of her stemmed from some other cause. Whatever Thomas had said to her in the hall, Rob would wager it had not presented the true case at all.

Rob knew he must go now, find her and try to explain. Not a task he relished or was even certain he could handle well, given his difficulty in understanding her words at times.

He was improving there, he thought, or else she had taken Wee Andy's admonition to heart and was attempting to alter her way of speaking. She had certainly done so for his father and, apparently, had decided to continue it for his benefit.

Was it possible that she already knew about him? Had someone told her or had she guessed as Trouville said she would? Nay, the forthright Mairi would have brought up the matter already if that were so. He would have to tell her, and he would have to do it sometime today.

Or he could wait for tonight. That would give him the day to think on it and decide how to tell her.

It would not be an easy thing to say, or for her to hear. He dreaded it now, having waited for so long. He wished to heaven her father had done his duty by her and informed her well before Rob had arrived at Craigmuir.

Then again, had the laird done that, Mairi might have sent Rob away at the gates and he would never have

known her, much less married her. And then what would
he have come home to find? Jehannie, all willing to wed
him, after all.

He rubbed his cheek, now recovered from the blow she
had dealt, and could all too readily imagine what marriage
to her would have been. Like their childhood, fraught with
temper fits and her always having her way. At least Mairi
would be more subtle in getting hers.

If she decided to stay.

His life, spinning along uneventfully enough until a fortnight past, had suddenly become a madly tangled skein of
yarns, Rob thought, shaking his head.

Henceforth, he promised himself, he would never again
mislead Mairi. Or anyone else. Even though he had not
told her the lie outright, Rob knew better than anyone that
words had not been necessary. He must tell her the truth
and, unlike the lie she believed, this truth would require
an explanation.

Bracing himself for his task, Rob entered the hall again,
his duties weighing heavily upon him from all directions.
The most difficult needed to be dealt with first.

Mistress Morgan stood near the back exit of the hall.
She looked up just then and threw him a rueful, gap-
toothed smile.

Where is my lady? Rob signed to her.

Her smile swiftly died as she removed her hands from
her ample hips and jerked a thumb toward the door of the
solar.

Rob made way across the hall, ignoring those who attempted to halt and beleaguer him with questions. Without
knocking, he entered.

He had expected to find her alone, worrying over her
encounter with Thomas. With a nod toward the two maids
assisting her at fitting candles into assorted containers, he

dismissed them. After they scurried out, he closed the door and leaned against it.

"We'll need much light for tending…" she began.

Rob held up a hand to silence her and watched her carefully set down the candle she was fixing into a small metal cup.

She waited for him to address her, so he did. "Say no more," he ordered. "Listen."

Mairi nodded once, her lips tight. She looked as if she expected chastisement from him. Since her argument with Thomas must be on her mind, he thought he might as well address that lesser problem and be done with it.

"About Thomas," he began.

She started to speak and then caught herself.

He continued, feeling that she had every right to know the cause behind his steward's enmity. Surely that would help her to understand his friend's resentment. "I was to wed," he explained, measuring each word. "His sister. Jehannie de Brus."

Her eyes probed unmercifully for answers, though she minded his request and held silent. How he wished he could bring himself to close the distance between them and take her in his arms, to reassure her that she had naught to worry over where Jehannie was concerned. But that would unleash the flood of questions she barely restrained, and he knew he would not be able to grasp all she would say.

So, he answered as best he could what he thought she should know. "Jehannie's grandfather objected."

Mairi raised a brow.

"The contract's nulled."

She looked away from him for a moment as though absorbing the information and what it might mean to her. Then she faced him again, encouraging him to go on.

"She was here," he added. "You saw her."

Rob knew the exact instant Jehannie's identity dawned upon her. Mairi's mouth rounded to an O and she blinked as if reliving the memory of that ill-fated encounter when they'd first arrived.

Her nod of acceptance came slowly.

"Thomas loves her," he declared, hoping she would take that as reason for his steward's churlish behavior.

He saw that she did. Bless God, he could almost always read her eyes, if not her lips.

With a shrug, he assured her, "Thomas will amend." Had he said that correctly? Should that have been *amend to* or *make amend?*

Damn, he could not think straight when looking into her eyes. It seemed all his hard-won knowledge leaked right out his ears.

Though she did not ask him questions, he knew she wished to. Worry clouded her features as she stood there, hands clasped tightly together as though trying to comfort herself.

Did she believe *he* still loved Jehannie? He did, of course, in a way. His childhood friend would always be dear to him. A wife would hardly welcome that news if he admitted it. Neither could he deny it, for he had promised himself he would not lie to Mairi again. His guilt must show.

Words failed him, of course. He had not thought out and rehearsed any that would make clear the difference in his lifelong friendship with Jehannie and the new and overpowering feelings he now had for Mairi.

It certainly would not do now to simply blurt out the thing he had come in here to tell her, that he could not hear. Following his declaration that he had been rejected as a husband for Jehannie, surely it would seem to Mairi that she was second choice.

True enough, she had been. She would conclude that his factor had found it necessary to search for the bride so far away that Rob's reputation would not have reached her family. And that no one else would have him, so why should she?

He could not do this. Not yet. Somehow he had to concoct a way to tell her that would not throw him in such bad light. Devil take it, he must think some more.

Rob knew he had best absent himself and do just that. The hour grew late and darkness was falling. He still had matters to attend outside.

Once they had finished the evening meal, he would take her abovestairs to their chamber and have her to himself. When that time came, he would delay no more from his duty to the truth. He would know by then what he must say and exactly how he would say it.

And in some small, secret place within his mind, Rob took comfort in the knowledge that it would be too dark then for Mairi to leave him. He would have the entire night to convince her that his lack of hearing did not matter and to persuade her to remain his wife.

Though she still watched him, Mairi stepped toward the table with the candles and began securing the one she'd abandoned into its holder. By resuming her task, she was giving him tacit permission to leave.

He could not do that, however, as long as she wore that look of distress upon her face. It troubled him too much to leave it there.

"Mairi?" he entreated, reaching out to touch the back of her slender wrist. "Do not worry."

She lowered her gaze to his hand and then slowly raised her eyes and smiled.

Rob realized then how enigmatic Mairi could be when she wished. Just when he thought he could discern all that was in her mind by looking into those clear pools of blue, she blinked and became a total mystery to him.

Chapter Thirteen

Mairi had done all she knew how to prepare for whatever threat might come. It had done little to distract her from that dreadful meeting in the solar with Rob.

At first she'd believed he had come to make an end to the deception that lay between them. With Rob caught fast in his pretense, and with her assuming the role of witless wife, they made quite a pair.

Now she wished she had come right out with the question days ago when she first suspected. But nay, she'd thought to spare his pride. In so doing, she had contributed greatly to her own misery and probably prolonged his. He wanted to tell her.

Instead of resolving that, he had thrown another, even greater problem into the mix. Jehan de Brus. All had come clear when Mairi heard who the woman was, his former intended. Rob must love her very much to allow her to strike him and steal his horse, then show no ill will toward her when he spoke her name.

Mairi chose not to confront him about it. In truth, she did not blame Rob at all. He must have loved in good faith, then suffered when denied the de Brus woman's hand. How could she fault him for that? He needed an heir for all this, she thought as she glanced around the well-appointed hall.

She just happened to be the one chosen by the brother of Rob's true love. Either Sir Thomas had sought to make amends for his grandfather's rejection of his lord by finding another bride, or else he worried Rob would toss him out if he had refused to do so.

Mairi supposed it did not matter. Thomas hated her now, and Rob was only honoring the marriage contract as best he could. To his credit, he seemed to be trying very hard to make things work for them, despite his disappointment. Mayhaps even because of it.

She would try, too. He did care, and did not wish her to be unhappy. He wanted her body, she did not doubt that. If she were a good wife, he might one day come to love her. If Jehan de Brus would stay away.

Rob arrived at table for the evening meal a few moments early. Had he groomed himself expressly for her, or was it his usual custom to do so before supper? she wondered. He had bathed somewhere, for his damp hair was neatly combed back from his face and he smelled of herb-scented soap.

Mairi suddenly recalled the day they had left Craigmuir when she had tumbled into the burn and he had rescued her. Afterward, she had seen him wet all over, water droplets shining like gems upon his magnificent body.

The memory made her shiver, thinking what might transpire later this night. There would be no more talk of the Lady Jehan, that was for certain. Mairi meant to dismiss that woman from his mind if she possibly could.

Later. But first they must endure this meal. Hunger would have been preferable, considering the attitude of those arriving to quell theirs.

She knew hardly any of her husband's people here, even

the ones she had ordered about today. The two young maids she had conscripted to help her this afternoon had introduced themselves. Then there was the unfriendly Mistress Morgan and the contentious steward, Sir Thomas. None of them ogres, certainly. But none of them friends, or ever likely to be.

As latecomers straggled in, she watched eagerly for Wee Andy, hoping he would appear. Any hospitable face would have proved more than welcome at the moment.

At last, she saw him enter and take his place at the lower table. He nodded her way, but gave no indication he was happy to see her again. She could have wept.

Rob stood and offered his hand to her as soon as everyone had gathered and was seated. She rose and placed her palm upon his as he expected.

''Welcome my wife,'' he demanded, pausing to observe each face at the upper and lower tables, then added, ''Lady Mairi.''

Apparently he awaited their good wishes. She feared he might grow old and wither in place before he got any of those.

No one looked particularly happy about the marriage or willing to wish him so. A few had the audacity to exchange glances among themselves, as if to reckon whether they should even acknowledge her.

She would be infinitely glad to end this meal and quit the hall, even if it meant climbing those stairs and spending the night with a man who loved another woman.

Jehannie. The name resounded in her head like a repetitive taunt. Not *Lady Jehan,* but *Jehannie,* Rob had named her at last reference. Had that been a slip of tongue, or had he wished to make even clearer his close acquaintance with Sir Thomas's sister?

As a belated reaction to Rob's announcement of their

union, Mairi now noted his knights and squires bending at the waist, right arms over their middles. Cramping bowels? More likely her husband had given them some sign of his displeasure and she had not noticed.

The women made little bobs such as one might if almost losing balance after too much wine, though none had yet been served.

If she were wholly generous and thinking optimistically, Mairi might have considered those tardy gestures bows and curtsies. Most of the folk simply nodded their reluctant acceptance.

Though Rob's face darkened and she heard his low growl of dissatisfaction, he seated her and took his own chair without further comment.

Immediately, he turned to Sir Thomas, who was seated at his left. "Tom?"

'Twas an obvious cue, for he then leaned back to allow Sir Thomas access to address her. The steward spoke as if by rote. "Let there be peace between us, my lady, for my liege has willed it so."

"If 'tis truly meant, Sir Thomas, then we have no quarrel," she answered, darting a look at Rob to see whether that would suffice.

Her husband seemed willing to accept the lip service she and his knight gave to the truce he had ordered. She promised herself that she would try to establish accord with his man. But if that dolt brought his sister back to Baincroft to live, Mairi much feared her response to the event would make anything her cousin Ranald might concoct seem tame as target practice.

The unfamiliar knight seated to her right never spoke a word to her. He remained half turned away and in deep conversation with the man at his other side.

Rob, of course, had nothing at all to say. He offered her

one morsel after another from their shared trencher. Also, he was feeding her much too quickly, as though she were in dire need of sustenance and he, her only source of food.

While the victuals were probably tasty, Mairi hardly had the time to taste any of them with anything approaching appreciation.

The young page who served those seated at the dais giggled incessantly behind their backs, jumping forward to refill the wine cups with all the alacrity of one set to a race with his fellows. She would have called him to account for it, had she known his name. Mayhaps it was as well she did not. The poor lad was the only one in the hall with his humor intact.

Lord, she wished herself elsewhere this eve, Mairi thought, as Rob held yet another sliver of venison beneath her nose. She bit into it and chewed furiously, willing the endless meal to be over.

And so it went until all the courses had been served—there were but four—and the food had been cleared away at last.

Rob stood immediately. "Good evening," he called out to no one in particular.

A few muttered their good-nights and tossed several halfhearted waves in his direction.

Sir Thomas cast her a small, mirthless smile that could have meant anything at all. Gloating, she decided, for he remarked, "I will wish you good-night, my lady." His voice fair dripped with tainted honey as he added, "For I am bound to do so."

"Never fear, sir. I shall make it better than good," Mairi replied, inclining her head as if to thank him, "for I am bound to do *that*. And there is naught to hinder me, is there?"

His gaze dropped away, affording her a momentary satisfaction.

With Rob's hand at her waist and her own clasped before her, they traversed the width of the hall to the stairs.

Winning the kind regard of Baincroft's people might not lie within her power, after all, Mairi thought with regret. She much doubted she could even win her husband's. But she would not admit defeat until she had tried.

Whatever Thomas's sister had done to make Rob love her, Mairi determined to do better. If only she knew what that was. She would lay wager it had not consisted of slapping him regularly.

Had they made love together? Many a man and woman did whilst betrothed. It was not frowned upon, and at times, was encouraged. Yet Rob had not rushed after the woman when she had stalked away and rode out in anger. Surely that was a good sign.

They reached the door to his chamber and Rob pushed it open, ushering her inside.

Someone had unpacked her clothing, shook out the wrinkles and hung her gowns on wall pegs. The wooden stand in one corner supported Rob's polished chain mail while his broadsword and shield graced the wall behind it. Whoever had seen to all of that had also laid the fire for them.

Mairi watched as Rob bent down, touched a slender piece of kindling to the blaze and lit the candles on the small table at the bedside.

She rubbed her palms up and down her arms and shivered, though it was not cold in the room. She knew not what to do next. Should she undress or wait for him to do so?

"Come, sit," he suggested as he positioned a chair by the fire.

She brushed against him intentionally as she moved to do as he directed. Her hand touched his, and his fingers caught hers. The bright heat and longing that flared in his eyes warmed her with hope.

Before doubt could take hold, Mairi stood on tiptoe and brushed her lips against his chin. He was so tall, that was as high as she could reach.

His surprised intake of breath was audible. That and the crackle of the fire were all that broke the silence.

Then, just as she'd wished, his head slowly lowered so that his lips rested for an instant upon her forehead, trailed slowly over her brow and down to her cheek. It felt so natural to turn her head a wee bit so that her mouth met his.

Ah, how warm and inviting was his kiss. He tasted of wine, spicy and drugging to the senses. His hands sliding through her hair and caressing her so fervently, made her dizzy with delight. And hope.

She reveled in his urgency, the way his body shifted hard against her own, announcing his obvious need of her. This very day, she had promised him and herself that if he did this again…

His groan of pleasure stoked her daring. Mairi clutched his hips, moving her lower body sinuously, trying to guide that part of him where it needed most to be.

Rob tore his mouth from hers and cradled her face with his hands. He fastened the full intensity of his hungry gaze upon her face and spoke her name, his breath shuddering out of him with the deep, soft sound. Music to her ears, for now she knew he did not pretend she was any other woman as they did this.

She could say nothing, for her lips were busy awaiting the return of his, open and ready, past willing. Her only reply was to arch herself into him again, closing her eyes on the ecstasy that surge created.

When he took her mouth again, his low, wordless growl reverberated through her like sweet thunder and she echoed the sound. She felt his strong fingers gathering her skirts until the wool and linen bunched at her waist. He broke their kiss only long enough to drag both her garments over her head, then returned to it with vengeance.

Dimly she heard his belt clink as it hit the floor. Her mind swirled as he lifted her, crushing her to him as he carried her the short distance to the bed.

There, he halted, propped her against the edge of the mattress and held her captive, first with his body, then with a deep and searching kiss that seemed to go on forever. Rapid as an act of magic, he dispensed with his clothes.

Skin to skin, he held her as they delighted together in the sweet, heated friction. Mairi savored the incredible feel of him, unlike any other sensation she had ever experienced.

His scent, rife with spice and the heady musk of desire, filled her with such deep longing, she knew she might die of it. The harsh rasp of his breathing and the undecipherable sounds he made from inside his chest told her more than words how fervent his need and how he recognized her own.

His hands fitted to her waist and lifted, even as he climbed, writhing with her until they lay full-length upon the bed, entwined.

Without ceasing, he slid one knee between hers and covered her swiftly, giving her no pause to think or to wonder what he would do. His hand moved between their bodies and he touched her. Mairi gasped with surprise, since she was long past fear.

A heartbeat later, he guided himself into her. Swift and

true as a well-honed sword, he thrust through her token of resistance.

Rob filled her so completely, her soul felt vanquished, and yet victorious, exquisitely owned, and yet the captor. How could that be?

She opened her eyes and stared into his, seeking answer. Her heart near stilled at the expression of anguish he wore. Unsure what had caused it, but moved to soothe him, Mairi raised her hand to his face and touched his lips.

"Mo cridhe," she whispered and smiled. *My love.*

As though she had unloosed some invisible tether that held him still, Rob began to move out of her. Her inner muscles clenched in protest, determined to hold him within.

As if to offer surcease, he thrust again, deeper, yet very gently this time. Sheer joy, it was, yet not enough. Once more, he retreated, near to leaving her distraught, only to give again all she would seek and more. There was more, she knew it.

On and on, the sharp, unspeakably sweet torture commenced until Mairi grew mindless, grasping, compelling him to hurry. The speed with which he moved increased in tandem with her demand, as if a shared inner force guided their movements without thought.

She could not think. Of a sudden, bright colors burst within her and stars showered down around them, shocking where they touched, and touching everywhere.

Her body quaked, her breath arrested, her heart thudding so loud it filled her head with sound. She felt run through with a pleasure so intense she could not bear it.

Rob reared above her and plunged deep, issuing her name in a wild and prolonged growl that flooded her heart, even as he poured his warmth into her. She could feel the pulse of it even after he stilled.

"Ah, Mairi…" he whispered, sounding so sad, withdrawing from her, shifting his weight to one side, yet holding her as close as his spent strength would allow.

Had she heard regret in his voice? If so, was it that they had coupled or that it was now over? No matter, she would not let it intrude upon the bliss she had just come to know. The morrow would be time enough to discover whether he was pleased with her or no.

Mairi closed her eyes and feigned sleep at once.

Rob sighed deeply and she could feel his gaze upon her, waiting for her to open hers. But she did not. Cowardly, it was, she admitted to herself as she carefully evened out her breathing. So be it, she did not care. Her day had mirrored hell itself and she had borne it with courage enough.

This lovely night was hers, and savor it she would.

Rob closed his eyes to temptation. A bit late for that, he thought, silently castigating himself with every curse he had ever learned.

God help him, what had he done? Did his honor stand no chance against his lust? Never in all his years as a man had he so disregarded the right of a thing, especially not for a few moments of fleshly pleasure.

Nay, it had proved more than that, he admitted. So much more than pleasure, there were no words to describe it. At least, none that he knew.

This woman completed him, made him more than he was or ever thought he could be. And Rob felt he had betrayed her. Now Mairi would have no say in whether they remained husband and wife.

She possessed no maidenhead to offer another man now. He had seen to that with his selfish taking. They could have made a child together just now, he thought, horrified to feel such joy in the possibility. What if she hated the idea once he told her about himself? What if she still decided to leave him in spite of it?

He should wake her now, tell her and have done with it. At least then he would know. Nay, he could not. What he had done was cruel enough. She should sleep first, recover. Allow him time to recover.

Even now, his traitorous mind would not fully claim regret as it should. No matter how he tried to deny it, Rob reveled in having Mairi well and truly trapped into this union. Foul delight, most foul.

He shook his head, then looked at her again, somehow unable to resist. Damn his eyes, even this soon afterward, he wanted her again. Craved, more like, with the taste of her still upon his lips and the scent of her enveloping him like an aphrodisiacal mist.

His ever-darkening mood followed him right into sleep. Dreams of indistinct yet dire consequences troubled and woke him twice before he finally found rest.

At last came a measure of imagined absolution to ease his trammeled conscience. The soothing caress of a soft hand, Mairi's, or so he dreamed.

Gentle fingers trailed over his heart, down the center of his body and settled lightly, tentatively around the very source of his dismay. Soon it ceased to be that, and became the center of his existence.

Rob shifted uncomfortably, wishing a braver touch, a firmer grasp, a clearer promise of fulfillment.

In the realm of dreams he could have her freely and without reserve, had enjoyed her there before, so many times since their first meeting. So why not exult in it?

But there…ah, she grew more bold than ever, raising his delight to pure delirium.

Dimly, Rob battled the realization that this time seemed

all too different, too real. Yet he could not relinquish this. He was almost there, to heaven with Mairi.

Her body slid along his, light as feather down, smooth as silk, her softness flowing over him like forgiveness. Rob sighed, cherishing the roundness of her breasts against his face, tasting their small budded roses graced with honeyed sweetness.

He groaned at the way her remembered nest of golden curls cradled his manhood, teasing him at her entrance and then allowing him in. Rob felt found, redeemed.

Then she began to move, taunting him with the slowness of her undulation, silently threatening him with waking should he dare increase the motion. He could not bear that loss, so he abandoned his need for surcease in favor of the prolonged pleasure.

Let it last for all time, he begged fate, for he never wished to emerge from this euphoria. Not ever.

The rush of his completion took him unaware, all too soon. He fought letting go the vivid dream so desperately, his own struggle awakened him.

The slight weight upon his body did not dissolve into the ether. She remained, wrapping around him, lips pressing a kiss upon his chest, hands tangling in his hair, legs resting along the outside of his.

No dream!

Rob released a long sigh of resignation. There was nothing he could think to himself or say to Mairi that would justify what he had done and he knew it.

A moment later Rob came to a practical decision, not in the least hampered by the fact that he remained inside her as he made it.

So long as he had thrown away the opportunity to play fair with her, and the decision was no longer hers to make, he would try to give her no cause to despair over it. He would please her so infinitely, she would never even think to leave him no matter what she learned.

He embraced her fully and sought her mouth with his for a kiss without reservation. Already aroused and enclosed within her, he loved Mairi for all he was worth and more. What did he have to lose?

This he could give her, for he did not need hearing to judge a woman's response to the touch of his hand or his mouth upon her. Her sweet purrs and cries of satisfaction he could feel right through her skin. They set him afire and kept him burning, brighter and hotter as the night progressed to dawn.

Rob awoke to a hand shaking his shoulder.

Mairi. His eyes flew open as she was leaning over him, looking worried, speaking.

"What's amiss?" he asked, raking a hand through his hair and giving his head a shake, but never taking his attention from her busy lips. Lord, he wished she would slow her speech! Did all Highlanders run on this way?

She cast a frantic glance toward the window where the bright sun beamed through with a vengeance, while she struggled to impart her message. Her lips were too swift, but he had other means of reading her.

Sleeping later than usual would not have upset her this much. Yet something outside the window had caused her alarm. The only other thing he could reckon was that she had heard the horn announcing someone's arrival.

Suddenly she bounded from the bed and snatched one of the pelts off of it to cover herself. Before he could move, she darted to the door, unlatched and flung it wide.

The shy Sir Olin McKinnon appeared too taken aback by the tousled, barely garbed Mairi to speak. He shrugged and shifted from one long leg to the other, trying unsuccessfully not to look at his lady.

She was a sight to behold with her mass of golden ringlets obscuring half her face, her lithe body wrapped in fur, shapely legs exposed and one cold little foot warming the top of the other. Rob wished he had nothing more to do than appreciate his wife this morn, but apparently that was not to be.

Since Mairi must have heard the horn, Rob already suspected what news his knight was bringing.

Short of death in the family or fire in the rooms below—neither of which was very likely—there could be only one reason for this intrusion.

The enemy had arrived.

Chapter Fourteen

Ranald MacInness smiled with anticipation as the distant horn sounded a warning to those inside Baincroft. They had been spotted, though they still had a half league to travel before reaching the gates.

He admitted now that he had worried whether his force would be sufficient or his skills equal to reclaiming his cousin. The men who had escaped death at Craigmuir swore they did not exaggerate the MacBain's ferocity when it came to a fight. From all they had said, he had wondered if the man might be as proficient with a blade as Ranald himself.

However, now he had no doubt his quest would end in success and with no blows suffered on either side. He glanced over at his hostage as they approached the bend in the road that would take them directly up to the castle.

"I've brought ye home to yer lover, Jehan. Can ye no' summon a wee grin of thanks?" He laughed at her glare.

"You lied!" she accused as she struggled with the man who shared her saddle. Ranald had chosen his strongest vassal to hold her since she was a vicious lass and prone to bite. He had the teeth marks to prove it.

"What do ye care? Ye'll be rid of her, and have the way clear so ye can wed MacBain."

"You'll kill her!" she exclaimed, and continued to fight.

He could not understand why she objected to his plan. "Take her to the back of the column and surround yerself with the others," he ordered Red Clem. "I do not want her seen afore I'm ready."

What a stroke of fine luck to have found her. His scout, Duncan, who had fought at Craigmuir, had recognized MacBain's mount grazing near the burn. They thought they'd found the man himself until Ranald rode in to challenge him.

Only there had been this wee lady, weeping fit to die. What could a man do but offer sympathy, especially when it would gain him knowledge of the enemy. The woman did have MacBain's horse, so Ranald figured she must know him well.

Right forthcoming she was, too, once he told her that MacBain had stolen his betrothed. The tale of her own plight seemed an omen of the very best kind. MacBain loved her, not Mairi, she'd told him. Only her grandfather had betrayed them both. Now the man she was fated to wed had found another woman just to spite her. Both she and Ranald had been sorely wronged, she'd declared. Ranald had agreed. At that point, a simple exchange had seemed ideal. Jehan for Mairi.

She had told him of the MacBain's deafness then. The man needed her to make his life easier, she'd said, something no other woman could do, for she had been trained all her life for it. She had been most willing that he suggest a trade.

Only later when they were camped for the night, did she happen to overhear him speaking with Red Clem about

Mairi and the true purpose for getting her back. No matter. The trade would still work.

According to the lass, MacBain had known her since their infancy and loved her well. Her own brother was steward at Baincroft and the people there were devoted to her. MacBain would not dare refuse to ransom the Lady Jehan, with Mairi as the payment.

And then Ranald could eliminate the final obstacle betwixt himself and the loyalty of Craigmuir's people and the entire MacInness clan. Mairi. He had hoped to take her to wife and use her to gain the power he wanted, but now knew she would prove too unwilling. Her father's people might overthrow him as laird if he returned with her. She would have to die.

With all the free-booters he had hired these past few months to serve under his command, he would soon rule the Highlands. Craigmuir would be the perfect lair from which to conduct his methodical plan to conquer every major stronghold in the north.

His legend, his lands and his retinue of men would increase with every victory. He might one day rule all Scotland, Ranald thought, by might if not right. There was that ancient MacInness connection to the crown, and anyone would be preferable to the present king. Even now, he could imagine the thrill of power, the respect, the wealth. And only his cousin Mairi stood in his way.

He clicked his tongue and nudged his mount into a canter, eager to meet his rival and make the exchange.

Mairi rushed to dress, tugging on the chemise tossed aside last eve and grabbing the blue woolen gown someone had removed from her pack and hung upon the wall. She quickly fastened a braided belt around her hips as she stepped into the soft leather shoes made for wear indoors.

Her sturdy boots seemed to have disappeared, and there was no time to search.

Behind her came the clink of chain mail as Rob removed his hauberk from its stand in the corner. The rasp of the metal links struck fear in her heart. Baincroft could well suffer the same fate as Craigmuir if Ranald's men found a way inside the gates.

This time, she could not bar herself within the armory and wait it out. Rob would need her help. Someone had to watch his back. Mairi quailed, remembering that there had been no one to do that for him in that other battle. 'Twas a mighty wonder he had survived it. Anyone could have approached him from behind and cut him down.

On that thought, she clutched her small eating knife encased in its scabbard and attached it to her belt. If only she had a real weapon. Not that anyone would afford her one. Women were not expected to do battle, even in the Highlands, and especially not here.

"Stay," Rob ordered her on his way out.

"Like one of yer hounds? Ha! Not bloody likely," she replied, knowing very well he did not hear her rebellious words. In his hurry, he never turned around to see whether or not she obeyed him.

Three steps behind, she followed him down the stairs to the hall, all but running to keep pace. "Slow down, ye long-legged beast!" she rumbled.

Directly through the keep, down the steps and into the bailey, she trailed after her husband. These folk who depended upon him for their safety might be willing to let him ride out and face that wretched cousin of hers, but Mairi was not about to allow him to endanger himself that way. She'd throw herself in front of his horse, if need be.

Much to her relief, she soon saw that was not his intention. Instead, Rob marched to the wooden steps of the

battlements and climbed them two at a time. She picked
up her skirts and dashed right up behind him.

"What do *you* here?" Sir Thomas demanded of her
when they reached the wall walk.

"I might ask you the same," she replied, tossing back
her unbound hair.

Her defiance withered a bit when Rob glanced back and
finally noticed her. Yet he looked more exasperated than
angry.

Thomas ignored her then and tugged Rob's sleeve. The
moment Rob turned, the steward's hands flew this way and
that, with no attempt at subterfuge.

The steward surprised her when he spoke the words, as
well. Not for benefit of her understanding, she would wager her life on that. Several other men stood near, mailed
and armed as Rob and Thomas were. Mairi supposed the
words were for them.

"MacInness has twice the number of men at his back
as we have within our walls. A rough-looking lot. He demands you send out his kinswoman," Thomas was saying,
with a nod in her direction.

"No," Rob replied.

"He says she is his, by right of law, and you must return
her to him. She was his betrothed, and therefore is not
your legal wife."

"He lies," Rob declared, then calmly moved to look
over the wall.

"Get back!" Mairi exclaimed, trying to pull him away
from the opening. "He'll have archers!"

No one paid her any mind at all. Rob stepped upon a
block obviously placed there to grant access to the embrasure. He climbed up and stood between the stout teeth of
Baincroft, his hands resting upon the merlons on either
side of him.

"MacInness!" he shouted. "Parley?"

"Nay!" Mairi argued. "Do not let him in!" She turned to Sir Thomas and pleaded, one hand grasping his gauntlet. "I implore you, stop him!"

Thomas held up a palm to silence her, and she heard Ranald's voice. "Whoever ye be, tell the MacBain I have his woman here, and will trade her for mine!" her cousin announced.

Rob stepped down without answering, and leaned back against the wall, his face pale with a terrible anger mixed with what looked to be fear. Not fear for himself, Mairi knew.

She could guess who Ranald held as his hostage. It could be none other than the fool lass who had galloped away from Baincroft yesterday.

"Lady Jehan!" she gasped.

"No!" Thomas cried, trying to maneuver the step up to the wall so he could see. He could not manage with his broken leg. Rob stopped his attempt, holding the smaller knight easily in his grasp.

"Think, Tom!" Rob demanded of him. "Keep your head!"

The steward stilled, drew in a sharp breath and shook off Rob's hands. "You will trade," Thomas declared fervently. "You must!"

"I will parley," Rob countered. "Arrange it."

"They've brought her forth, Tom. I can see her," said one of the older knights who had leaned forward enough to see below. "One of his men holds her astride his horse in front of him. She's red in the face and looks fit to kill the bastard. He has a blade at her throat."

"God save her," Thomas gasped, burying his face in one hand, propping himself against the wall with the other.

"Galen, go. Make a parley," Rob demanded. It was

obvious that Sir Thomas was too overset to do anything, so worried was he for Lady Jehan's life. Mairi felt a pang of sympathy for him. Though she did not like Thomas, she respected the love he had for his sister.

Galen, the other knight, climbed upon the step and occupied the space Rob had vacated. "My lord would speak with you on it, MacInness!" he shouted down.

"Naught to say! We exchange!" Ranald replied in a loud voice that carried all too well. "The woman has told me of yer devil-cursed lord and I know he canna hear me. Tell him I will slay this one if he refuses to trade."

Sir Galen twisted around and told Rob, "He'll kill her else you agree."

"I will go out. Fight him. One to one," Rob instructed. "For both women."

"Fool! You cannot ride out there!" Mairi exclaimed, throwing out her hands in dismay. "His men will slay you ere you draw your sword! Stay inside. We can withstand a siege." Too late she remembered what that would mean for Ranald's hostage.

Rob was watching her thoughtfully. Studying her. She wondered if he might be considering an exchange, after all. Then he spoke. "I will fight." His face softened with apology. "She is my friend."

Mairi remained still, examining his face. The resolution there prevented any further argument. And, in good truth, she could not deny that woman needed rescue. Ranald would kill her if Rob let matters stand as they were.

Mairi nodded her acceptance, knowing he wished her blessing on this, even if he did not require it. "Go. Save her."

"I will win," Rob vowed, his steely gaze full of certainty.

Never once did she imagine that Rob would lose a fair

fight with Ranald. Her cousin was as large, mayhaps even heavier than Rob, but she had seen her husband in action at Craigmuir. But Mairi did worry that Ranald would employ treachery.

She touched his forearm. "Beware his tricks. But I know you will best him," she replied carefully, slowly, and even summoned a smile.

The full force of his smile was so arresting in its beauty, Mairi had to look away to think properly.

He encouraged her to go down the steps, but he did not follow. Behind her, she overheard his man address him, "He mocks you. Calls you...devil-cursed."

The knight's words were jerky, barely whispered under the breath, as though spoken to himself. Though she did not turn her head to look, Mairi was certain that signs accompanied them. So, those who used the signals said the words as well most times, she deduced. She wondered how Rob had intended to negotiate with her cousin if Ranald had agreed to it.

"When you speak, play to pride," Rob suggested to Sir Galen, the older knight Rob had set to arrange matters. "Challenge his skill," he ordered, pausing. "Against my...evil."

"Aye," Galen responded. "I'd wager he's vain as a rooster. I'll say the tale will spread. His fame..."

The man's voice drifted off and Mairi figured that they had resorted to signals alone.

Sir Galen then clattered down the stairs, passing around her to be about the business of taunting her cousin into a duel. This plan would probably work. Ranald could never resist preening.

Rob took her arm and guided her the rest of the way down into the bailey. "Go inside," he ordered brusquely, pointing toward the keep.

Mairi made as if to do so, then halted the moment his attention settled elsewhere. She must find the means to remain outside in order to see what went on. And if Rob left the safety of these walls, she meant to go with him.

The barracks would be deserted, she thought, and dashed for the low building set against the walls.

Inside she found the men's quarters in disarray as if everyone had dressed and armed on the instant, which no doubt they had. Mairi grabbed up a pair of abandoned braies and a simple gray tunic from one of the pallets.

Concealing herself behind the door, she hastily shed her gown and chemise and donned the male clothing. A quick search located a woolen cap that would hide her hair.

Unfortunately all the men's weapons were gone. She borrowed a leather strap someone had discarded on the floor, using it to cinch up the too large tunic and strap on her eating knife.

With all the bravado she could summon, Mairi left the barracks and sauntered out to join the men milling about near the gates. Carefully, she kept Rob within view, but remained out of sight behind him.

She only hoped no one else noticed her and remarked on it to her husband. If they did, she would stand her ground.

At the moment everyone's attention was directed at the unbolted access door beside the gates, a heavily reinforced portal barely large enough to accommodate the size of a dismounted man leading a horse.

She heard raised voices from without. Mairi recognized the tone of Sir Galen's as one of the speakers. So the negotiations had begun.

The words were indistinct, however. At least, from where she stood. She waited impatiently with the others until he reappeared within the walls.

"Tomorrow morn," he announced to all. His hard, uncompromising features took on a sardonic smirk while he waggled his thumb toward the enemy. He folded his hands under his chin and glanced soulfully heavenward. "MacInness would have the night to *pray!*"

Peals of laughter greeted that. Mairi almost laughed with them at the thought of her wicked cousin on his knees in holy supplication. The most that wretch should expect from above was a well-deserved bolt of lightning.

"Poor Jehannie," came the worried groan just behind her. She turned to see Sir Thomas's pained expression.

Mairi felt moved to comfort, despite their differences. "Surely Ranald will not harm your sister," she said, gently touching his arm.

He started at the sight of Mairi in her borrowed clothes, but otherwise did not remark on her appearance. "Do you know the man well?" he asked.

She shrugged and grimaced. "Not well, I fear. I but saw him each time he came to Craigmuir. My father kept me well out of his reach, worried Ranald would force his attentions on me and thus a match between us."

Too late, Mairi realized what this implied, that Ranald was prone to rape. True though it might be, she regretted voicing it as she had. Sir Thomas was worried enough about his sister without hearing that.

The steward shook his head, desolate. "He'll take her, I know it, just as he knows Rob has taken you." He said, exhaling harshly, seeming drained of all hope, "If he has not already done so."

Mairi shook his arm. "Sir Galen said she looked fit to kill, aye?"

"Yes," he admitted, meeting her gaze with question.

She forced a smile. "You see? Ranald has not broken

her spirit! If he had shamed her, would she not be hanging her head, afeared and broken?''

A bit of hope dawned in his dark eyes, so she fed it as best she could. ''And the *good* Sir Ranald will not broach her tonight, now will he? Nay, not when he is holding vigil for tomorrow's trial, eh? Celibate as a monk he'll stay, for the look of it, if not for righteous reason. His men will expect it, aye?''

''You think so, truly?'' he asked, desperate to believe it.

''Aye, I do!'' she exclaimed, though she did not believe it. Ranald would do as he pleased, but Sir Thomas was in a bad way and needed shoring up.

She continued, ''He'll want to make a bard's song of this. How would it be sung if he spent the night's vigil debauching an innocent maid?'' Mairi could not help asking, ''And she is that, is she not?''

''Of course,'' he answered absently, busily digesting all she had said. Then it seemed to occur to him how strange it was that she should be here, speaking thusly. ''Why do *you* seek to ease my mind about this?''

Mairi patted his arm maternally. ''Because I am lady to your lord and friend, Thomas. My loyalty to him and to Baincroft extend to you, whether you will it or no. And, believe as you will, I wish your sister no harm at all.''

He appeared upset by her pronouncement, uncertain what he should say to it. Mairi was not surprised when he simply shot her a look of patent disbelief and walked away. Despite that, she felt better for having pulled him out of his despair. Rob might need him, and he'd been no good to anyone in his former mood.

A hard hand landed upon her shoulder. No question whose it was. Mairi sucked in a fortifying breath, assumed an expression of manly confidence to suit her clothes and turned around to face her husband. She would attack first.

"Aye, well, I might be disobedient, mistrusted an' generally of no account around here, but with yer good interest at heart, m'lairdie, I shall do as I see fit, no matter that ye order me about as if I were some mindless nithing to ye," Mairi said, secure in the knowledge that her rapid speech was completely lost on him. It rather freed her to say what she pleased, which was the singular benefit to her of his predicament.

He quirked his mouth to one side and leveled her with a remonstrative look.

"I will do what I must," she declared plainly, and so that he would not mistake her this time.

Her pronouncement delayed his chastising her publicly for this display of will, which was exactly what she intended.

Though she had heeded his commands on the way from her home, he might as well learn now that she had a mind of her own. She was a woman to be reckoned with.

Several of his men had halted in their tracks, only just now realizing who she was. Mairi raised her chin and addressed them, "Is it not time to break fast?" Not waiting for an answer, or even expecting one, Mairi strode off toward the barracks to fetch her gown and chemise.

Rob's canny ability to judge a person's thoughts did not work with his wife unless she willed it so. He had thought so before, and now was certain of it. Mairi was a law unto herself, one of a kind, so unique in her thinking, likely a seer would have trouble divining her turns of mind.

She would do what she must? What the devil did she mean by that? She had not minded his orders today. Not a one of them. Instead, she had gone off and dressed herself in that ungodly fashion, no doubt intending to follow the men out, had that kinsman of hers decided to fight him this day.

Thank God, he had not. If Mairi dared venture outside these walls, her cousin would likely have her slain the moment he saw her.

Or had she been disguised to run away once she cleared the walls? A distinct possibility if there were an exit left unguarded, and God knew she had reason.

She knew everything now. Thomas had given no thought to signing openly as he spoke when they were upon the battlements. And she would have heard her cousin's taunts.

Rob wondered exactly how explicit Ranald MacInness had become with his accusation about the devil-granted powers. Had Mairi heard it all? Had the lout spewed that old belief that the dark one demanded a price for unnatural abilities? That price being the relinquishment of one of Lord Baincroft's senses, of course. And forfeiting that, why not the soul itself?

Rob had heard this before, out of the mouths of laymen and priests. Even in writing from Jehannie's grandsire. *In league with the devil.*

The thing that rankled so much was that Ranald MacInness probably did believe that God would favor him in the morrow's trial against a devil's minion. When Rob took down the wretch, would any of those watching the victory fear that evil truly had triumphed over good? None of *his* people would think that, for they knew better.

But Mairi might believe it. A tingle of dread rippled up his spine. What had she said to him before she stated her intention to act as she thought she must? Had she added her denunciation to that of her cousin?

Rob pounded a fist into his palm, a small concession to

his overwhelming frustration. He could ask Thomas if she had said anything about it once she found out. They had been speaking together just before he confronted her.

But Rob did not trust Thomas to relate what Mairi had said without adding his own slant to it. Not that his friend would lie outright, but it was obvious he had a dislike for Mairi and might have heard only what he wished to hear.

Salvaging what he could with Mairi would have to wait until the business with her kinsman was completed. This evening and the night long, he must spend in vigil within the chapel. MacInness had stated a similar intent, so Rob must do likewise.

How would it appear if his enemy passed the night on his knees with prayers on his lips while Rob marked the same hours ostensibly enjoying earthly pleasure with Mairi in their bedchamber? As if he truly were the devil's own?

Rob trusted his strength and ability without question when it came to competing upon any field against any opponent, but his people would expect him to carry out this trial with all of the ceremony common to such. And it was a trial, no mistaking that. The rituals here would be even more important than when he first stood before them accepting his knighthood.

He would bathe, fast, prostrate himself upon the stones before the altar, confess and lay his soul bare to the mercy of his maker. That way, none here would suffer any doubt who had been granted the might of right when Rob slew Ranald MacInness.

Beside that consideration, divine assistance in all the matters that plagued him, would be most appreciated.

No matter how he dwelt upon the preliminaries for the coming event, he knew he could not lay aside his concern about Mairi. Could he avoid her all day? A brief explanation of his lie of omission and what the deafness might mean to them in the future would hardly help settle anything. He could never justify keeping such facts from her, even in his own mind.

And what had happened between them last night, Rob could neither explain nor understand. Or regret, God help him.

It would take time to make amends for all of it, to regain her trust and begin again. Assuming she would allow it. Aye, he would pray. He must.

"Tom! To me," he shouted when he spied his friend walking dejectedly back toward the keep.

Thomas immediately reversed his direction and approached, obviously trying hard to maintain his composure.

Rob clapped him on the shoulder. "I'll win the day, Tom."

"I hope." Thomas then inclined his head toward the hall. "She is mad, you know."

"Mairi? Mad, you think?" Rob asked with a short laugh. "With anger or...?" He tapped his temple.

Thomas shifted one cane, mirrored the gesture and nodded in answer.

Rob fell to signing, for he was weary and it was easier. He did not care that Thomas must hang his canes upon his arm and balance on one foot to answer in kind. Served him right for making such an accusation. *What makes you think she's daft?*

She dressed as a male, Thomas answered, running the backs of his fingers up his tunic and then tugging his forelock. He frowned fiercely as he propped one fist up with his palm and then crossed his fingers like swords. *She comforts her enemy.*

"MacInness?" Rob demanded, disbelieving.

Nay, me! Thomas signed emphatically, then shook his

head and brushed his hands together, flinging off any attempt to understand Mairi's behavior.

And? Rob asked, still hoping Thomas would mention what Mairi had said in her last exchange with him, without his having to ask.

She confuses me apurpose. Never does the expected. And she provokes you with words when she knows you cannot hear. The woman is mad.

Well, that would neatly account for everything, would it not? Only Rob knew it was not so. Whatever strange things Mairi did or said, they were his own fault, Rob decided.

He had married her under false pretense, whether by his intent or no. Then he had taken her maidenhead while wholly aware that there was no way out of a consummated marriage other than death.

But he also felt fairly certain that Mairi would not accost him fully for any of that until after he had saved her from her cousin Ranald, and had also avenged her father in the process.

Alienating the one man who could do that for her would make no sense. Mairi might do the unexpected when it suited her, but she certainly was not a fool, nor was she mad.

"Vigil tonight," he told Thomas. "Draw lots for guard duty."

"Now that is madness!" Thomas declared, almost dropping his canes as he repositioned them to support him.

Rob grinned at his oldest friend. "A heathen's whim, Tom. Indulge me."

Chapter Fifteen

Mairi pointedly ignored the curious looks she received upon reentering the hall dressed as a man. She carried her own clothing draped over her arm as she strode past them, trying to maintain a dignified bearing.

Changing again in the barracks would have been risky after the men had dispersed from around the gates, so she had chosen to not attempt it.

Besides, after being so hastily roused out of her bridal bed this morn, she now needed to bathe, brush out her hair and properly set herself to rights.

Her soft shoes scuffed against the stairs, the stone bruises on her soles reminding her of the folly of not locating her boots. She must look ridiculous, Mairi thought.

What cared she how these people saw her garbed? They had determined they would not like her no matter what she did. They still clung fast to the hope that Rob would supplant her with his steward's sister.

She sighed as she pushed open the door to Rob's chamber and flung her raiment upon the bed. Even as she tugged off the rough-spun tunic and braies, she seriously considered keeping them on and leaving this place.

Mairi had expected Rob to confide in her once she had

given herself to him. Should her willingness not prove her intent to be a wife to him in all ways? Had she not done all she possibly could to gain his trust and make him love her?

In all fairness, however, she admitted there had been little time either last night or this morn for him to explain himself. He might yet do so.

Though enamored of Rob, she knew that the emotion was likely due to the powerful pull of the passion that flared between them. Their desire for each other had been evident from the very beginning, but that alone hardly constituted real love.

Mayhaps she had no right to expect deep feelings from him so soon. And she admitted that she might even be misnaming her feeling for him in the afterglow of such recent ecstasy. Nay, it might not be love at all. It might be only lust, though there seemed more to it than that.

Suppose all they ever had was the pleasure of the marriage bed? Though that was naught to discount as unimportant, she thought with a sigh.

Indeed, her Rob proved far better than adept at his husbandly duties, and she believed she had satisfied him, as well. The wondrous memories of his hands upon her, followed by the recollection of that wicked, caressing tongue of his flew through her mind unbidden. Simply reliving it in her mind sent prickles along her skin and shivers through her body.

It would prove difficult to live without him after last night. Aye, it would be nigh impossible to give that up for her pride's sake.

Mairi drew a cold, wet linen cloth over her face and neck, dunked it again in the bowl of water and squeezed out the excess to finish her ablutions. But washing away Rob's scent and cooling her body's memory of their loving did nothing to banish her wish to have him again tonight. And every night hereafter.

Desire to share his bed and the wish to have his children, to see to his comfort and happiness in every way she could were not merely duties. They had become her dearest dreams. But Rob held the power to dash those dreams against the rocks of reality if he could never love her.

She would always want him so. That would never change, but it might not be enough to satisfy either of them in the years to come.

What if he began to wish she were the Lady Jehan? And what if she grew to resent him for it? Honestly, she resented him now for his concern over Ranald's holding the woman, even though she worried about the same thing herself.

Waiting to see what happened after he dealt with her cousin and saved his former betrothed made more sense than sneaking out the postern gate.

'Twas possible the guards there would not allow her to pass, even disguised, she reasoned. They must know everyone within Baincroft and would discover her ruse in an instant. They likely had orders to not open the gates for any reason. Even if they did let her go, Ranald might catch her.

But suppose she did succeed in leaving. Would she not always wonder whether she acted too hastily to give Rob a proper chance to confide in her?

Last, but not least, Mairi had no notion where to go if she should leave here.

She might return to Craigmuir, of course. It would be safe enough. After tomorrow, Ranald would surely be dead by Rob's hand and her father avenged, just as she had wished.

The clan would welcome her home, but Mairi also knew

they would immediately choose another man to be laird. There would be a gathering to decide who would serve, and then she would have to take her place as a mere clanswoman. She would no longer possess special privilege as the laird's daughter.

Yet how could she remain here as wife to one who did not trust her, and as lady to folk who held her in contempt?

All things considered, however, Mairi realized the only prudent choice was to stay where she was. At least for the time being.

After Rob had rescued Lady Jehan, she would see how the wind blew between those two.

She glanced at the stolen clothing she had discarded on the floor and decided she must use it again. Come the morning, she would dress more carefully and go out with the men to witness the fight. So long as Rob did not see her, no one would care if she were there, even did they recognize her. In so doing, she would be able to see Rob's face in the moment he was reunited with his former beloved.

If he gave any indication then that he still preferred that one over her, she would act accordingly and quit this place. For as much as she believed she might love him, she would not reduce herself to accepting scraps of his attention and competing with another who held his heart.

Mairi flung the cloth into the bowl and wiped her damp hands over her face to quell the sudden flash of anger. She could always make her way somehow if need be. Craigmuir had been short of weavers when she left.

She felt like hiding herself away for the rest of the day, but knew that would not do. The people here would like her no better if she became a recluse. They already thought her strange enough, she suspected. So long as she did reside here—be that one day only or as long as she lived—

she would act her role as lady. As their baroness. This was her right.

So, as soon as she dressed for that part, Mairi confidently marched down to the hall and set about organizing the commotion there into productive activity. The folk of Baincroft might resent her, but unless her husband, their lord, ordered them otherwise directly, Mairi knew they were bound to follow her direction.

Though she had believed that work would make the day pass faster, she soon realized she was wrong. The interminable hours dragged by.

Rob and half the men had come in for midday meal, wolfed down their food and gulped ale while still standing. Then they'd hurried out again to allow the others who stood watch their turn at eating.

All within the keep and the bailey seemed poised for action. Though all of that was scheduled to take place outside the walls, who knew what Ranald's men might do once he was defeated? There could still be a battle. And Rob's men were outnumbered. Mairi had heard Sir Galen say so.

After Rob had finished his meal and the second group of men came in to eat, Mairi managed to corner the distinguished Sir Galen. He was a giant of a knight of roughly five and thirty years, balding, and possessed of the finest length of mustache she had ever beheld.

The reason she chose him to speak with was that he had tossed her a half smile upon entering the hall. There was that to recommend him, and it was certainly more than any other had offered her. Also, he had been the one to speak with Ranald and make the arrangements.

Mairi supposed him to be the captain of Rob's guards, though no one had actually introduced them. He looked the eldest of the lot and wore his confidence well.

She took her own ale cup and joined him where he stood, leaning against the back wall. "What is to happen when my lord slays the MacInness? Do you think the rest of that rabble will depart in peace?"

He shrugged and spoke around a mouthful of bread. "Nay, my lady, they will not. But no matter."

"No matter?" she asked with a huff of disbelief.

Sir Galen swallowed and grinned, showing a fine set of even, white teeth. "Lord Rob sent to Trouville for a company of his men, you see." He shrugged again. "'Twill put the odds in our favor and then some."

Thank God. She took a sip of ale, then asked him, "Why not simply surround and overpower the lot and be done with it? Why must my husband fight Ranald alone?"

He quirked a brow. "Lord Rob's honor, of course. You'd not dismiss that so casually, would you, my lady?"

She shook her head. "Never, but my cousin has none of that. No honor at all. He ordered my father slain and plans the same for me. 'Tis that, or widow me and wed me himself," she said with a mirthless laugh.

"I note no fear in you of either fate," he commented with a full-blown grin. He again bit off a hearty portion of crust he held and chewed it as he watched her.

She met his eyes in all seriousness. "I trust in my husband's ability, for I have witnessed it firsthand." Then she added, "However, I would have a blade worth the name in readiness should anything go awry."

"Mine will be handy, make no mistake," he declared.

"A most comforting thought, sir. But do you suppose you could procure me one? Not a broadsword, of course, but something sharp and substantial?"

He glanced at the small eating knife she wore at her waist while he took another small bite. He pointed toward it with the remainder of the crust. "Sharpen the one you have. It would do for opening your veins if the unthinkable happens and the bastard wins you.''

Mairi laughed again, this time with real humor. ''Oh, I do not think to kill *myself,* good sir! All I ask is a well-balanced blade longer than the length of my hand. I shall feel safer.''

Holding her gaze, he reached down to his boot and withdrew a bone-handled dagger at least thrice the length of her own blade, black as sin and with a deep blood runnel cast in it point to hilt. A wicked thing, it was. Just what she needed.

''Have care this is not misplaced,'' he warned with raised brows, his great mustache quirked to one side.

She smiled at him with deceptive calm as she accepted the dagger and held it within the folds of her gown. ''Aye, I shall place it truly should the need arise, you may be certain. Many thanks, Sir Galen.''

He looked her up and down as if to judge her worth. When he had done so, he nodded once as though satisfied she measured up. Then the big knight quaffed the remainder of his drink and sauntered away.

Holding it concealed, Mairi hefted the weapon he had given her, testing its weight. She might never need to use it, but at best now she did not feel quite so vulnerable as she had since leaving Craigmuir.

Aye, and she would be accompanying Rob outside the walls tomorrow. She must chance it, for she could not wait inside the gates for someone to relate to her what had happened.

Though she did not doubt the outcome between the two men involved, Mairi must see for herself how Rob greeted the Lady Jehan once he had saved her from Ranald. She needed to observe them just after his moment of victory to discover Rob's true feelings for the woman.

Once she knew that, she would know what to do. And if she had to leave here, she would be already dressed and armed for the journey.

With that decided, Mairi took the dagger upstairs and hid it, along with the braies and tunic, beneath the mattress so Rob would not see them and take them away from her.

The remainder of the day, she would spend among the strangers belowstairs, trying to act as lady of their keep.

Mairi worried when Rob did not appear when the supper was served. All of his knights, including Sirs Galen and Thomas, were missing, as were most of the other men.

Even the shy young priest she had met briefly during her day's duties was absent. She had not expected all of them to be present, but the fact that *none* of them was troubled her.

Mairi presided at table, hardly able to choke down a bite with all the watchful looks focused upon her. They must blame her for causing all of this. Though she had not wished it on them, she admitted they had good cause in holding her accountable for it.

If Rob had not wed her and brought her here, he would not be facing Ranald in a fight to the death. And Baincroft would still be the peaceful place they had always enjoyed. As soon as she felt it proper to do so, Mairi left the table.

In Rob's chamber, she waited for hours, hoping he would come to her with further assurances that he could not fail.

He had obviously been there while she was out. Or someone had, for his clothes chest stood open and someone had laid a fire for her.

She had quickly checked to see whether anyone had removed Sir Galen's dagger and the borrowed clothing that she planned to wear on the morrow. To her relief, they remained beneath the mattress where she had left them.

If only Rob would come to her now and they could make love together once more.

Now was the time for him to trust her with the truth about himself, even though he must know by now that she had guessed the secret. It hardly remained a first priority, given the other more immediate problems facing them, but they should speak of it, nonetheless.

When half the night had passed and Rob still had not joined her, Mairi decided she would go and find him. If nothing else, she should wish her husband victory and tell him again that she believed in him.

She donned a fur-trimmed woolen chamber robe that she had never seen him wear. Mairi luxuriated in the scent of him within its soft folds. Her leather slippers scuffed almost silently against the stones as she made her way downstairs.

She intended to search for Rob among those sleeping within the hall. But when she did so, she found there were none but the women occupying pallets there. Were all of the men standing watch?

Mairi pulled open the hall door, hurried down the steps and went out into the bailey, drawing the warmth of Rob's robe around her against the biting coolness of the night. All was quiet, though she felt surrounded by an air of expectancy.

There was a very small number of sentinels upon the battlements, Mairi noted with surprise. Two guards patrolled the main gates and another two manned the postern. That seemed strange, this being the eve of what could be the first battle they had seen here in decades.

She glanced around at the buildings within the walls. While the full moon loomed bright enough to cast shadows, the barracks appeared a sinister and forbidding place, not one a woman should enter in the middle of the night with so many men on the edge of a fight.

What if they attacked, believing her someone bent on treachery by stealth? She quickly rethought her intent to search in there for Rob.

Flickering light emanated from the chapel door. Mairi crossed the open ground to reach it, wondering what was taking place. A meeting of the men? She heard no voices.

Upon entering the open portal, her breath caught on a gasp. Hundreds of candles threw their collective glow upon the somber crowd within.

Some of the men stood, some knelt and some crouched in corners. Only a few eyes turned her way. Most were closed, either in sleep or prayer.

It looked as if all of Baincroft's male occupants, save the few guards she had just seen upon the wall, were attending a night-long, silent service of some kind.

Dressed entirely in white, Rob lay like a pale cross within the aisle, arms outstretched to either side, his feet to her, head toward the altar with his chin propped upon the cold stone floor.

Mairi quickly dropped to her knees and crossed herself. She had never seen the like in all her days. What was this?

She met Wee Andy's eye as she looked around. The portly fellow knelt only an arm's length away and was peeking sideways, looking horrified to see her.

Mairi was about to beckon him to follow her outside and tell her what was happening, when she felt a nudge at her elbow.

Thomas. With a jerk of his head, he urged her to get up and follow him out.

Mairi forgot about Andy and accompanied the steward.

She was so sharpset with curiosity, she cared not who explained, so long as she found out what was going on.

As soon as they were out of earshot of those in the chapel, she demanded, ''What is that? How long does it last?''

''The night through. He is at vigil.''

''So he'll conveniently fall asleep while my cousin guts him? Where is his mind, Thomas?''

Mairi flung out her arms and rolled her eyes heavenward in dismay. ''Can he not say a prayer and be done with it? You can wager your mortal soul my cousin will not forego his entire night's sleep!''

Thomas chuckled, a mean, wee laugh that grated on her patience. ''Ah, so you are a practical woman. None of this useless prayer and nonsensical fasting for you, eh?''

''Good heavens, has he not *eaten,* either?'' she exclaimed, grabbing his arm. ''This is not necessary, I tell you! Nor is it in the leastwise prudent!''

''So I advised him, for all the good it did,'' Thomas said with a rueful shake of his head. ''But Rob will be Rob. Once his mind is set, naught save a killing blow can change it. He will do this, for he believes he must.''

''But *why?*'' she pressed softly. ''Does he worry he will lose?''

''No, of course not!'' Thomas sighed and ran a hand through his hair. ''He wants there to be no mistaking who fights on the side of good tomorrow. Rob would turn aside the old belief that he has made pact with Satan, that he sacrificed the sound of his world for evil powers.''

''Good my Lord! What madness is this?'' Mairi demanded and tossed her hair over her shoulder. ''His own people would think such of their lord?''

''Apparently your Highland man believes it,'' Thomas

explained, then paused for effect. "And Rob fears *you* might, also."

"Of all the half-witted..." Mairi groaned with annoyance and turned smartly about to return to the chapel and tell her husband how wrongheaded he was.

Thomas grabbed the back of the robe and fell against her as he almost lost his balance. She quickly whirled about to prop him up, catching his free arm with one of hers. "Fool!" she chided. "Go sit down somewhere before you do yourself worse hurt!"

"Come with me, then," he suggested through gritted teeth, "for you cannot march in there and interrupt."

Mairi stood her ground. "He had no need of vigil when he fought at Craigmuir. Of a certainty, God took Rob's side in that without all of *this!*" She flung her hand toward the chapel and scoffed.

Thomas moved even closer and spoke harshly. "Lady, I warn you, do not make mock of what he does in there. I will suffer anything but the mocking of him, do you understand me?"

He tightened his grasp on her and his fingertips bit into her flesh through the fabric of her sleeve. "Robert is a brother to me."

"Not in blood," Mairi countered, enduring his painful grip to feed her anger. "But ye'd have it made so by marriage, aye?"

"I would," he admitted vehemently. "Were it left to me, I would send you out tonight and welcome my sister home again where she belongs!"

"Then I must thank God for that broken leg, so that I can best ye if you try!" She grabbed his wrist and shoved his hand away from her, nearly oversetting him with the act.

He straightened and regained his stance, but did not

touch her again, obviously realizing he had best not injure her. "I regret I said I would send you out. I did not mean it," he said grudgingly.

"Of course ye meant it," Mairi snapped.

But her fury deflated as an overpowering weariness claimed her. Thomas was right, she could never persuade Rob to abandon the vigil. It would do more harm than good if she tried. Should she shame him so before his men, he'd not forgive her for it. Neither would he sleep afterward, for he would be too angry.

Rob likely knew his strengths better than she, and must feel confident that he could prevail tomorrow despite the lack of food and sleep. Mairi had to trust him that far, for she had no choice.

"Leave it be, Thomas. I will return to the keep. You go and watch over him, since I cannot. Try to make him rest awhile and eat before he fights."

He merely glared at her as though she had suggested the unthinkable. Mayhaps she had, for she knew naught of these men's doings. Highland men were different. Even so, she could not help worrying about Rob.

Mairi trudged back to the steps and climbed them. At the landing before the hall doors, she turned and watched Thomas limp into the chapel, wondering exactly how much sway the steward had over her husband. And more to the point, how much the sister held.

Tomorrow, she would know.

Chapter Sixteen

The weak, gray light of predawn crept into the chamber and chilled Mairi to the marrow. She knew she must rise and make ready, but she clutched the covers to her chin and stared at the underside of the plain, linen canopy above her. How she dreaded this day.

She jerked her gaze toward the door as it opened quietly. Rob entered, treading lightly. He carried the white garb he had worn the night before over one arm and was now clad in his chain mail.

The edge of the quilted gambeson he wore beneath it peeked crookedly above the metal links at his neck. His hair looked mussed and flyaway, waves of it tumbling over his brow. He was dressed, though his feet were still bare. Long and narrow they were, yet strongly made as the rest of him.

He had left his sword and belt below somewhere, probably to avoid the clink and rattle of them so as not to wake her. She wondered who had told him about the racket those made. A lover, she supposed.

Mairi sat up, startling him.

"Good morn," he said then, adding haltingly, "I need hose...and tunic." As if to convince her of that, he bent,

plucked a dagged-edge green wool garment and matching
hose from his open clothes chest and tossed in the white
ceremonial raiment.

She rose, pulling his robe around her, and went to him.
When he closed the chest lid and turned, he looked as
weary as she had feared he would.

Mairi frowned up at him. "You need sleep."

"Do not fret," he said gruffly.

Mairi would have kissed him, had he looked willing. It
could be the last she had of him if she saw he preferred
Lady Jehan.

Belatedly, she recalled the ceremony that had most
likely been some sort of purification ritual. Ah, well, she
would not want him to think she mocked that. Thomas's
warning last night had affected her more deeply than she
wished to admit.

"Win the day!" she said slowly but succinctly, trying
to remain stoic and hide her concern. He might interpret
that as fear that he would not win against Ranald.

"I shall," he assured her, studying her face with that
intensity she had come to expect. "You will watch?"

"Aye," she said, nodding, though she knew very well
he was imagining her hiding behind the walls, peeking
through an embrasure or an arrow slit. "I'll watch!"

Suddenly he embraced her, his mouth taking hers with
a ferocity she had not expected.

His tongue invaded, his arms crushed and his lower
body pressed against her with near desperation. Before she
could recover from the surprise of it all and respond to
him, he released her and backed away.

Mairi reached out with one hand to detain him, to explain her hesitation, but he turned too quickly and departed
the chamber, closing the door behind him.

She stood there, transfixed for some moments, touching

her lips, reliving the kiss and wishing there had been more to follow.

Mairi realized then that she had little time to lose. The men would be gathering even now and as soon as the sun rose fully, would be going out to see the deed accomplished. She had to be there.

A hesitant scratch sounded upon the door. "Come," she called.

"My lady?" came a frightened squeak. "'Tis Elfled."

One of Rob's squires, she recalled, a gangly tow-haired lad of around thirteen summers. He had helped her count candles. "Aye, enter then."

He did so, wearing only a yellowed sark that hung almost to his knees and a pair of ragged braies that were too small for him.

His voice cracked high and low as he informed her, "Sir Galen said I might come and…uh, collect the clothes."

"Clothes?" she asked innocently. "What clothes?"

Elfled ducked his head. "Those you…uh, borrowed. They are mine, you see, and I wished to…uh, wear them."

His hands tugged the hem of the old sark and his braies barely covered the upper half of his gangly legs. "I would look my best today," he added.

She should have realized the person who owned the garb she had borrowed might own little else, especially if he was a servant or a squire picked from one of the poorer families. Yet she was not yet ready to return good Elfled's clothes, since she had need of them herself.

"Look at you!" she commented, shaking her head. "That sark needs a cleaning and the braies are too small. Come with me," Mairi ordered, grasping his shoulder and turning him about smartly. They ascended several steps.

"But, m'lady…"

"Get you into the garderobe, laddie. You cannot expect to dress yourself in my presence, now can you?"

She marched him to the door set into a wall cavity that served as the privy for this level. "Remove that sark and I'll fetch you one cleaner, though it might be too large. With your own clothes over it, no one will notice. Give me those braies, as well. They could use patching. Get in there now and hand them out to me."

Mumbling a protest, he did as she commanded.

Mairi rushed back to Rob's chamber and quickly tossed off the robe. She pulled Elfled's sark over her head and added the rest of his good clothing to it. She hid the old braies, though she knew he would not dare reenter the lord's chamber if she were gone.

She hated leaving him naked, but at least he would be out of the way. And she might even be taken for him, should the rest of the men not look too closely or notice that poor Elfled had shrunk half a hand in height. She cinched up the tunic and tucked Sir Galen's knife beneath the leather belt.

Luckily, she found her boots sitting side by side beneath the bed. With the jaunty cap covering her hair and the borrowed blade at her waist, she had naught to worry about other than keeping her head down so that no one would see her face.

As she exited the chamber, she heard a timid knocking from the garderobe door. "M'lady?" came the hesitant plea. "M'lady, please? Where'd you go?"

Mairi blew out a breath of regret for the necessity of the trick, shook her head and promptly dismissed Elfled's predicament from her mind. There were far more important matters at hand than the plight of a half-grown squire. She would sew him a whole new set of clothes if she were fortunate enough to remain lady here.

Mairi fled down the stairs, trotted across the nearly deserted hall and out the door. Just in time, she caught up to the men as the last few began to exit the gates.

Archers stood with arrows nocked, daring any of Ranald's men to approach the open portals while Baincroft's force came out, Rob exiting first.

Across the open field that surrounded Baincroft, they strode, each altering his step until they marched shoulder to shoulder. They halted as one when they neared the opposing force. Ranald's men had awaited, just out of easy reach of the bowmen's threat.

These several hundred yards from the castle walls, the troop formed a large half circle, a full score of warriors, if she included herself. Rob had assumed the center position, while Mairi remained on the end to his right.

She marked that Ranald's men numbered at least ten more than Rob's. Behind the enemy, however, she watched a line of nearly thirty mounted men quietly appear at the edge of the forest. They halted there, still some distance away, yet close enough to ride forward should there be an all-out fray. Trouville's standard whipped above the horsemen in the early morning breeze.

Mairi grinned. Ranald would be furious about this unexpected turn of events. She deduced that Trouville's men must have taken the Highland horses by stealth sometime during the night, since none of Ranald's men were mounted. So much for her pious cousin keeping a prayer vigil, she thought with an inward chuckle.

Ranald wore no dark circles beneath his eyes. That good night's rest had cost him dearly, however. He had no prayer of escape from here without mounts. She looked forward to his comeuppance. To seeing her father finally avenged.

Mairi's anticipation faltered when she spied Lady Jehan.

Her captor imprisoned her about the waist with one beefy arm. Her long, dark hair hung loose about her shoulders and her gown had been ripped to expose the upper curve of one breast. She appeared haughty even in defeat and at threat of death. A dagger much like the one Sir Galen had loaned Mairi glinted just beneath the woman's chin. One had to admire her courage, Mairi admitted.

"Bring out Lady Mairi!" Ranald demanded.

No one answered him. Rob simply stepped forward and pointed to Jehan. "Set her away. Remove the blade."

"Nay!" Ranald countered, shaking his head. The one who held Jehan did not move.

A standoff, Mairi thought. What now? If Rob slew Ranald in this fight, his man would slit the woman's throat. That would neatly solve Mairi's problem regarding her marriage, but she could not bear to see it happen. Yet revealing her own identity now would do naught to insure that Ranald's man would release Lady Jehan.

"If you harm her," Rob announced, his voice deep and deadly as thunder, "all will die."

Ranald glanced behind him where Trouville's men blocked any escape. If the sight surprised him, he managed to hide the reaction.

He looked pointedly back at Rob for a moment, then shifted his gaze to Sir Galen and addressed him instead. "Tell this devil's lackey I would have our mounts returned to us. Tell him I shall not proceed until all the spoils are displayed upon the field. Bring Mairi MacInness out. She and this one may stand together as the prize." He raised his voice, "Tell MacBain—"

Rob took another step forward, drew off his half helm and tossed it behind him. "*You* tell me, MacInness! Knight?" He spat upon the ground with disgust. "I say *knave!*"

Ranald drew his sword and began sweeping his gaze across the line of Baincroft's defenders. Mairi quickly ducked her head.

"Hear me, all present!" her cousin commanded. "When I defeat MacBain, both women are mine! God will curse any man who does not honor this pact. MacBain has given his *word!*"

His dark, close-set eyes flickered with menace. And mayhap desperation. Ranald had to know he would never leave this field alive. Even should some dark fortune grant him victory over Rob, the men of Baincroft and Trouville's men would surely cut him down where he stood.

Or would they? No one had yet protested her cousin's most recent demand. Would these men actually honor the terms set forth? Would they surrender both her and Lady Jehan to Ranald's dubious mercy if luck ran the wrong way?

She suddenly wondered whether she also should have spent last night on the floor of the chapel, praying for herself.

Jehan suddenly groaned.

Mairi's eyes flew to the woman. The man shifted the blade, jerking it outward as Jehan collapsed and fell to one side in his grasp. He had nicked her chin, but there was little blood spilled. Now that she hung there, dead weight, he had to use both arms to support her or let her fall to the ground.

Mairi felt like applauding. Neatly done, but at great risk. Not for an instant did she believe Jehan de Brus really had fainted away.

One of Trouville's archers had a nocked arrow aimed directly at the captor's back, but had not loosed it. 'Twas obvious he could not see the less-threatening position of the knife from where he stood. Mairi prayed the missile struck true when the moment came.

The harsh rasp of metal against metal drew swift attention back to the combatants. Both had swords drawn.

Rob and Ranald faced each other now, taking measure, circling, blades at the ready. The only sound on the early morning air was the soft, almost musical clinking of their chain mail and the scrape of their boots against the pebbled ground. Mairi held her breath along with everyone else.

Suddenly, with a hellish war cry, Ranald attacked. Blades clanged as Rob easily deflected the blow, pivoting calmly into position to receive another.

"You are *loud!*" Rob conceded with a smile of mock appreciation.

Her kinsman lunged. Rob caught the powerful thrust on his shield and bounced it harmlessly away.

"And clumsy!" Rob added with a chuckle. "Giving up?"

Ranald cursed and rushed him again. Rob neatly stepped aside, eyebrows raised as if it were a close miss. "Oo-oh!" he crooned. "Better!"

Mairi heard more inflection in Rob's voice than ever before. He was enjoying every moment of this, she realized. Exulting in it. Damn him, he should be seriously intent instead of taunting. Ranald was obviously not the swordsman Rob was, but his sword *was* sharp and this was no game!

Again and again, Ranald leaped forward, striking from every conceivable direction, grunting with each effort, perspiration streaking down his face and dripping off his chin.

Each time her husband met Ranald's blade with his own, reducing the threat to nothing. Yet he did not retaliate. Not once did he launch himself, either in anger or in determined assault. He continued to smile and add the occasional comment to make Ranald furious.

The rest of the Highlanders looked on warily, shifting uncomfortably, eyeing the fight with growing apprehension. Ranald tired eventually and backed off the offensive to recoup.

"Yield?" Rob asked cheerfully, plaguing his opponent with a wolfish grin. He propped his sword tip on the ground, holding it exactly as Thomas held a cane.

Ranald ran at him, blade whipped up and extended, only to have his own weight propel him right past when Rob dodged. For Rob it looked effortless. For Ranald, humiliating.

Mairi wished Rob would get on with it and stop playing about. Who knew when Ranald might sneak in an unexpected strike?

They faced off yet again, Ranald huffing, exhausted, absolutely enraged.

Even Rob grew serious now, as if he might be ready to end matters once and for all. She watched him flex his hand upon the hilt of his weapon to strengthen his grip.

Unconsciously, Mairi also gripped hers, the knife borrowed from Galen.

Ranald spoke through gritted teeth, his voice low and deadly as he said to his man, "Kill the bitch, Davy. Do it now."

Mairi gasped, her gaze flying to the brute who held Lady Jehan. He was hefting her about on one arm so he could ply his blade with the other hand. Her eyes flew wide, terrified, as she struggled.

With no thought but to prevent murder, Mairi bent, snatched up a stone and threw it with all her strength. It bounced off the man's forehead, only distracting him. Jehan jerked away and toppled from his arms.

She hit the ground on her hands and knees and with a speed that astounded all who watched, scrambled madly across the open area toward the Baincroft contingent.

Almost simultaneously, the man who had held her prisoner arched forward. When he fell, Mairi saw the arrow protruding from his back. *Thank God!*

Mairi quickly looked toward Rob, fearing the distraction had served him ill. That's when it happened. Ranald's seething gaze collided with hers. In a livid rage and past all thought, he flew by Rob and ran at Mairi full-tilt, his sword extended to impale her.

She had no time to back away, no time to run. Mairi yanked Galen's dagger free of her belt as she ducked under Ranald's heavy blade.

Even so, she felt the steel's glancing bite graze her shoulder. With all her remaining strength, Mairi struck upward beneath his breastbone. His chain mail caught upon the sharp point, gave way and the entire blade sank home to the hilt when his weight fell against her.

She landed on her back, fair crushed beneath him.

"Ha!" she huffed, as much surprised at her success as Ranald must be. Then her breath would not return.

Rob's deep voice shouted her name. The heaviness lifted off her. Mairi struggled upward to no avail. Her limbs would not move. Her lungs would not work. *Nay, she had won, not Ranald! She had avenged her father. This should not be happening!* Her vision swam and blackness threatened. She tried to fight it.

Dying, she realized. So quickly done. Already her eyes would not blink open and her body grew cold. She did not hurt. Fear did not set in as one would think. Only regret. Such powerful and all-consuming regret, she could not bear it. Rob would never know she loved him, would never hold her again.

At least she had helped save Jehan for him. Mairi wanted to laugh wildly at the irony of her deed, to mock the unfairness of the result. But she could not breathe.

Thunder rumbled all around her, pierced with the cries of the damned. Hell, already. And dark it was.

Rob ignored the writhing body he'd pulled off Mairi's and fell to his knees beside her. There was little blood, only a deep scratch that had barely parted the skin beneath the sliced fabric. He pushed gently on her chest, slid his hands beneath her ribs, lifted, then pushed again. Ranald had knocked the breath from her.

Jehannie scrambled next to him, trying to push him away. He glared at her.

"Poison," her lips formed. "On his blade."

"Jesu, nay!" Rob cried, bending again to embrace Mairi, to hold her against him, to will her to live. He squeezed her tight and felt the soft rush of her breath against his face. He wept with relief as he lightened his hold and then squeezed again.

"Inside!" Jehannie cried, pointing. *Hurry! Take her!* She signed as she jumped up and took off at a run.

Rob scooped Mairi up, staggered to his feet and followed, vaguely noticing that all hell had broken out behind them.

He prayed as he ran through the gates and on to the keep. Jehannie would know what to do. Her mother was a healer. Please, God, Jehannie would know.

Not for a moment did he doubt she would do all in her power to save his wife. While she might lack good sense on occasion, Jehan de Brus did not lack honor.

Mairi had helped save her from the Highlander's knife by throwing that stone, and Jehannie owed her for that.

"Deed for deed!" he reminded her as he laid Mairi

upon the table in the hall. Though he trusted Jehannie, he left no chance that she would forget her debt.

She ignored him and spoke to the maid Gunda who stood hovering nearby. The lass scurried away, nodding, while Rob watched Jehannie's nimble fingers tear away Mairi's bloodied sark and tunic.

To his horror, she began squeezing the wound, causing it to bleed more. Then he understood. She was ridding Mairi of as much poison as possible. Rob took over when she indicated he do so, though it pained him to make Mairi bleed.

Soon Gunda returned with leeches and Rob was shoved aside to allow the creatures to do their work. Even as he watched, the dark slugs drew out more blood, swelled fat and fell away. Dead, he expected, or soon would be, from the poison. He blessed them, every one, if they could save his beloved that fate.

Jehannie quickly crushed the herbs the lass had brought her and stirred them in some liquid. With one hand, she patted the air, palm up. *Lift her.*

Rob slid one arm beneath Mairi's lax shoulders and cradled her upper body against his. Forcing her head back and her mouth open, Jehannie poured a bit of the mixture in and rubbed Mairi's throat, repeating the process until all the concoction had been swallowed.

Rob worried it had all trickled into her lungs and she could not cough it up. He glanced at Jehannie, who appeared as concerned as he felt.

"Will she die?" he asked, pleading with his eyes for hope. Just some small measure of it to cling to.

Jehannie shrugged and shook her head. It was obvious she had done all she knew to do. With a sag of her shoulders, she placed her hand on his arm and squeezed to offer him comfort.

"I heard MacInness's plan," she said as he looked at her. "The poison is monkshood."

"And this?" he asked, nodding at the empty cup.

"A mix of things. Foxglove, water lovage, other herbs to stir wakefulness," Jehannie replied, looking doubtful that she had done enough. Or mayhaps had given too much. The herbs she had used were poisonous as well if taken in large amounts. Every child knew that.

Jehannie rubbed her chest with one palm, directly over her heart. *So sorry.*

Rob did not reply. If his Mairi died, it would not be intentional on Jehannie's part. He trusted her.

He lifted Mairi and carried her from the bloodied table to put her in their bed upstairs.

Jehannie followed, tugging at his sleeve. "Wake her, Rob," she ordered. "Give her much water. No wine. No ale."

Rob nodded, leaving Jehannie behind to tend the others who might be wounded this day for his cause. He understood that Mairi's destiny now rested with him and with God. And the Almighty must be terribly engrossed with other issues today since He had permitted this to happen.

He kicked the door open and placed her upon the bed and brushed the tangle of hair from her face. Her incredible pallor had increased and her skin felt damp and cool to the touch.

"Come awake, Mairi!" he demanded, shaking her body gently, then much more forcefully. She did not stir in the slightest. "You must try!"

Gunda came in, bearing water for Mairi and ale for him. Rob thanked her and sent her out, knowing she would remain nearby if he needed to send for anything. He wished to be alone with Mairi for what could be her last hours alive.

He spent those next hours ordering her to wake, trickling water down her throat, and hauling her about the chamber in his arms. The toes of her small boots dragged upon the boards and her head listed to one side as he attempted to coax her to wake up and walk. If only she could sweat the remainder of the poison out, he thought.

Rob paused only to press his fingers to her neck, to reassure himself that the weak pulse was still there. When he could not find the beat, he would wet his own lips and hold them close to hers so he could feel her breath.

"I cannot lose you!" he cried at last when his own strength gave out and he lay beside her on the fur coverlet to rest a moment. He held her close, his face buried against her breasts as he wept. "I cannot!"

In the utter stillness that followed, he felt a slight tremor in her chest, as though she had groaned. He quickly lifted his head and stared hopefully at her face.

Chapter Seventeen

Surely she had made a sound, Rob thought, renewing his efforts to rouse Mairi. His own limbs trembled with exhaustion as he jostled her upright and tapped the side of her face with his fingertips. Her head lolled on her shoulder as though she were a broken poppet.

Rob sighed with defeat. After a while, he placed her back on the pillows, propped himself on one elbow and rested for a moment. This was not working.

He felt her neck for the pulse again. Though it was not that strong or yet quite rapid as it should be, the beat of her heart did seem steadier. That must count for something, though it was not nearly enough.

All of this was his fault. If only he had not gone to such lengths to impress Mairi with his skills and sought to deal out an additional measure of insult to her wretched cousin, this would not have happened.

Why had he not simply finished the business at the outset? Not killing MacInness immediately had caused Mairi to suffer this terrible hurt.

Rob had known Mairi watched him, for she had declared she would. He could not even claim that he thought her watching safely from inside the walls, for he had seen her tricked out in young Elfled's clothing.

The sighting had come too late to send her back without revealing who she was, however, so he had thought to strut like the cock before the hen. One final attempt to prove his ability as a warrior, his worthiness to have her as his wife.

Winning at once would have been child's play, considering MacInness's debilitating rage combined with lack of proper training. With a single blow, Rob could have dealt with him and prevented what had occurred. But that also might have insured Jehannie's death at the hand of Ranald's man.

In addition to impressing his wife, Rob had thought that if he played for time, the one guarding Jehannie might become distracted, that Trouville's archer might find an opening to strike.

And so it had happened as he had hoped, with a bit of assistance from Jehannie herself and his wee, brave wife's quick thinking.

What a price Mairi had paid for that act of courage. He only hoped that she did not finish paying with her very life.

Rob stood up, leaned over and shrugged out of his mail shirt, letting it fall to the floor. He pulled off the sweaty quilted gambeson he'd worn beneath it and dropped it on top of his mail.

Next he retrieved the dagger from his boot and gently cut away the remnants of the bloodied sark Mairi wore, slipped off her small boots and the rest of her garments.

How young she looked lying there, he thought with a catch in his throat. How pale and lifeless and cold. Quickly he fetched a chemise and pulled it over her head, threading her arms through the sleeves as one would dress a babe.

Would he ever hold her close and enjoy the beauty of their loving again? She had claimed his heart as surely as he had claimed her body. If only he were given another chance to show her how deeply he cared for her, how much he admired her in all ways.

Rob ran his hands over her, smoothing the soft fabric as he went. Then he covered her to the neck with furs to warm her. ''Do not die, Mairi,'' he whispered.

''How does she?'' Jehannie asked him as she slipped into the chamber carrying a small flagon in one hand.

Rob shook his head and pressed his forefingers together side by side. *The same.*

She set the flagon down on the table and signed, *Take heart, she lives.*

He pressed a hand to Mairi's uninjured shoulder and pleaded with Jehannie. *Do something!*

She poured liquid into a cup—another infusion of herbs, he guessed by the scent—and handed it to him. Together they worked to make Mairi drink it.

Though her eyes drifted slightly open then, Mairi simply stared, blankly as a corpse. Rob's own blood ran cold at the sight. He feared she had expired and rushed to test her heartbeat yet again. ''Thank God,'' he said, finding what he sought.

Jehannie watched him as she scooped up the clothing he had removed from Mairi and took it outside.

When she returned a moment later, she wore a wry smile as she signed. *I found Efled in the garderobe. Naked and furious. Mairi stole his clothes.*

Rob attempted to smile back, but he could not manage. Jehannie joined him again at Mairi's bedside. She seemed tireless in her attempts to wake their patient, while his own energies began to flag seriously. Lack of sleep and food, in addition to waning hope made him clumsy and nigh useless.

"You should rest," Jehannie declared.

"When she wakes," Rob promised, enduring her reproving glance.

Gunda appeared in the open doorway with a tray piled high with food. Her curious gaze settled on them, but she said nothing.

Jehannie spoke to her and motioned to the table and chairs beside the fire. When Gunda had departed, Jehannie pushed Rob's hands away from Mairi and settled the coverlet over her.

"Let her be for a while and hope the herbs will do their task. Come." She beckoned as she strode across the room to where Gunda had set the tray. "Eat."

Rob had no taste for the food, but he did as she suggested, hoping that the victuals would fuel his strength for the hours to come.

All the while he kept an eye on Mairi, willing her to shift, to open her eyes again and see this time. He wished she would do anything that would signify she might soon come out of her deep and motionless sleep.

When he had finished eating, Jehannie touched the back of his hand and signed. *Not your doing.*

Rob stood, turned his back to her and went to gaze out the window, unwilling to let go his guilt. He felt her arms slide around his waist, saw her fingers lace in front of him and felt her lay her face against his back. He sorely needed the comfort of a friend, but knew he should not turn to her for it.

Grasping her wrists, Rob broke her hold on him and stepped away. When he faced her again, he saw only her sympathy.

Her eyes questioning, she gently placed her palm over

his heart and then turned her hand toward Mairi. *You love her?*

Rob nodded, his lips tight, his gaze blurred.

Jehannie nodded, as well, and then embraced him, resting her head against his chest. He could do naught but hold her, unable to reject the solace she offered.

She understood. As simply as that. Jehannie would do all she could to help him save Mairi, not only because she owed her a debt, but also because she would not want his heart to break. No matter what came to pass, she would always be his friend.

After but a moment she pulled away, patted his face with her efficient little hands and smiled up at him. "Together, Robbie," she said. "Like before."

"Imp," he replied, using the name he'd called her when she used to urge him or Thomas to attempt some impossible scheme or other. He prayed this endeavor would succeed.

"Ogre," she answered in kind with a saucy grin. "Let us to it, then!" She took his hand and urged him toward the bed where Mairi lay.

To his amazement, when they reached her side and looked down upon her, Mairi's eyes were open and alert. Two round, blue flames blazing with accusation, magnified by tears.

"Ah, nay," he exhaled on a wearied sigh. Her thoughts were no mystery to him now. Rob knew exactly what she must be thinking.

Mairi could not bear the look of sudden dismay on her husband's face. He must have expected her to die. She shifted her gaze to Lady Jehan, who appeared to be fading away even as Mairi looked on.

"Robbie!" the woman cried, her fingers clutching Rob's arm. "She has wakened! You see?"

Rob saw, Mairi thought with a grimace of misery. He appeared to be wondering what he might say to explain his behavior just now. As if he could. "Tell me why. I dare ye," she muttered. But he couldn't hear her. Useless to talk to him.

Did he hope she'd not question his embracing another woman? A woman he had once loved and wished to wed? Those feelings were not a thing of the past. Very well. Mairi yawned.

She shook her head to clear it, but her thoughts would not settle into any order. Grimly, she grabbed at one.

What a sight to greet her when she finally broke through the dark blue haze that had imprisoned her. God's mercy, she had not even breathed her last and they were at each other already. Anger roiled through her and left her just as rapidly as it had come. Did she care?

Aye! This was not to be borne, but she was in no mind at present to fight for or even argue her rights as his wife. Mairi squeezed her eyes shut and willed a speedy return to that cloudy netherworld she had fought so hard to escape. It was near, beckoning.

"Do not sleep!" Rob thundered, shaking her. He had one knee upon the bed now, depressing the mattress beside her hip.

"Get off her, you oaf!" Lady Jehan commanded angrily, pushing at him.

Oaf. Mairi wanted to laugh, but could not recall the jest.

Rob had seated himself close and was prodding her neck with his fingers. It hurt. Everywhere he touched pained her, for her skin felt afire. Why was he doing this?

Her head ached abominably. Her tongue felt dry as tinder and tasted foul as sour wine dregs.

"Water," she said, not really expecting either of them to comply with her plea.

They nearly drowned her. Mairi sputtered and choked when Rob yanked her up from the pillows and Lady Jehan emptied a cupful into her mouth.

She tried to bat them both away, but her arms moved as though encased in heavy steel. Out of self-defense, she gulped the cool liquid until there was no more.

"Leave me," she gasped, breathless from her efforts. "Go away."

The woman laughed, a low, dulcet sound that made Mairi wish to retch. "Not likely we shall do that after all this work," Jehan said with a chuckle. "I fear you must suffer some torture first."

Rob hastily brushed the tangled hair from Mairi's forehead and then snaked his arm farther beneath her shoulders to lift her higher. She welcomed his touch, though it hurt. Nay, she should not allow it. His strength, that was it. She wanted that of him, for she had none of her own. None.

Before Mairi knew what had happened, they had her upright, supported betwixt them.

"Walk!" Rob ordered gruffly.

"You must sweat," Lady Jehan explained. "Soon we shall let you sleep all you want. The foxglove and lovage are working, I believe. You've been poisoned, you know."

"Poisoned?" Mairi groaned, wincing at the incessant pounding in her brain. They had *poisoned* her?

Aye, they had! And everyone else would believe she died of the wound Ranald gave her. That injury must have been too slight to do the job in itself. But who would believe this if only these two had the tending of her?

But she trusted Rob. Didn't she? She could not recall just why, but she had put her life in his hands.

'Twas the woman, Mairi thought with a groan. The sorceress with evil herbs. Had she plied Rob with potions, too?

Mairi sighed, helpless to do more than sag between them as they hauled her around the chamber. Her thoughts bounced wildly. First she wished to crawl away from Baincroft, curl up and hide, then to fall back into bed and die there.

In truth, she wondered why they would not let her rest in peace. Of a sudden, she was past willing to give up and do so. Let them have each other. She wanted nothing but sleep. Sweet oblivion.

"Please," she moaned, praying they would allow her dignity, if not her life.

"Do not worry," her rival assured, the musical voice imbued with obvious delight in the way things were progressing. "The worst has passed. We only need to be certain the herbs have done their work upon you."

Mairi did not bother to cry mercy. She put one foot before the other and did as she was bid. Should the poison mix prove a goodly dose, there was little use fighting it.

However, her mind did seem to be working better than it had a few moments past. Was it moments? Or hours? Her head ached worse than ever, but the feeling in her limbs increased with each step she took. Mayhaps they had misjudged how much it would take to kill her.

If she could fool these two into thinking they had achieved what they set out to do, she might yet escape death. Mairi continued to cooperate until she felt she had the strength to walk on her own.

Then she purposely collapsed, hanging limp in their arms.

"Enough?" she heard Rob ask.

"Aye, that should do," Jehan answered.

Mairi said nothing.

He guided them back toward the bed, lifted her in his arms and put her back upon the mattress.

The woman pressed her hand to Mairi's neck and seemed satisfied with what she felt there. Through slitted eyes, Mairi watched that same hand motion something to Rob. He nodded, appearing relieved.

Then Jehan left, but not before she pulled Rob down and kissed him softly upon his cheek. It took all Mairi's will to remain silent. Had she any strength to spare for it, she would have clouted them both.

Instead, she feigned sleep until she heard Rob move across the room and poke at the fire. The chair creaked. Only a short time later, his evenly measured, deep breathing told her he slept.

Someone had replaced Elfled's sark with her own chemise. That was all she wore, for they had also removed the braies from her. The lad's clothing had disappeared. Quietly as she could, she slipped off the bed and found her boots tossed carelessly against the wall.

Struggling to maintain her balance on unsteady legs, Mairi made it to the wall where hung her woolen gowns. She chose the sturdiest she owned, the dull green camlet, and slipped it over her head.

Fortunately for her husband, she no longer had that knife Sir Galen had loaned her. She much feared she would be tempted to use it if she had.

Her anger knew no bounds and she held fast to it, knowing it would mask the heartbreak she could not afford to give way to at the moment. If only her mind did not reel so, she could make short work of this and be gone. *Somewhere.* She would decide that later, Mairi thought.

With shaking hands, she rolled Rob's furred cloak into a bundle to take with her. Though the weather remained fair and unseasonably warm, her body felt as though icy water filled her veins.

Her thinking still seemed muddled, but she did understand that this might be the only chance she had to get away. Quietly as a thief in a counting house, she stole barefoot down the stairs and kept to the shadowy corners of the great hall. She ducked into an alcove and donned her boots.

It seemed everyone who lived at Baincroft had gathered there. Several wounded men lay upon floor pallets around the far edge of the huge chamber and women were tending them. Many of the men congregated in groups, drinking ale, laughing and talking loudly amongst themselves.

Trouville was still here, Mairi noted, and thought briefly of approaching him to ask his aid. She quickly thought better of that, however. He might believe she lied about the poisoning or else support Rob's decision to get rid of her. Jehan might hold special favor with Rob's parents, since they knew her so well.

Either no one had noticed her arrival downstairs, or they did not care. There was much traffic in and out of the hall, so the doors had been propped open.

Mairi spied a gray shawl someone had left lying on one of the benches along the wall and quickly snatched it up. She draped the threadbare thing over her hair, leaving the edges to half cover her face. Though she was fairly certain no one would try to stop her.

Why would they care if she left? Now that she thought on it, Rob would probably have given her a horse and provisions, had she stated her intent and asked for them.

But then again, he might think he would be much better off rid of her permanently. If she were dead, he would be free immediately to wed that woman. That witch.

Slowly, head down and taking measured steps, she made

her way to the portal and went out. Though 'twas nearly dark, the bailey teemed with the restless Trouville mounts, stable lads and squires. The entire party must be planning to leave for their home soon. That would explain why the gates now stood open and virtually unguarded.

Those men who stood near the gates paid her no attention when she approached, engrossed as they were in recounting the morning's battle.

For a few moments Mairi lingered, listening to their bragging accounts of the victory. They mentioned Ranald's death and her part in it. She remembered that and her heart felt even colder. Mairi had killed him. That should bring, if not pleasure, then certainly satisfaction. Instead, she felt sorrow, both for taking her cousin's life and for his greedy soul that had forced her to such a deed.

The men even laughed as they remarked on Lord Rob's savage little Highland wife.

She had driven the blade home, so she supposed they were right. With her free hand, she touched the wound her cousin had dealt her. A scratch, nothing more, but he would have cleaved her in twain had she not ducked. And if she'd not stabbed him, his next blow would have been fatal to her.

They were saying now that Ranald's men had fought doggedly that morn until only a few remained standing. Those had surrendered and were being held prisoner until Lord Rob decided their fate.

At least Mairi now had a destination. She could return to Craigmuir, after all, and be safe there. All she had to do was figure out how. She possessed no food or coin for the journey. But she did still have her life, for what that was worth.

Mairi exited the gates, her steps slowing with exhaustion. The heartsickness over her failed marriage and Rob's ultimate betrayal were worse than the effects of the poison. But she could not dwell on that yet. 'Twas hard to dwell upon any one thing at the moment, for her mind skipped about like a hopping toad.

She gripped the rolled-up robe against her chest and veered off the main road. It would not do to have Trouville discover her on his way home and demand an explanation. Mairi headed for the forest that lay west of Baincroft.

'Twas there she found the Highland pony, his lead rope trailing as he grazed near the edge of the woods. God was with her. Trouville had missed this one.

"Mairi!" Rob thundered as he slammed the door of the empty garderobe. Where the devil was she?

He hardly touched the steps in his hurry to reach the hall. It lay dark and quiet in the midst of the night.

He woke every soul sleeping there, nudging first one, then another with the toe of his boot. He shook shoulders and yanked pillows from beneath heads, shouting all the while, "Wake you! Help search!"

Flint struck tinder in several sections of the hall as torches were fired. The hall came to life before him.

"My wife is gone!" he announced, struggling to remain calm in the face of his fear for her. "She is ill. Find her!"

He dashed out to the barracks and woke his men. A thorough search ensued. Every hidden corner of Baincroft was laid bare and gave up no sign of his lady.

Rob grew more frantic with every report. Mairi was nowhere to be found within the walls. No one had seen her. She had simply disappeared.

The accusation in her eyes when she had first awakened still haunted him. She had seen him embracing Jehannie and he had not explained that away. Instinctively he knew

she had left Baincroft willingly—more like desperately—
to get away from him.

Ill, angry and feeling betrayed, the poor lass would
never heed the dangers of the night as she should. Wild
animals and exposure to the chill were his main concerns.
Thieves and rogues rarely haunted the lands around Baincroft, for none wished to chance his wrath. However, that
threat remained a possibility, too. Rob forced himself to
not think upon it more, lest he go mad.

He wished to heaven that his father and his men had
stayed the night. Rob could send for him to return, but he
could not wait for help. He must act now.

One of the stable lads brought his mount and Rob lost
no time. He took a lighted torch, as did the others, and led
his men out.

"She will go west," Rob informed Sir Galen, who rode
beside him.

Then he recalled something she had written on the
parchment when they were getting to know each other.
There was her lifelong wish to see a city. "Or east to
Edinburgh," he added to Galen. *If* she even knew that city
lay east, Rob thought.

God's mercy, he knew not where to begin.

Clouds hid the moon. They had little hope of finding
Mairi unless they stumbled over her by sheer accident. He
sighed at the futility of the search, but could not abandon
it so long as there was the slightest chance it might succeed.

Mairi had not intended to sleep. After guiding the pony
she'd found into the cover of the trees, she had tethered
him there so that they were both well hidden from pas-
sersby until Trouville and his men had left Baincroft.

While she waited for them to leave, a short rest to fortify

her for a night-long ride had seemed prudent. But she had not awakened when she'd meant to. 'Twas morning now and the sun was peeking over the castle walls as she looked east.

The gates still stood open, she noticed, and wondered whether Rob's father had waited until this morn to depart.

Just behind her, the pony whinnied, shifting restlessly beneath his rough saddle and tugging at the rope she had looped 'round a stout branch. He wanted exercise, she supposed. Heaven knew he had found enough to eat. His belly was so distended, he looked about to foal.

Mairi shrugged out of the cloak that had kept her warm enough to sleep throughout the night. It still held the scent of her husband, not a welcome thing after all that had gone on. She quickly rolled the garment and tossed it across the saddle.

The surrounding forest seemed to welcome their presence, her and her newfound beastie. Birds warbled, obviously unafraid of the intruders, and she could hear the nearby bubbling of water over rocks.

Thinking to refresh herself and water the pony, she untied the reins and wandered a bit farther into the woods to find the source.

Mairi knelt beside the brook and drank of its coolness, splashed her face and dried it on her sleeve. Then she began to think rationally for the first time since the battle.

The cobwebs cleared from her brain and left a realization that she did not like at all. This escape of hers suddenly seemed cowardly and not in any way befitting of a woman who had faced down her greatest foe and prevailed.

"Why should I run?" she asked the pony. He snorted, stamped one hoof and lowered his head again to drink.

"How dare he think to be rid of me and yet keep what's mine? I'll have my dowry!"

The beast snuffled.

"Right you are, ye wee scruff!" She stood and clasped one hand to her chest. "I am not some simpering slow-wit who fears the likes of the MacBain and that mean-spirited witch!"

The pony returned her glare with a placid blink.

Mairi paced three long strides to the right and turned to pace three more, tossing a didactic nod at her new companion. "I am Mairi of the MacInness, you know! And since I choose not to remain here, I'll yet have what's due me ere I leave! If the MacBain wants shed of me, then he can bloody well return my dower lands!"

She threw up one hand to make her point. "Aye! Why should I lose in this? I've done naught but what a good wife should! How could I think to go back to Craigmuir and act a servant to my clan when I have lands of my own to tend, eh? I'll *not!*" she declared.

"Poison *me,* will they? We shall see about *that!*" Mairi grasped the pony's lead rope and tugged him back through the trees toward the road. Before she lost the impetus that drove her, she mounted up and rode hard for the open gates.

Chapter Eighteen

Openmouthed stares greeted Mairi as she galloped through the gates into the bailey. She heard frantic blasts from the horn that signaled her entry. "Aye, I am here!" she shouted. "Let him know it!" She reined up in front of the steps to the keep and quickly slid off the pony, landing on her feet with a thump.

This must needs be quickly done, she decided. Stalking up to the hall doors, she pushed her way inside and came face-to-face with Sir Thomas on his way out.

"God's blood!" he exclaimed, his eyes round with surprise. "Where have you *been?* Everyone has—"

She shoved past him, demanding, "Where is Mac-Bain?"

"Out searching for you!" he replied, reversing his direction and following her back into the hall.

Mairi figured Thomas was the one she needed most to see anyway. He had arranged the match between Rob and herself. He could bloody well undo it. "Where are the marriage documents? I wish to see them."

He shook his head firmly. "Only your husband can—"

She dismissed his objection with an angry flick of her

hand. "Do not play games with me, Thomas de Brus!" Mairi felt herself trembling with fury. "Get them, I say!"

"She's back!" came a cry.

Mairi glanced to her right and saw Lady Jehan dashing across the hall toward her. Thinking only of the woman's attempt on her life, Mairi quickly reached out and snatched Thomas's eating knife from his belt.

Propped on his canes, he moved too slowly to prevent it. She wheeled on Jehan, waving the blade in front of her. "Do not think to kill me this time, ye spiteful witch! Ye're welcome to MacBain, but I will have what's *mine!*"

The woman halted an arm's length away and leaned back from the knife. Her bright eyes darted from Mairi to the weapon and back again. "Of…of course you shall," she said in a small, uneasy voice. Then she seemed to digest what Mairi had said before that. "*Kill* you? What do you mean?"

"Foxglove!" Mairi exclaimed as she tossed her braid over her shoulder to get it out of her way. "Also lovage, eh? Ye admitted ye poisoned me!"

Jehan backed up a step. "But—"

Mairi felt a steel grip on her wrist. "Drop the knife, my lady," Thomas warned as his fingers cut off the feeling to her hand. The blade clattered to the floor and he released her.

Jehan dived for it and Mairi instinctively kicked it from her reach, falling atop the woman to prevent her scuttling after the weapon. "Not this time!"

She grasped a handful of hair and wound it tight, her other hand blocking two flailing fists. Jehan clawed, kicked and bucked Mairi off, reversing their positions, and cried, "Ah-*ha!* Take that, you ungrateful…"

Mairi's head reeled from the open-handed blow, but she returned it full-force. The resounding smack felt wondrous.

Jehan screamed with rage and would have struck again, but Mairi twisted free.

She forced her opponent back upon the rushes and straddled her, one hand still clutching hair, the other at the neck. Her reach was longer than Jehan's. She had won.

But what had she won and for how long? Thomas could clout her on the head and 'twould be all over. She risked a glance at him, noting that he stood dumbstruck.

"Do not approach!" she warned him, looking again to judge his reaction. "I will cut off her breath!"

He gave a jerky shake with his head and held his peace.

Mairi deliberately took a deep breath, tried to stop shaking and at the same time retain her grip on Lady Jehan. Fortunately that one had realized her struggles were useless and now lay still.

"W-what is it you want?" Thomas asked.

"My dower back," Mairi said firmly. "I wish the marriage dissolved and my dower returned so that I will have a home."

She glared down into Jehan's reddened face and narrowed her eyes. "There was no need to kill me. Be assured, I'd have no man who wants another!" To her chagrin, she watched her own tears dropping upon Jehan's bodice, leaving spots upon the rich yellow brocade.

"Rob does not want *me!*" Jehan declared, far from calm, but no longer fighting. "He loves *you!*"

"Ha! Then why would he wish me dead?"

"He does not, you lamewit! He never did!" She wriggled and grimaced. "Now get *off* me!"

Mairi loosened her grip on Jehan's throat, but kept her hand in place. "Ye expect me to believe that? Ye named the poisons! And I saw ye—"

Suddenly someone grasped Mairi beneath her arms and

jerked her away. Her back landed against a hard body. She knew immediately who held her.

"What goes here?" the familiar voice rumbled.

She craned her neck to look up at him, terrified of what he might do. Rob did not look happy to see her, but that was no surprise.

Jehan scrambled to her feet, brushing her tangled hair out of her eyes with both hands. She sniffed and sucked in a deep breath. "It was Ranald MacInness who poisoned you, Mairi. His blade was tainted with monkshood. I gave you the foxglove and lovage to save you from it."

Ranald! The enormity of her mistake hit Mairi like a fist in the face. All that she had heard in her sickbed made sense now. All she had seen happen between Jehan and her husband did not, but at least they had not tried to kill her.

Rob lowered her so that her feet touched the floor and turned her to face him. "Are you well?" he asked, his eyes hard as flint.

"Nay," she answered breathlessly, tugging at her garments to straighten them, feeling foolish and ill at ease. And oh, so wrong. She bit her lips together, wondering what she should say.

Could it be true that Rob wanted her? She could not forget that he had embraced Lady Jehan. The woman had kissed his face and he had not seemed to mind.

He stared at her so intensely, Mairi wished she could disappear. "You believe her?" he asked softly. "It is true."

Mairi shrugged. Rob obviously had understood Lady Jehan's words to her just now about the poison. But Mairi was uncertain how to explain to Rob what had convinced her they were guilty.

Her mistaken judgment of them had been due in part to

her muddled thinking, but not entirely. There was affection between Rob and this woman. A long-standing affection, at that. But was it love or simple friendship? They had been betrothed.

Even if Mairi loved Rob, that feeling would not be enough to see her through the years she must spend with him if he truly loved his first betrothed. It would only mean misery for all three of them.

But how was she to know which one he loved? Or whether he loved them both? She looked up to meet that cold, gray glare again, but now saw something else in his eyes. *Hurt.* She had wounded him with her accusation. Pride was there, too. He would not ask her to stay. But he wanted her to. He tried to disguise it behind that pride of his, but Mairi saw.

Jehan spoke up, her hands moving in concert with her lips. "She will never trust you, Rob. So how will you trust her? You cannot depend on *her* to look after you."

Mairi saw red. "*Look after him?* Ye think he needs looking after? Have ye ever *seen* this man in a battle?" She huffed as she backhanded his arm. "Not that mincing dance of yestermorn, but a true life-or-death fight? None can match him, I tell ye! None!"

Lady Jehan inclined her head as she held up a hand to interrupt. "I do not speak of his skill at that, Mairi. But he must have a wife who can speak for him in matters—"

"Matters of *what?*" Mairi demanded, throwing up her own hands in disbelief. "Of business? What wife has say in that, I ask ye? Not one that I've heard of! He has a steward for it, though I vow he did right well without yer dear brother at Craigmuir when he came for me. Not one person questioned my husband's words! Nor his worth!"

Rob's gaze was fastened on her mouth. She could not

tell how much he gleaned from what she said. Nor did she care at the moment. She was not speaking to him.

Her rival glanced up at Rob, then placed her fingers in front of her lips when next she spoke. "Rob is used to our help, Mairi. He cannot—"

Mairi's temper snapped completely. "Aye, he *can!* He can do anything he wishes to do, and without yer interference! There, ye hide ye words behind yer hand, so he canna see and be offended. Protecting him, are ye? Puir wee Robbie?"

Jehan made to speak, but Mairi hushed her and went on. "Aye, ye think him still a bairn, is what! Ye and Thomas! For all yer years, his mother taught ye to treat him so! To speak for him, do for him, thrust yerselves betwixt him and the world!"

She grabbed Jehan's arm and shook her. "He is a man now, Jehan! And, by God, he is *my* man! Ye'd best not forget it!"

Jehan bit her bottom lip and looked up at Rob for a long moment. Then she jerked her arm from Mairi's grasp and marched past them out the door.

Mairi wanted to think good riddance and begone. This woman did not know Rob nearly as well as she thought she did. How disastrous it would be to leave him in Jehan's keeping. Just as she'd declared a moment ago, he did not need to be *kept!* He needed a wife to love him, believe in him, stand at his side. That was all.

But Mairi could not let Jehan go this way in spite of all that. The woman had saved her life when it would have behooved her not to do so. All she'd had to do was to let the poison work unhindered, yet she had not. Mairi owed her, and a MacInness always paid a debt.

She nudged Rob's arm and spoke slowly. "Wait here. I will be back."

Hands clasped behind him and his expression now un-readable, he nodded once.

Hurriedly, she went after Jehan, intent on making peace with her rival, no matter how inconvenient it might prove to be, having her around. Somehow she would find a way to tolerate her.

"Do not go," she called from the top of the steps. "Ye need not. Let us speak more and settle this between us. I did wrongly accuse ye of the poison, and I'm sorry for it."

"'Tis settled!" Jehan replied, tossing Mairi a saucy grin and a wink.

"Ye can stay," Mairi called.

Jehan shook her head. "I but waited to see if you suited our Robbie. You do!"

Mairi started to protest again her leaving, but Jehan fore-stalled her. "Thomas will have related your little speech by this time," she informed Mairi. "I'd advise you to learn the signs, Highlander. My brother will not be there to translate for you in the marriage bed."

Mairi rolled her eyes at that impertinence. "Where will ye go then?"

"To Lady Anne!" Jehan called out as she marched backward toward the stables. "Do not worry for me! Robbie has a fine brother in France! I expect he'll need some looking after." Laughter trailed behind her as she turned and trotted out of earshot, though it sounded a wee bit forced.

One had to admit, as a face saver, it worked quite well and must be admired.

Mairi shook her head in amazement while she retraced her steps and went inside to face her husband. This day had turned up nothing she had expected thus far. Not one thing.

He would probably punish her, and she surely deserved
a setdown if anyone ever had. Rob's two closest friends
hated her, and with sufficient reason. His people did not
want her here, but she was staying despite that. All those
trials to bear, and still her heart felt light as goose down.
It was a wonder.

Rob waited impatiently for Mairi's return, hardly able
to believe what had happened. She had returned to Baincroft of her own accord.

At first she had requested her dower lands and a dis-
solution of the marriage, so Thomas said.

She had accused Jehannie and him of the poisoning.
That much he'd understood, and it would explain her first
demand. She believed better of them now. At least, he
hoped she believed.

However, the most confusing thing was when she had
defended him to Jehannie. Or so Thomas told him she had
done. Rob had only understood the last part. The most
important part. When Mairi had declared he was hers. *Her
man.*

Rob's hope for them grew. They might work things out
in time, he figured, if Mairi truly felt they belonged together. *Why* she had decided that so suddenly would determine the outcome of all this, however.

Sympathy for him or her sense of duty would not be
enough to build their lives upon. He wanted more from
her. And Mairi deserved much more from him than he had
given her thus far.

"It is time," he said to himself as he watched the doorway where she had disappeared. "Past time."

Thomas hobbled around to face him. "Time for what?"

Rob merely smiled and raised one brow.

"Oh, that," Thomas said, and rolled his eyes.

Rob motioned across the hall to young Gunda and ordered her to take food, wine and hot water to his chamber. He'd had a long night roaming the countryside searching for Mairi and he felt famished. Mairi must be worse off than he was in that respect.

Truth told, all his hungers plagued him, not least his need for Mairi. The possibility of assuaging that stirred a restlessness he could not contain. But he must be patient, he warned himself. There would be much to discuss before they loved again. *If* they loved again.

Thomas leaned his back against the wall for support and propped his canes beside him. *You are in for trouble,* he signed.

Rob questioned that with a barely curious look.

Everyone will call her a hellion, your wife.

They have said worse of me, Rob admitted. *And you.*

For a while they stood there, contemplating each other, until Thomas threw up his hands, obviously exasperated. His signs were curt and without grace. *I lied. They will love her. She is strong and honest and intelligent. Like you.*

He turned his face away for a moment, then resumed. *And she is right.*

About what?

His friend sighed, his shoulders slumping, his expression resigned. *You no longer need us, Jehannie and me.*

I will always need friends, Rob assured Thomas. *Mairi will need you, too, no matter what she thinks now.* He was already assuming she would stay, he realized.

She does not like me, Thomas signed.

You do not like her, either, but that shall change. Rob raised a brow in warning. He would have this change if Thomas remained here.

Thomas picked up his canes and pushed away from the

wall, but he spoke so that Rob could not miss his reply. "Very well, your lordship. If you say so."

Mairi reentered, hesitating in the doorway with her hands clasped tightly together. She was smiling her most innocent smile, but in her eyes, Rob could see wariness, fear that he would punish her because of her display of temper.

By all rights, he should make her pay for those accusations, for fighting with Jehannie, and for throwing him such a scare by disappearing as she had. But he knew he would not. He was too happy to have her safely home.

"You made peace?" he asked, knowing he must ask that much of her if she had not.

She nodded, then cast a quick glance at Thomas who stood watching them. "Your sister goes to Lady Anne. She says we should not worry for her."

"We have more to fret over than my wayward sibling, I should think," Thomas replied with a grimace. "Your husband demands that we be friends."

Mairi shrugged and pinched her pretty lips together for a moment, though she wore a wide-eyed look of pure devilry that Rob found enchanting. "Aye, well then," she said, forming her words slowly, very properly. She did so more to taunt Thomas than for Rob's understanding, he was certain. "So long as you heed all I say and do everything as I wish, I am certain we shall get on quite well, sir."

Rob watched Thomas's face drop in comic disbelief. 'Twas time to intercede before these two came to blows. They would never see eye-to-eye and he might as well accept it.

He hoped there would be many lively years ahead in which to settle what lay between them, but he did not mean to begin this instant. He had more important matters to attend.

"Come with me," he ordered Mairi as he took her arm and threaded it through his, leaving her no choice. He did not miss the vaunting smile she threw over her shoulder to plague the frowning Thomas.

Once they entered his chamber, Rob noticed she had lost her bluster and swagger. A meek Mairi seemed almost unnatural.

"Sit, eat," he told her, pointing to the food Gunda had brought for them.

Obedient for a change, she fell to it, tearing off a portion of fresh bread and offering to share. Rob took it and the cup of wine she poured for him and sat across from her in the other chair.

The meal progressed rapidly. Mairi said nothing as they ate, but regarded him as carefully as one would a predator about to strike. She obviously expected some form of retribution for her mistake, but surely she did not fear him.

He tossed back the last of his wine, set down his cup and rose to stretch. She watched him, brushing the crumbs from her fingers and chewing thoughtfully.

There was no further excuse to delay. They would have to come to an understanding now. He must know that she remained with him for the right reasons and not out of duty or pity.

He knelt beside his chest and drew out the parchment and charcoal in the event they should need to write. When he placed them on the table Mairi had just cleared, she frowned at the implements.

"Nay," she said, her eyes meeting his. She pushed back from the table and left her chair. When she reached the bed, she turned toward him again. She leaned back, crossed her arms over her chest and said, "Let us speak."

Resigned to the effort, Rob began. "You were duped."

She inclined her head in agreement. "Aye." Then she narrowed her eyes. "Did my father know?"

Rob nodded. "Forgive me, Mairi?"

"Aye, if ye forgive me. I always judge too quickly. And I behaved badly." She shrugged one shoulder and her smooth forehead furrowed. "I was so angry. Afraid. Worried."

"Are you now?" he asked, wanting to reassure her somehow.

"Nay," she replied with a hesitant smile. "I am content."

"Content with me?" Rob questioned.

Her words spilled out too swiftly then, so he held up a hand to silence her. "Speak slowly, please," he demanded.

He approached her then and lifted her to sit upon the edge of the bed. He stood before her so they were face-to-face, her hands grasping his shoulders, his resting upon her waist. "Now, begin again."

Haltingly, she told him that she had suspected the truth the night she was attacked in their camp, that she had seen the exchange between him and Wee Andy when they thought her asleep. Later, she had doubted her suspicions, but had them confirmed just before they had reached Baincroft.

To his great surprise, she also added how it had made her feel. She spared him none of her worries as to how his not hearing might complicate their marriage and her life.

Rarely had anyone ever spoken so openly to him of this. Mairi was direct. Yet in the end, she vowed she did not mind the deafness. She had grown used to it, she said. Rob almost laughed, wondering whether he ever would.

He did have to smile at her concerted attempt to have him understand her. She exaggerated and used the most simple words, doling them out one at a time, most likely speaking louder than was normal for her, believing that would help.

To Mairi's credit, she met with success. He did grasp nearly every word and was able to add in the missing ones from what he did ken.

In time, he would grow accustomed to her manner of speech, just as he had so many years ago with Trouville and Henri. *If* Rob were granted that time. He must know whether he would have that.

"You want free?" he asked, keeping his own voice soft, little more than a whisper.

"Oh, *nay!*" she answered, shaking her head in vehement denial.

"Why not?" The crucial question here. He had expected her response. Mairi was not one to break her vows. But he would not have her keep them if she felt they had been sought under false pretense, or if she regretted them now.

She cast about for an answer, appearing at a loss, then recovering. "Because...I...care!" Her fingertips bit into his shoulders almost desperately.

Rob leaned forward and brushed a kiss across her brow, then drew back, as ready as he ever would be to offer what he must.

"You may go," he told her. "I will provide. Gold. Servants. Your own home."

Her small hands trembled when she cradled his face between them and looked deeply into his eyes. "Oh, Rob. *This* is home. I want it. I want *you.*" With a heavy sigh, she asked, "Do you ken?"

Rob smiled as he touched his lips to hers. "Aye, I ken."

Relief swept through him like a cleansing tide. Mairi wanted him. She cared. He knew it was not pity or duty or some misbegotten sense of honor that held her here. Thank God.

She must have concerns, however. Any woman would. As much as he wanted her and as ready as he was to claim her forever, Rob still waited. He placed a hand over her middle. "Our babes," he said, hoping he could reassure her. "They will hear."

Though she asked no question as to how he knew they would not inherit his deafness, he could see it in her eyes.

"I once heard," he explained, smiling at the few faint memories he treasured and at Mairi's avid interest. "My mother's songs. My dog barking. The wind."

"Whistling at the windows?" she asked, warming to his revelations.

"Through the trees," he corrected, holding up his hand, waving his fingers for the tree sign, then curling them into a fist at the corner of his mouth. "And the horn."

She bobbed her head, urging him on. "Aye, on the wall! When someone approached!"

"I was two...mayhaps three," he told her. "I had fever."

Her face darkened as she frowned. "Nothing now?" she asked, gently touching his ears, running her fingers along their outer curves.

Rob reached up and grasped her hands, bringing them to his lips to kiss. "Drums. Whistles. Flutes," he told her.

"Ach! I knew it!" she exclaimed with a brief laugh. "The dancing! Yer quite good!"

"I know," he admitted, laughing. "Better than you!" Which earned him a mocking punch.

"May I learn the signs?" she asked eagerly, twisting her hands in motions that made no sense.

"You had better," he replied, shaking his head ruefully

as he gently thumped one of her hands. "Such *naughty* signs!"

Mairi glanced down at her offending fingers and worried her bottom lip before she realized his jest.

She laughed with him then. God, how he loved her laughter! It looked so joyous and free. It must sound like music, he thought.

Inspired by that, Rob fanned the fingers of one hand as if plucking upon a small instrument. "'Tis your name," he explained. "Like harp strings."

Mairi repeated the new sign a few times, seeming delighted with it, then asked, "What is *yours?*"

She watched intently as Rob tapped three fingers midchest to signify the MacBain device he often wore there. "This is me."

"Who makes them?" she asked of the signs.

"My mother first," he told her, carefully teaching her more as he spoke. "Now everyone does."

"Three words," she said curiously, her fingertips tracing his chin, then his mouth. "You rarely say more. Why is that?"

"I told you." He grinned, nipped one of her fingers and quipped, "Three are enough."

"I suppose," she said, inclining her head wistfully. "*If* they are the right three."

Rob tipped up her chin and looked squarely into her eyes, all jesting aside. He crossed his palms over his heart, then opened them to her as he declared with feeling, "I love you."

She sighed deeply with pleasure, as he'd hoped she would, and leaned to kiss him tenderly on the mouth.

"I love you," she repeated, offering him her own heart exactly as he had offered his.

Volumes might be spoken between them in the coming

years, but everything of importance had been voiced just now.

He leaned into her, deliberately brushing his body against hers, a definite promise implied in what he did not say.

"Wait! I believe I know that gesture!" she exclaimed, laughing softly and so sweetly, he could swear he heard the sound. Her fingers threaded through his hair and she leaned back upon the coverlet, drawing him with her. "It means *come to bed,* aye?"

He answered her as eloquently as he possibly could, considering both his mouth and his hands were fully engaged.

'Twas a discourse never to be forgotten.

Epilogue

Three Years Later

"Cease that noise this instant!" Mairi cried, cupping her hands over her ears. Wee Ned chased his twin, Harry, who dodged around a chair and threw himself into the safety of his father's arms.

"Da! Save me!" the two-year-old screeched as he climbed up the front of Rob's new surcoat and latched on to his neck.

Ned followed him up. "Got ye!" he cried, pounding his brother's back with the short ring of jester bells he'd found in the hall.

The racket was unbearable. Some days she envied Rob his silence. There was racket a'plenty in the hall already, with the preparation for their visitor. The horn had sounded his arrival and he would be entering at any moment. Three years wed and Mairi had yet to meet Rob's brother, who was just come from France. What would he think of his two boisterous nephews clinging to their father's neck like wriggling limpets?

Rob chuckled merrily, tickling the boys' ribs until they

slid out of his lap, weak with laughter. Mairi caught both
by their belts and hauled them to the long stool beside the
hearth.

"Sit, Ned!" she commanded, snatching the japer's bells
away from him. "You, here!" She plunked him at one end
and grabbed Harry. "And you, there! A moment of quiet,
please! And do stay clean!"

Harry pulled a tiny wooden horse from inside his jerkin
and smiled his father's smile, taunting his brother, "My
horsey." Then he added a singsong patter of words even
Mairi could not fathom. Ned answered in kind. Their
strange conversation continued as they decided to share
the toy, clacking it along the bench between them.

Mairi shook her head and turned to her husband. "Why
do they speak so, Rob? I try to teach them! What is wrong?
They insist on this...gibberish."

"Mercy!" His hands flew to his face as he gasped in
mock horror. "'Tis not Gaelic?"

She laughed in spite of her dismay over the children's
speech. "Nay! *That* I could ken!"

"Not French?" he demanded, appearing even more
worried.

"Nor English! Nor Latin!" she replied with a sage look.

Rob sat back, grinning up at her. "Watch this. Lads?"
he said firmly, gaining their attention. "Tell me. Who is
Harry?"

Harry waved his forefinger as if teaching a lesson.
"Unca Henri..." he paused, teasing them, then pointed to
himself and added a very loud. "And *me!* Harry."

Rob nodded his approval, then queried, "Who is Ned?"

"Gran'pere Edouard and *me!*" Ned announced.

Rob regarded Mairi with boastful silence and signed.
You see? Why worry?

Mairi nodded. She knew he was right. Their sons were

as near perfect as any two noisy wee hellions could be. Some days it seemed her life was too happy, that something must go wrong in it. Rob was teaching her to live each day and to expect happiness on the morrow.

The hall door swung open and Mairi alerted Rob. "He's here," she said unnecessarily, for the tall, dark lord strode toward them wearing a grin of absolute delight. So much like Trouville, she thought, though missing the father's staunch formality.

"Robert le Rogue!" he shouted with a hearty laugh as he threw his arms around Rob.

"Harry the Hapless!" Rob answered gruffly, slapping his brother upon the back as they embraced. "Well come, brother."

Mairi waited patiently for her introduction, though her wee'uns leaped around the two men's legs like eager puppies.

With a final thump, Rob released Henri and turned. "My wife, Mairi," he said, beaming at her. "Here is Henri."

Thinking he would take her hand, Mairi extended it. Instead, he stepped right up to her, kissed both her cheeks, and offered a copious stream of words in his native tongue.

"I do not speak—" she began.

"French. Father warned me," he said suggestively. "Neither can *he* speak it," Henri said, inclining his head toward Rob. "This way I could secretly tell you that you are in danger of being swept away to France by a rascal who loves you madly at first glance. Will you come away with me, my beauty?"

Mairi rolled her eyes heavenward, falling in with his foolery. "Oh, aye, my lord. I and my gently reared bairns here shall make your life heaven! Meet Harry and his brother, Ned!"

Henri immediately knelt and took each lad by a shoul-

der, examining them as he might hounds to be purchased.
''So. Shall you come to France and be my knights? We'll
conquer the English!''

The twins shrieked their assent and climbed into his
arms as if they had known him all their lives.

Mairi rescued Henri after a few moments of the rough
play, and offered him a tankard of ale in exchange.

''You should father your own knights,'' Rob suggested,
reclaiming his chair. ''When do you wed?''

''I!'' Henri exclaimed. ''No need. Harry can be my
heir.''

Mairi beckoned to Gunda to take charge of the little
ones before they became too boisterous to bear. The maid
sat them back upon the bench and offered them each a
bannock to nibble.

''They are beyond wonderful!'' Henri announced.

Mairi could almost swear she saw tears glaze his dark
eyes. She noticed Rob watching his brother thoughtfully.
Both men were looking a bit sad for such a happy reunion
as this. Did it have to do with the reason Henri would so
willingly leave his legacy to a nephew instead of having
sons of his own?

''We are happy to have you here with us, my lord,'' she
said brightly, as much to change their mood as to make
him feel at home. Baincroft had been his home for a longer
time than she had lived here.

The dark cloud lifted then and conversation turned
pleasant as they enjoyed their visit and the evening meal
that followed.

Afterward, they sat beside the fire in the hall where
Henri charmed them with amusing tales of his travels.
Even the lads sat spellbound, propped against each other
on their bench and nodding with exhaustion. 'Twas bed-

time for all, but Mairi hated to end the day. Having a
brother was a new and wondrous experience for her.

"Now, you must tell me of the Highlands, Mairi,"
Henri demanded, "for that is one place I have never
seen."

She quickly complied, her enthusiasm growing as she
thought of her clan. How content they were now with Ranald's nephew as laird, a good young man whom they had
chosen to lead them.

She told of how Rob had come to the Highlands for her,
embellishing his fighting skills with outrageous exaggera-
tions that made Henri laugh and Rob blush.

Of a sudden, Rob reached out and grasped her hands,
stilling her emphatic gestures. "Please, Mairi!" he cautioned her with a pained wince. "Not in front of the children!"

"What?" she cried, opening her palms as if her inad-
vertent message in signs might be written there. "Whatever did I say?"

"That I am the greatest lover in all Scotland," he admitted with a self-conscious, lop-sided smile and an embarrassed shrug.

Henri nodded, all seriousness. "And that he might only
be surpassed by a Frenchman better equipped and with
years more experience." He added, though his dark eyes
twinkled, "And that you are frightfully tempted to—"

Mairi threw up her hands. "I am *frightfully tempted* to
swat the both of you!"

"Not a good sign," Henri commented with a quirk of
his brow.

"I know," Rob agreed. "She needs lessons. Excuse
us?"

"Certainment!" Henri exclaimed. "I bid you good
sleep."

Mairi smiled over her shoulder as Rob led her to the stairs, behind Gunda and the lads. "Thanks to the challenge you presented him, *Frenchman,* I much doubt there will be any sleep tonight!"

"What did you say?" Rob asked, since he had not seen her lips as she spoke.

She smiled up at him with all innocence. "I wished a good night, my love. A very *good* night."

*   *   *   *   *

*Be sure to look for Lyn's
next historical,*

HENRI'S STORY,

coming in the Fall of 2001!

LYN
STONE

A painter of historical events, Lyn decided to write about them. A canvas, however detailed, limits characters to only one moment in time. "If a picture's worth a thousand words, the other ninety thousand have to show up somewhere!"

An avid reader, she admits, "At thirteen, I fell in love with Bronte's Heathcliff and became Catherine. Next year, I fell for Rhett and became Scarlett. Then I fell for the hero I'd known most of my life and finally became myself."

After living four years in Europe, Lyn and her husband, Allen, settled into a log house in north Alabama that is crammed to the rafters with antiques, artifacts and the stuff of future tales.

HH551

Travel back in time to America's past with wonderful Westerns from Harlequin Historicals

ON SALE MARCH 2001

LONGSHADOW'S WOMAN
by Bronwyn Williams
(The Carolinas, 1879)

LILY GETS HER MAN
by Charlene Sands
(Texas, 1880s)

ON SALE APRIL 2001

THE SEDUCTION OF SHAY DEVEREAUX
by Carolyn Davidson
(Louisiana, 1870)

NIGHT HAWK'S BRIDE
by Jillian Hart
(Wisconsin, 1840)

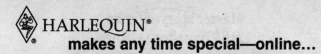

HARLEQUIN®
makes any time special—online...

eHARLEQUIN.com

shop eHarlequin

♥ Find all the new Harlequin releases at everyday great discounts.

♥ Try before you buy! Read an excerpt from the latest Harlequin novels.

♥ Write an online review and share your thoughts with others.

reading room

♥ Read our Internet exclusive daily and weekly online serials, or vote in our interactive novel.

♥ Talk to other readers about your favorite novels in our Reading Groups.

♥ Take our Choose-a-Book quiz to find the series that matches you!

authors' alcove

♥ Find out interesting tidbits and details about your favorite authors' lives, interests and writing habits.

♥ Ever dreamed of being an author? Enter our Writing Round Robin. The Winning Chapter will be published online! Or review our guidelines for submitting your novel.

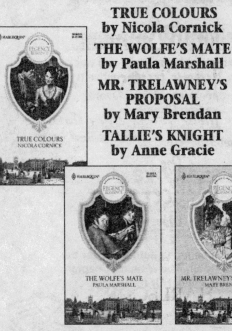